A MATTER OF JUSTICE

A LEWS CANON CRIME NOVEL

HERBERT GROSSHANS

ISBN: 978-1-68046-613-3

Melange Books, LLC
White Bear Lake, MN 55110
www.melange-books.com

Published in the United States of America.

Cover Design by Ashley Redbird Designs

PROLOGUE

MY NAME IS LEWS CANON. I'm a Private Investigator. A Dick.

If you're wondering about my name, let me assure you, Lews Canon is my real name. Actually, it's Lews Bullseye Canon. Given to me by a man with a strange sense of humor.

My father.

What do you expect from a guy whose name is Bigg Canon and who is only five feet, three inches tall in elevator shoes, is as skinny as a third-world refugee and has a head as bald and big as a watermelon? Fortunately, I didn't inherit his genes. I'm five-eleven and I have a healthy carpet of hair on my head. It is carrot-red, but otherwise I'm a normal-looking guy, except for my eyes.

One is brown, the other one blue. Courtesy of my grandfather, Bullseye Canon.

That's right. Bullseye! That's how I got my middle name.

I have no kids and I may never have any. It seems this leg of the Canon line will end with me. Perhaps lucky for those unborn potential children. But, should I for some reason have children, I would never give them names like Bigg, Lews, Bullseye, or any other similar cute name. I'm not married, probably will stay single until the day I die. What sane woman would want to marry a guy who is hardly home, who spends his evenings sitting in a car, listening in on other people's

1

phone calls and watches husbands cheating on their wives or a wife screwing another man instead of her husband?

Unless she's Sonya. Sonya McKinnon. She tends bar in the nightclub across from my office. I can't figure out why a gorgeous chick like her would even think about marrying a guy like me. She could have any of the guys who are constantly hitting on her. Most of them are married, the majority of them are drunks and gamblers, but a few are actually upstanding citizens and would probably make good husbands.

She's never shown any interest in any of them. The only one she's interested in is yours truly. Don't ask me why. I've told her many times that I'm not the marrying kind. I had a taste of it once and it didn't work out for me. Don't get me wrong, I like her and we're good together. She's a passionate woman and holds nothing back. However, I can't see myself tied to only one woman for the rest of my natural life, which may not be that long, considering the work I do. Possibly, that is another of the reasons why I don't want to commit myself again.

Like I said, I'm a Dick. Sounds so crude. *Private Investigator* sounds so much more sophisticated, more glamorous. It conveys a life full of danger and adventure.

Believe me, it is nothing but. Most of the time it's boring.

There is nothing glamorous about watching a bored housewife screwing a guy in the backseat of his car and trying to snap a picture that shows her face and the face of the guy she's banging.

Sometimes I take videos. Anything to give the husband the weapons he needs for a divorce to end in his favor.

When it comes to child support and support in general, the courts still seem to rule in favor of the wife. A husband who is cheated on needs concrete evidence to support his claim.

Sometimes the guy a woman is cheating with is also married. That's when it becomes messy.

Stating my job is boring holds true for most of the time. However, there are times when it does get somewhat exciting. When I say exciting I don't mean adventurous or fun to experience. In fact, while some cases are easy and end well, some turn downright ugly. Take the case of Frederick Titman. It started out like any normal case. Titman, a fifty-five-year-old stockbroker, was married for five years to a woman twenty-five years younger. Marriages like that seldom work out.

She used to be a model. A successful model. Everyone in the fashion world apparently knew Julia Brenner. She gave up a promising career when she married Mr. Titman.

Their happiness lasted for the first couple of years, but then the magic left; at least that's what Mr. Titman told me. He suspected she'd been cheating since then.

One look at the picture of Julia told me enough. A good-looking dish like that will never be happy with one man, especially not with a man like Frederick Titman; according to my own experience and observation, of course.

Some women marry for love, but plenty of them marry for money. That's what I thought at first about Julia. How else to explain why a woman like her would marry a man who was no more than five-one, if that, nearly bald, with watery eyes, a nose like a pear, and a belly that has seen too many hamburgers and fries and way too many beers. He was not a handsome man. And to top it off his last name was Titman. I'm an old-fashioned guy. I believe a woman should change her last name to that of her husband. However, with a name like that even I would not object should a woman decide not to take her husband's last name and keep her own.

Of course, as it turned out, my assumption was way off its mark. It wasn't the first time, either, that I was wrong, but I'm usually a little reluctant to admit that kind of thing.

ONE

"WHAT MAKES you assume your wife is cheating, Mr. Titman?" It was my standard question and I expected the usual answer. His answer was close enough.

"Well, a couple of weeks ago, she told me she was going shopping with one of her girlfriends. She phoned later in the evening and informed me she'd be spending the night at her friend's place because they had celebrated a little too much. When I dialed call-return the woman on the other end answered with *Silver Moon Motel*. Does that sound like some sort of clue, Mr. Canon?"

"Not necessarily. Maybe your wife and her friend spent the night in the motel." I said it but didn't believe my own words.

He shook his head. "No. I phoned Erika; that's her girlfriend's name. She confirmed my suspicion. Julia was not there. She had not been with her all day."

"Hmm." I studied Julia's picture again. "Do you have another picture of your wife? I mean more than just her face? I can't tell if she's fat or skinny, tall or short."

He chuckled. Then he pulled out his wallet and removed a picture, which he had folded in half. I had to suppress a whistle. Now—this was more like it!

He must have noticed my staring eyes, because he reached for the

5

picture and fairly ripped it out of my hands. "Now you see what I mean?" His voice sounded almost apologetic.

When I looked at him, I noticed the color that had crept into his cheeks. I couldn't blame him for being somewhat embarrassed. It's not common practice for a man to show a nude picture of his wife to another man; especially not one like the one Mr. Titman had shown me. I've seen less revealing pictures on porn sites.

Not that I'm looking for any, but anyone surfing the internet inadvertently stumbles across them at one time or another. Sometimes more than once. I'm not exactly a prude. Looking at a picture of a nude woman isn't something a healthy man should deny himself.

"I can provide you with a different picture, if that's what you wish, but I can give you her statistics." He smiled crookedly. "I know them by heart. 36 - 25 - 35. She's five-four and weighs one hundred and thirty pounds."

That image of her nude body stayed with me for a couple of days. Not often do I have the privilege of looking at the nude picture of a woman as stunning as Julia Titman. Lucky Mr. Titman, or perhaps not so lucky. To find out that the woman you love is screwing another man cannot be considered a lucky discovery.

"What do you want me to do, Mr. Titman?" I asked. It was just a routine question. I already knew what he wanted. After all, I'm an investigator.

"Bring me proof my wife is cheating. That's what I want you to do. You're a detective. Isn't that the kind of stuff you find out?"

"I do. Tell me, Mr. Titman. What if I find out your wife is unfaithful? Do you have any plans as to what you're going to do with that information?"

"What I'm going to do with it?" He looked at me with a blank expression on his face, his watery eyes magnified by the huge, dark-rimmed glasses. He looked like an owl ready to swoop down from its perch to catch a mouse. Then he shrugged. "I don't know yet. Let's worry about that when you find out."

"I don't know if I can spare the time, Mr. Titman." I gave my head a shake and pressed my lips together to show him my doubts about finding a timeslot for his case. He didn't need to know that my calendar was never full. There was always room for another case. To be truthful, right now my calendar was empty. I'd learned a long time ago that you never advertise you're in dire need of money. It always brings down the price. "I'll have my secretary check my schedule. If you leave me your card, I'll have her call you."

"You don't understand, Mr. Canon. I won't take no for an answer." His owl eyes stared at me. "This is too important. I was told you're the best. If it's a question of money, that should be no problem. I'm not exactly a poor man."

I cleared my throat. That was assuring to hear. It's always a question of money. There are quite a number of people who expect me to work for free, or for next to nothing. After all, theirs is the most important problem in the universe and the world is coming to an end, according to them, and it's my duty to help them out, notwithstanding the fact that even I have to eat, pay expenses and the rent on my office, as shabby as it is.

"I never doubted that you had money, Mr. Titman," I said, soothingly. "I usually don't discuss money with my clients. That's my secretary's job. She's the one who handles all that money-stuff. I devote my time to solving my cases."

Mr. Titman left his card behind and a check in the amount of two thousand dollars after I promised him that I was quite positive I'd find a bit of time to take on his case. He called me again the next day. He seemed pleased. "Mr. Canon, I spoke to your secretary and she assured me you'll look after me. She sounds like a nice young woman. I sent you a picture of Julia in an e-mail attachment. Your secretary asked for one. Like I said, she seems quite competent. I can usually tell what people look like by the sound of their voice, and your secretary has a lovely voice. So soft-spoken and melodic. It can only belong to a petite, beautiful blonde. Am I correct?"

I didn't have the heart to tell him that he wasn't even close. Tusnelda is six feet tall and built like a fridge. Nobody ever argues with her. Especially not after looking at the Colt 45 she carries strapped to her hip for all to see. If it's not the gun then it's one look into her icy blue eyes. She scares even me sometimes. She's into mixed martial arts, which means she can smash a man's balls with her foot so deep into his belly that even a surgeon may have trouble finding them while at the same time shoving his false teeth down his throat with her fist, providing he has false teeth. If he doesn't, he'll have them after an encounter with Tusnelda. She must have the largest feet and hands I've ever seen on a woman, or a man, come to think of it. And I'd swear her bones are made from iron. If there were such a thing, one could easily believe she wasn't quite human. She's like a cyborg. One of those half human, half robot creatures you see in science fiction movies. She could probably play in one of them without putting on a disguise. Or perhaps she's some kind of alien, a foundling. It's a good thing I don't believe in those things.

She's no beauty, and she never will be, even with a gallon of makeup, but she's the best partner anyone could have. I always call her *my secretary* when I talk with prospective clients, because it sounds professional and is more impressive, but in reality she's my partner. She's the daughter of a good friend of mine, who passed away in 2010 of cancer, and I promised him to look after his daughter once she was released from jail. Juvenile sent her there for beating up a couple of guys who tried to rob her at gunpoint. Both needed corrective surgery. The judge called it overkill. The punks were sixteen and seventeen years old. It didn't make any difference to her; she doesn't take kindly to being threatened by anyone. By the way, she hates to be called *Tusnelda*. She never forgave her parents for giving her that name. I call her Nelda.

I'd say there is a certain kinship between Nelda and me, because we both have names we hate. Why didn't we ever change our names? It's one of those things. Our names are who and what we are. Even if I would change my name, I would always know who I really am.

Lews Bullseye Canon. That's who I am. No change of name would fix that. The mistake was made by our parents and once you're branded like that the damage can't be undone. Then again, perhaps the forces that control this universe had a reason for giving us these names, as obscure as those reasons may be. I'm not a great believer in coincidences. As far as I'm concerned, nothing happens without some kind of purpose.

Since I had no other case to work on, I dove right into finding out more about Julia Titman. I called Mr. Titman back and asked him if he had any idea where his wife might be the next day. Apparently, she had an appointment with her hairdresser at 9:00 a.m. He gave me the address. The next morning I drove there in my Cadillac.

That's right. My Cadillac. I am a Cadillac driver.

Mind you, it isn't a new car; actually, it's quite old and has seen better days. A buddy of mine fixed it up for me and covered all the rust holes with putty and sprayed it with a coat of paint. It runs fine. Usually. Sometimes it doesn't want to start, or the motor might stop running for no good reason at all, but after giving it time to let the motor cool down, it keeps on going. I don't have to waste time with oil changes, as long as I add a quart of oil every couple of weeks. Unfortunately, it is somewhat hard on gas, but that is to be expected from an eight-cylinder. The interior is still nice, though, and the trunk is large enough to transport a couple of bodies if need be.

I received it as payment a few years ago from a widow who was swindled by some con-man. I tracked him down for her. She didn't have much money left, since that son-of-a-bitch took it all from her and spent it, so she gave me her late husband's old car. She didn't have a driver's license anyway and no use for it.

I was happy to get that Cadillac because my own car was stolen just a few days prior and I needed another car badly. By the way, the cops never did find my car and the thieves who stole it. When I told them my car was a 1994 Toyota, they actually laughed and said they had better things to do than tracking down a sixteen-year-old jalopy. They also suggested if I were a patriot I'd drive American cars, not some foreign garbage.

Well, I'm driving an American car now and it reminds me every day why I stayed away from them till now. But then again, why look a gift horse in the mouth?

Julia Titman arrived at the beauty salon a few minutes before her appointment. I have no idea what kind of work she had done, but she was in there nearly two hours. It must have been the hottest day in July that day, and it was still early in the morning. My car doesn't have air-conditioning, and even if it had, I couldn't afford to have the car running for two hours, not with the price of gas these days. So I sat with my window open, swallowing dust, breathing exhaust fumes, and sweating like a pallbearer wearing a dark suit and a tie waiting for the eulogy given by a longwinded relative to end.

When Julia finally stepped out of the salon, she looked like a million bucks. She had her auburn hair pinned up to reveal her ears and the diamond earrings dangling from her small earlobes. The short skirt she wore showed off her well-formed calves and more of her thighs than necessary, and she had undone the top button of her blouse to give anyone who was looking a good view of her creamy breasts. She didn't wear a bra and it was obvious she didn't need one.

How did I know all that? Well, it helped to have a good pair of binoculars. I remembered, though, to snap a few pictures before she got into her brand-new BMW.

Oh, how I longed to be sitting in that car with her. Not because I wanted to get between those lovely thighs she had displayed so boldly, which I wouldn't have minded, either. No, my mind was on something much dearer to me at that moment. It would have been heaven to slide onto those smooth leather seats and to breathe the cool air blowing from the air vents.

She pulled into traffic and I knew it was time to get my car started and follow her. But it wasn't going to happen. My car decided to throw another tantrum. The motor hummed a little, and then all the lights started blinking, but the car didn't start.

Now, I know as much about the workings of a car as a city slicker knows about survival in the desert. Probably even less. I know how to put gasoline into the tank, how to add oil to the engine, even top up the radiator. I've learned how to check the tire pressure and how to make sure there is enough fluid in the windshield washer, but that pretty much sums up my knowledge of car engines and cars in general.

I lifted the hood and stared at the motor, gingerly touching a few things here and there. Everything seemed in order. Nothing was out of place. Nothing seemed to be missing, as far as I could tell.

"Trouble, Mister?"

I turned around to look at the black kid standing suddenly beside me. He was perhaps twelve or thirteen years old. Skinny and tall for his age. His clothes were a couple sizes too large, probably inherited from his older brother, but then I remembered that's how kids wear their clothes these days. I looked for an earring but didn't see one. Give him another couple of years, I thought, and he'll have one, possibly even more than one.

"Car won't start," I said. Taking off my baseball cap, I wiped the sweat from my forehead. If the stress with the car wasn't going to be death of me, this damn heat was surely going to do the job.

"Maybe I can help," the kid said.

"What do you know about cars?" I gave him a doubtful look.

"What do *you* know about cars?" he countered.

I shrugged. "Not much."

He gave a little, almost contemptuous, laugh. "I figured."

"Why do you say that?"

"Because staring at the engine isn't going to fix anything. You'll have to get your hands dirty. What actually seems to be the problem?"

"All the lights are blinking," I told him.

He screwed up his face. "Sounds like a dead battery to me—or nearly dead, anyway." He spoke with an authoritative voice and suddenly looked much older than he was. "Do you have a battery tester?"

"A battery tester? Of course not. Who has a battery tester? I didn't even know the average person could buy such a thing."

He threw me a sidelong look. "How long have you been driving cars?"

"Since 1993 when I bought my first car."

"Wow, that's over twenty years ago." He shook his head. "One would think after all that time you'd know everything about cars."

"Well I don't. I'm not mechanically inclined and never really had an interest anyway. There are other things in life than cars."

He kept shaking his head. "For me there is nothing else. I can't wait to be old enough to drive one. Do you mind if I have a look?"

"Do you have a driver's license?"

Looking at me with pity in his eyes, he said, "Do I look old enough to you to have a driver's license?"

"You could be a midget," I said, lamely.

Without waiting for my permission, he opened the car door and climbed in. Sitting behind the steering wheel, he moved his hands over the dashboard. "Nice." Looking around the interior of the car, he said, "It feels comfortable and the inside is clean. Better looking than the outside. It seems you took care of at least the inside. What year is this?"

"It's a 1997."

"Pretty old. I love old cars. My uncle has a 1957 Chevy. Now that's old. They don't build them like that anymore. He works on it all the time. It looks like new. He belongs to a club, you know." He stroked the dashboard. "A Cadillac. This must have set you back a few bucks when it was new."

"It would have had I bought it new."

"I see. It was used when you bought it. That's actually the way to go if you want to save some money. New cars cost too much, and the moment you drive them off the lot you've already lost at least a thousand bucks."

"How do you know all this? Have you ever bought a car?"

"Kids my age don't buy cars." He gave me a shake of his head before he turned the key. For a moment I thought the car might actually start, but then all the gauges started flashing again. He let go of the key and nodded. "Yep, like I figured. It's your battery." He slipped back outside.

"What makes you think it's the battery? The car started fine this morning."

"Well, I guess you drained it while driving." He wiggled on the terminals of the battery. "They look okay." He gave me a sharp look. "Did you listen to your radio or play CD's?"

I laughed. "Son, this is an old car. CD players were not standard equipment in 1997. You were lucky to get a cassette player."

"What's a cassette player?"

"I thought you knew everything?"

"I'm only twelve, Mister. When I'm as old as you I'll know everything." He touched a few things on the motor, pulled on some wires.

"Maybe you shouldn't touch anything," I warned him. "You might hurt yourself."

"I won't. By the way, I think I may have found your problem." He pulled on one of the wires. "Was this wire always dangling around like this?"

I shrugged. "How would I know?"

"Geez, you sure are not too smart," he said. He crawled on top of the engine and fiddled around. With a satisfied little grunt he slid off the motor. "I believe I fixed it. That was your connection to the alternator. It came loose somehow. I pushed it back in."

"You pushed it back in," I repeated like a dumb parrot. "How the heck can you be so sure that's where that wire belongs? You can't just push wires into places where you think they should go. You may have screwed up even more."

There was nothing but pity in his narrow face. "My uncle is a mechanic. He knows everything about cars. He taught me a lot. I'll be a mechanic once I'm old enough."

"Is it safe to start the car now?" I asked.

"It would be if you had a full battery. Because of the loose wire the alternator didn't charge the battery. Now the battery is pretty much dead. It needs to be charged. That'll happen when you drive."

"Sounds so simple when you say it, but there is only one problem—how do I get the car to drive?"

He lifted his thin shoulders. "You'll need a boost or a tow truck."

"They'll charge a lot of money. I can't afford that."

"I kinda figured that too," he said. "Do you have a cell phone?"

"I do."

"Give it to me. I'll call my uncle. He'll give you a boost."

"How much does he charge?"

"If I ask him he'll charge you nothing. He's that kind of a guy."

"I can't believe that. Nobody works for nothing. There has to be a catch." As a detective, I'm not only curious by nature, but also suspicious of people who offer me something for free. Nothing is ever free.

"No catch. He believes in the principle of paying it forward, just like my dad did. You've heard of that?"

"Of course I have. It may work for some people, but most people don't believe in it."

"That's because most people don't want to do something nice for others. It works if you believe others will follow through. You must have faith in people, Mister."

"It's Canon, but you can call me Lews. What's your name?"

"I'm Billy Brandon, but I won't call you by your first name. That's not polite and shows no respect for a young kid like me to call an older man like you by his first name. I'll call you *Mister* Canon."

"That's okay, but I don't consider myself an old man. Anyway, Billy Brandon, you seem to be a smart, honest kid, and I've decided to trust you." I handed him my cell phone. "Here. Now don't run away with my phone. Call your uncle."

Billy rolled his eyes, and then he made the call.

His uncle pulled up in his tow truck within fifteen minutes after Billy called him. He was a big man, with a bit of a potbelly and a wild beard. Looking at Billy first and then at me, he said, "This little rascal tells me you've got yourself a bit of a problem with that car of yours."

"Battery is dead, according to Billy here."

"Well, if he says it's dead then it is so," he said. "He's a smart boy. Goes after his uncle." He laughed. "That's me. I'm Brandon Brandon, Jr. Most people call me Brand. My close friends call me Brandy. My pappy used to call me Junior."

I stared at him, ready to burst out laughing. "Brandon Brandon?" I repeated.

He must have seen it in my face. I've never been a good actor. "That's right. Something funny or wrong with that name?"

"Oh, hell, no. It's as good a name as any. I just wondered what your father's name was."

"I don't know why you want to know my pappy's name, but there is no harm in telling you. His name was Brandon Brandon, Sr."

"I thought so. By the way, my name is Lews Canon. Lews Bullseye Canon."

"No shit. Pardon me for saying so, but why would a man with Canon as his last name christen his son *Loose*? And Bullseye? Whoever heard of a name like *Bullseye*?"

"It was my grandfather's name." I smiled. "It seems you and I are sort of related in a way."

He tilted his head and looked at me with narrowed eyes. "How'd you figure that?"

"You know—*Lews Bullseye Canon* and *Brandon Brandon*? Makes you think, doesn't it?"

Shaking his head, he said, "I don't really see a connection there, especially since you being white and me black." He chuckled. "Bullseye. Loose. No parents should give a kid names like that. What's the world coming to?" He peered at me. "What's with your eyes? One blue and one brown. You wearing contact lenses?"

I sighed a little. "No contact lenses. They're natural."

He chuckled to himself. "No sir, we ain't related. Ain't nobody in my family with eyes like that. They don't look natural to me. Kinda creepy, if you ask me. No offense. Anyway, what is the problem with the car again?"

"Won't start. Dead battery."

"Oh, that's right. Dead battery. Don't worry; we'll get you going in no time." He rummaged around in his toolbox and pulled out a pair of long jumper cables. Handing me one end of each cable, he said, "Attach these to your battery's terminals. Make sure you don't get the polarity screwed up. Then we'll give her a boost."

It may be difficult for some people to believe, especially a mechanic or car enthusiast, but I'd never boosted a car before and had no idea what to do. I didn't want to appear like some kind of moron, so I pretended I knew what he was talking about. One of the huge clamps was red, and I guessed that had to be the plus side. I attached it to the terminal with the plus sign on it and the other clamp onto the remaining terminal. Billy, who stood beside me, supervising, removed the clamp from the negative terminal and clamped it against the frame of the car.

"You have a lot to learn, Mr. Cannon," he whispered to me so only I could hear.

"Go start the engine," his uncle told me.

I got into my car and turned the key. When the engine sprang to life I was as ecstatic as a TV-evangelist after receiving his first pledge. No flashing lights, just the rumbling of the motor. What a lovely sound.

When I climbed out of the car, Billy had already removed the booster cables from my battery. He winked at me. "I told you it was the battery. You should be okay. Just don't shut off the engine too soon. Let it charge up the battery."

Brandon must have been listening. He chuckled. "You'll make a fine mechanic someday, Billy. I'm proud of you." Turning to me, he said, "Too bad my brother isn't alive anymore. His head would be swollen with pride."

"What happened to your brother?"

"He was killed last year. Murdered, actually. They never found his murderers and the cops did nothin'."

"Why not?"

He shrugged. "Who cares about another dead nigger? I guess had my brother been white and somebody important, things woulda been different. No offence to you, Lews. That's just the way the system works. They told us to hire a private investigator. We can't afford that. Private investigators are expensive."

"They need to eat, too," I said, defending my profession.

"Everybody needs to eat but not steak every night in a fancy restaurant."

"Is that what you think PIs do? Eat steak every night? You may be surprised."

He eyed me curiously. "Why, you know a PI?"

"You might say so."

He rolled up the jumper cables and stored them away again. Looking back at me, he said, "It don't really matter. My sister-in-law hasn't got the money to hire one and neither do I." He held out his hand. "Well, good luck with that car, Lews Bullseye Canon. You should have her checked out some time. The engine runs not badly. May need a bit of fine-tuning, though."

"I think that piece of junk needs more than a bit of tweaking," I commented and shook his hand. "It never fails, when I need that car the most it decides to strike. Like the labor unions. By the way, how much do I owe you?"

He let go of my hand and waved it off. "You owe me nothin'. I don't mind helpin' people out when they're in trouble." He grinned. "Perhaps the Good Lord will smile kindly upon me when he decides to call me home." Looking up into the sky, he said, "Not too soon, I hope. I got a lotta livin' still to do."

"You'll get your special place in Heaven," I said, even though I wasn't exactly a believer. "You're a good man with a big heart. There aren't many like you left who'd to this for a stranger. Thank you so much." I hesitated, not really enthusiastic about what I was going to say, but something compelled me. "Perhaps I can do something for you, I mean for you and your sister-in-law." I looked at Billy. "And for him. A boy needs to know the truth about his father."

"What are you talking about?" Brandon gave me a puzzled look.

"I might be able to find out what happened to your brother." There! I'd said it. Now I was committed.

"That PI you know?"

I nodded. "I'm that PI. That's my job. In fact, I'm on a case right now."

He was still giving me that puzzled look, laced with an expression of disbelief. "You wouldn't be pullin' my leg, would you now?"

I lifted both hands. "I'm telling you the truth. Wait..." I reached into my pocket and pulled out a crumpled card. "Here is my business card."

He took it from me and smoothed it out. "Canon Detective Agency. Private Investigators. No job too big or too small. Call...." He stared at me. "I'll be damned. You're a Dick. Who would have thought? I mean—with those eyes and a name like yours and bein' so ignorant about cars..." His eyes narrowed. "How much would you charge us for that?"

Well, here we go. There was no turning back now. "Since you helped me out of a jam, it would be my honor to do it for free." My gaze rested again on Billy. "For you and young Billy here."

Brandon took off his cap and scratched his bald head. "This sounds too good to be true. It's like a miracle." Slapping the cap back onto his head, he pulled out a big handkerchief and blew his nose noisily. I had no idea people still used those. He shoved it into his pocket again. I didn't want to think about the germ factory in that pocket. "You know, just last Sunday in church when I was lookin' at Jesus on the cross, I saw my brother's face, right on top of the face of Jesus. He smiled and nodded to me. Now I'm sure I wasn't imagining things. That was a sign. The Good Lord sure works in mysterious ways." He grabbed my hand and pumped it enthusiastically. "You do this for us and I'll fix your car for free, Mr. Canon."

I felt suddenly embarrassed seeing such a big man so emotional and I felt like crying myself. "That's not really..." I stopped talking. What the hell was I doing? I've never done a job for free in my career as a detective, and here I had committed myself to what looked like a problem case. If he offered to fix my car for free, I'd be an idiot to turn it down. At least I'd get something out of it. Mechanics weren't cheap, either. This was a stroke of luck, a gift. If I were a religious man I might have waved my arms in the air shouting, *Hallelujah*.

Fortunately, he hadn't heard my near blunder. "I would really appreciate that," I said. "And, please, don't call me *Mister* Canon. It's Lews to my friends." I cleared my throat. "I need to know everything about your brother. A picture would help. Perhaps you can come by my office and we can discuss everything in detail." I pointed at the card still in his hand. "You have my number. Give me a call and we'll set up an appointment."

"I could swing by tomorrow, if that's all right." He seemed suddenly eager.

"Tomorrow would be fine," I told him. "Ten a.m. okay with you?"

"Ten is okay. I'll be there." He climbed into his tow truck. Watching him drive off, I wondered what I had gotten myself into. Now I needed to do some explaining to Nelda. She wouldn't be overly excited. We couldn't really afford to do pro bono jobs. They didn't pay the rent and didn't put food on the table.

I had forgotten about Billy. He was still standing on the sidewalk waiting for me to drive away, I guess.

I gave him a little wave and pulled away from the curb. He waved back and ran across the street. I could see him in my rearview mirror. It seemed he was heading for the beauty salon Julia Titman had left a while ago.

TWO

IT DIDN'T COME as a great surprise when Nelda told me she wasn't happy with the new case. "We can't afford to work for free, Lews. The rent for the office is due in a couple of days and our account is empty," she said, favoring me with one of her icy stares.

Shivering, I asked, "How old are you, Nelda?"

"What kind of stupid question is that? You know how old I am."

"I do, but I want you to say it."

"Why?"

"Just humor me."

She let out an exaggerated sigh. "Today I'm still twenty, but, in case you have forgotten, tomorrow is my birthday. And why would you bring up my age right now?"

"Because a young woman like you should not worry about money. You should go out having fun with other girls your age, or, maybe even better, a handsome man who has money."

Her eyes were like two buttons of glacier ice. "You know, Lews, you are quite something. First of all, I don't have any girlfriends, and secondly, how can I have fun when I don't have any money? As for a handsome man with money? Handsome men don't go out with a girl like me. If they did I'd wonder what was wrong with them."

I have a tendency of putting my foot into my mouth more often than not. I need to learn to keep my mouth shut before letting the wrong words escape. "You could look for an older gentleman. There must be a desperate old guy out there somewhere."

I didn't think it was possible, but a glacier couldn't be colder than those eyes of hers. "If you weren't my father's best friend and my partner, you'd be gagging on your balls right now, Mister. You sure know how to hurt a girl with your words. A desperate old guy—really? What makes you think I'd want an old guy? You should have become a columnist for one of those gossip-rags."

"Look who's talking. You're the one with the sharp tongue, young lady. Besides, you read too much into what I say," I protested, trying to smooth things over, but I knew the damage had been done.

"Perhaps you should listen to yourself talking sometimes. Record everything you say during the day the way you do with your clients. You may just be shocked to hear what comes out of your mouth at the most inappropriate occasions. Especially after you've had a few drinks. Have you been at it already this morning?"

I lifted my right hand. "Not one drop, I swear."

"Still a hangover from last night?"

"Nope. Didn't go anywhere."

"You could have fooled me. You've been slurring your words. By the way, how is it going with Mr. Titman's case?"

I shrugged my shoulders. "Not so good, I must admit. Things were starting to fall into place until that damn car of mine went on strike. That's how I got our new case."

She waggled one of her thick fingers slowly back and forth as if she were trying to hypnotize me. "Not *our* case—*your* case. I won't be getting any benefits from that one."

"Not directly, but there'll be fringe benefits, even for you. These days it's almost a necessity to have a good friend who is a mechanic."

"He is not your friend. He's a client. Don't forget that. Try to get as much out of him as you can."

"Not everything is about money, Nelda."

"Easy talk when you have it. We don't have any."

"Why would you say such a thing?" With a patronizing expression on my face—at least I hoped it was patronizing—I took out my wallet and removed the check Titman gave me. I handed it to her.

"Two thousand bucks?" I could have sworn there was a tiny spark of warmth in her blue eyes when she looked at me. "Are you telling me you actually asked for a retainer? That's a first."

"Mr. Titman insisted I take it. I think he was afraid I might turn him down. He's really concerned about finding out if his wife is cheating or not."

"Does it really matter if she does? That old goat should consider himself lucky to be married to a gorgeous woman like Julia. He's no prizewinner. Any fool can tell she married him only for his money."

"And that's precisely the reason he wants to know if she is a faithful wife or not. If she isn't she won't get a penny of his money if he divorces her."

Nelda laughed. I was always amazed how such a lovely sound could be produced by someone like her. "He'd be a fool to divorce her. He'll never find another woman with her looks."

"I'm not saying you're wrong with that statement. She is gorgeous," I agreed.

"Just don't get any ideas." Her sweet voice had somehow taken on a slight edge.

"Now I'm hurt. I've never been involved with a client. I know better than that. And you should know I never do."

"There is always a first. That woman could be your downfall. How are things between you and Sonya?"

"Things are fine between us. Why bring her into the picture?"

"You should marry her. You're not getting any younger, Lews."

"Come on, forty-one isn't old. I'm in my prime. Besides, I'm not really husband material; I found that out the painful way."

"No man really is until he gets married. His wife makes one out of him." She grimaced. "At least that's what I've been told. I'll probably never experience the pleasure of molding a man."

I made a sound that was supposed to signal my disgust, but it sounded like someone blowing his nose. "You don't have to be married to a man to try to mold him. You're doing it with me."

"It's because you need some tweaking here and there."

"I'm perfectly happy with the way I am," I said. "Why do women seem to think they can shape and control a man? I'm not a piece of dough a woman can knead into a loaf of bread."

She laughed. "Where do you find these strange expressions?"

"In my head." I glanced at my wristwatch. "Listen, Mr. Brandon is going to be here at ten o'clock. It's nine-thirty now. I know you're not interested in the case, but perhaps you can do me a favor and listen in. Make notes if you want."

"What for? Won't you be recording your interview?"

"Of course I will, but you may pick up on things. You're good at that. You know—things he says but doesn't really say. You may even want to ask your own questions."

She shrugged. "Sure. Why not? I don't have anything else to do anyway. Mind you, I could go shopping now that we have a little bit of money. My fridge needs stocking up."

"You can go shopping tomorrow."

She pulled her eyebrows together in a deep frown. I wished she wouldn't do that. It made her look like some kind of female ogre ready to smash something heavy onto someone's head—mine, in this case. Luckily, she didn't have a baseball bat or a length of pipe. She might just follow up on that. Of course, her fists were large enough for a good bang. "On my birthday? You want me to go shopping on my birthday?"

"What better day than your birthday. Buy yourself a small present. That should cheer you up."

"Why would I want to cheer up? Do I look like I need cheering up?"

"Never mind. You do what you want. Go shopping, don't go shopping. I'm not your keeper. Sometimes you act like a little child. An overgrown little child, mind you, but still a child." I walked over to the window when I heard a car door slam shut. "Here is Mr. Brandon now. He's not alone. He brought somebody with him."

Nelda joined me by the window. "Is that his wife?"

"How would I know? I've never met her." I made shooing motions. "Go, sit down behind the desk and pretend you're busy. I want to make a good impression."

"What for? He's not a paying client."

"But he may lead to one. You never know. That's how the universe works. Things are connected, you know. One thing leads to another."

Shaking her head in disbelief, she went over to sit behind her desk. "You should stop reading those weird books, Lews. They're making you say and do strange things. And that stuff about making a good impression? Have you looked around our office lately?"

When I heard the knock on the door, I went and opened it. "There you are, Brandon," I said brightly. "Right on time."

Actually, he was early, but that didn't matter.

He grinned and walked into the room. The woman accompanying him followed him slowly. At first, I thought she was white with a bit of a tan, but then I noticed certain characteristics proclaiming her of mixed color. I also noticed that she was quite beautiful. Her black hair fell in gentle waves past her shoulders and she carried her slim body proudly. She stopped when she saw Nelda sitting behind the desk, her dark eyes widened for a quick moment, but then she looked at me and said, "You must be Mr. Canon. I'm Shirley, Brandon's sister-in-law."

I shook her hand. "You're Billy's mother, I assume?"

She nodded.

"He helped me with my car. He's a bright young boy."

"That he is. Sometimes he sticks his nose into things he shouldn't, though. Not everybody's problem is his to solve, but he thinks it is."

"I'm glad he stuck his nose into my problem." I chuckled. "Who knows, without him I may still be standing beside my car, staring at the engine and wondering how I was going to get it started."

"He told me about you," she said, giving me a quick smile.

"I hope it wasn't all bad. He didn't think too much of my ability when it came to handling a car. I admit I've never had much interest in cars and most gadgets that have a motor. As long as I know where the buttons are that get them going I'm satisfied."

"Don't feel bad, I'm not really much of a mechanic, either," she said, looking at Brandon, Jr. "I don't have to be. I leave that up to Brandon."

"But you're a woman. You can get away with that. Men are supposed to know about cars."

"If everyone would be knowledgeable about cars I'd soon be out of business," Brandon said. "We need ignorant people like you."

With reluctance, I moved my attention away from admiring Shirley and turned to Brandon. "You'll get no competition from me; I can assure you of that." I clapped my hands together and made rubbing motions. "Well, I guess we should get to the business at hand. Did you bring me some documentation about your brother?"

"I brought a couple of pictures," Shirley said. Her expression changed suddenly from happy to gloomy. "I'm really grateful that you are going to look into my husband's murder, Mr. Canon. I've had no help from the police department."

"First of all, call me Lews. Secondly, perhaps we should all get a bit more comfortable." I pointed to the old couch in the corner. "Sit over there, please." I grinned sheepishly. "The couch is a bit lumpy, but it's sturdy. It's had its share of fat—I mean weight-challenged—clients sitting on it." Realizing what I had said, I reached out to touch Brandon's arm. "I didn't mean to imply you're in that category. It's just a general observation."

"That's okay, Lews. I've got a thick skin." He grinned. "I realize I'm not exactly a featherweight."

"I'm glad to hear you saying that. Some people are self-conscious about being heavier than regular, normal folks."

I glanced over at Nelda, who sat in her chair behind the desk, smirking and rolling her eyes. It wasn't difficult to imagine what she was thinking.

Shut up, Lews Canon, before more of these compliments come out of your mouth!

"By the way, that over there, behind the desk, acting busy, is my secretary, Nelda. She'll be sitting in as an observer, just to make sure we don't miss any important information."

"Hi, Nelda," Brandon said, lifting a hand as if he was going to wave, but then he moved it to his beard and tried to smooth it out with his fingers. "I'm Brandon Brandon, Jr."

"I know," Nelda said. "Mr. Canon, my wonderful boss, filled me in about your case. You're in good hands with Mr. Canon. He's the best."

"Good to hear. I hope he's a better investigator than he is an auto-mechanic," Brandon said, obviously thinking it was funny, because he laughed so hard his belly shook.

Nelda joined his laughter, clearly enjoying herself. "He's a dud when it comes to motorized vehicles, but as far as investigating goes, he's the man to get."

"How about murder cases?"

Making a wavy motion with one hand, she said, "I'm not sure about murder cases. I've only been with him since 2011. Most of his cases involve cheating wives. He's dedicated and will spend hours watching them make out in the backseat of a car or looking through an open window into a hotel room."

Thanks, Tusnelda!

Brandon looked at me. "Have you ever handled a murder case?"

"Let's not worry about whether or not I've had a murder case before. That's just a minor detail. Now, please, have a seat." There was no need for me to explain that there had been no murder cases during the few years I ran my own agency, but in my days as a cop I'd seen too many of them. None of them pretty or exciting.

Shirley was the first one to sit down.

"Oops," she said as she sank into the soft cushion. "I hope I can get out of this again." She chuckled. "I may just need some help." She crossed her legs delicately, exposing quite a bit of her naked thighs. Her skirt moved up to show even more bare skin. She smoothed out the thin material of her skirt and put her handbag into her lap. Opening it, she removed a couple of pictures and laid them onto the low table in front of her. "Here are the best pictures I could find."

Brandon took the seat beside her in the meantime. Lowering his bulk carefully into the cushion, he looked expectantly at me. "You're still willing to find out who murdered my brother, aren't you?"

"I promised I would. I never break a promise." I took the wooden chair and moved it so I would face them. Reaching for the two pictures, I studied them carefully. They showed a black man in a suit and tie, wearing a hat. He didn't look at all like his brother. Slim and trim, sporting a thin mustache, he almost looked old-fashioned.

"He liked to dress nice," Shirley said, watching me.

"Yeah, he was some kind of a snappy dresser," Brandon said with a little chuckle. "Didn't like to get his hands dirty. Sometimes I wondered if he was adopted or something. Come to think of it, he could have been related to you, Lews, excepten him being black and you white, of course. And those eyes of yours. Wasn't much interested in cars, either. Unlike Billy. One would never think Billy was Bart's son."

Shirley pulled out a tissue and wiped her nose. "He was a good guy and loved life. Loved to have fun, too."

"How did he die?" I asked. Perhaps a little bit abruptly, but it needed to come up eventually.

"He was stabbed," Brandon said.

"Stabbed? Where and exactly how did it happen?"

"It was late at night. He was waiting to catch his bus. That's all we know. Nobody saw or heard nothin'—apparently." Brandon sounded bitter and angry. "A couple of nurses found him shortly after midnight. He was already dead, lying in a pool of his own blood. They called it in. The cops didn't even search the area for clues. They told us nothin' could be done."

"Was he robbed?"

"He still had his wallet and driver's license. His wallet was empty. The money was gone, but not his credit cards. They didn't take those."

"So it could have been robbery."

"That's what the cops say. I don't believe it. Robbers would have taken his watch and his ring. And the golden cross he wore around his neck. Possibly his credit cards, too." Brandon let out a disgusted sound. "No, siree, it wasn't no robbery. He was murdered."

"What about debts? Did he owe anyone money?" I looked at Shirley.

She shook her head. "Just the usual stuff. Mortgage and credit cards. He never borrowed money from anyone."

"Did he gamble?"

"Oh no. He was much too stingy for that. Didn't like to lose money. He was no gambler."

"What did he do for a living? I assume he had a job."

"He worked for the Lucky Millionaire's Casino as a dealer." She chuckled. "Which is kinda funny, since he didn't believe in gambling."

"That *is* funny." I smiled. "I have to ask this, so don't take it the wrong way. Did he have a drinking problem?"

"Never touched alcohol. Didn't do drugs, either."

"It looks like he was quite a solid guy." Too solid if you ask me. I wondered what he did for fun. A guy has to have some type of vice; otherwise, what's the sense of living?

"He liked to read," Brandon said, as if he'd been reading my mind. "Books. He had a room full of books. Like some kind of professor."

"Yes, he loved his books." Shirley sighed. "That's where he spent his money. He didn't care much for those electronic readers. He needed to hold a real book in his hands."

"Actually so do I," I admitted. I didn't tell them that I couldn't afford one of those expensive readers. There were too many other expenses to take care of. "Nobody carried a grudge from earlier times? No old enemies?"

"None I can think of. He was well-liked by everyone. One could say he was a model citizen." Brandon laughed softly. "Even filed and paid his taxes always on time."

I grinned. "That is commendable." I leaned back in my chair, searching for the right words. I didn't want to discourage them, but at the same time I didn't want to give them too much hope. "In one way, it is too bad so much time has passed since the incident. It makes the case a bit more difficult."

"Are you telling us you won't be able to investigate it?" Shirley sounded disappointed.

"That's not what I'm saying. I promised and I will look into the case, just don't expect miracles. It may take a while. There isn't really much to go on."

Shirley looked at her brother-in-law. "Maybe we should tell him."

"Tell me what?" I asked, curious what they were holding back.

"I don't think it's important," Brandon said.

"Everything is important," I told him. "The tiniest bit of information could make or break a case." I looked from him to Shirley.

"Well, about a week before Bart got murdered, he witnessed something in the back lane behind the casino. He was struggling with his conscience if he should go to the cops or not. He wasn't fond of cops."

I got suddenly curious and just a little bit excited. Perhaps this might be the piece of important information that could put me on the right track, because so far I had no idea where I should begin with my investigation. "What did he witness?"

"A murder."

"A murder?" I repeated. "And you didn't think that was important?"

"Bart never did go to the cops and neither did I. I was afraid I might get into trouble since Bart had told me about it and I didn't mention it to the cops after his murder." She looked suddenly scared as if she had told me too much already.

"Your husband was the one who should have but didn't report the incident to the police. They can't charge you with anything."

"That's not what Mr. Titman said."

A shiver ran down my spine. I had to make sure I heard right. "Who's Mr. Titman?"

"Bart's boss. Well—ex-boss. Mr. Titman owns the Lucky Millionaire's Casino."

I turned my head to look at Nelda to see her reaction. She returned my look but didn't say anything. Instead, she opened the file she had on the desk and removed a picture. Getting out of her chair, she handed the picture to Shirley.

Shirley's eyes grew large when she saw the picture. "That's Julia Titman. Mr. Titman's wife. I just saw her yesterday in my salon." Her eyes searched mine. "I don't understand. Why would you have her picture? Is she one of your clients?"

"Sorry, but I can't tell you that. Did you say she was in your salon?"

"Yes."

"Are you working in that beauty salon on Fifth?"

She nodded. "I'm renting the building from Mr. Titman and he has a share in the salon."

I had to take a few minutes to digest all this new information. There was more going on here than what it looked like on the surface. This was one of those strange apparent coincidences that happened once in a while. Mr. Titman owned a casino and part of a beauty salon. I wondered what other properties he might own. According to the information he gave me, he was a simple stock broker. His only interests his stocks and the whereabouts of his wife.

"You're saying Mr. Titman was your husband's boss, right? Did he know about the stabbing that happened behind his casino?"

"Bart told him about what he thought he saw and wondered if he should report it to the police. Mr. Titman warned him not to mention anything to anyone, especially not the cops. He said he didn't need any bad publicity. He suggested Bart must have been mistaken when he thought he recognized the men who did the stabbing. If a stabbing actually occurred. There might just have been only a scuffle between a bunch of drunks. It was too dark in the back lane to make out faces and details. He also warned Bart to be careful giving false testimony by accusing innocent men of murder. It could have serious consequences."

"Serious consequences? Hmm. Makes me wonder. Did you talk to Mr. Titman about the incident?"

"After Bart's murder I called Mr. Titman and asked him for advice. I wanted to know if I should go to the cops with what Bart told me. He advised me also against going to the cops. It would only get me into trouble with the law. They might even charge me with withholding evidence, which is a serious crime. He asked if Bart had told me any details about the apparent stabbing he thought he witnessed. I said no he didn't. Mr. Titman said it would be best if I just forgot the whole thing."

"I find that interesting. By the way, did your husband tell you anything about what he saw?"

She hesitated, but then she shrugged. "It will do no harm now to tell you everything. Bart said that he watched a couple of guys he'd seen before stab a man several times. Then they threw the body into a dumpster. There was plenty of light in the back lane for him to make out details."

"Did your husband by any chance describe the men who he allegedly saw stabbing a man to death?"

"He didn't describe them, but he told me the name of one of them."

"Do you recall his name?"

She looked at Brandon. When he nodded, she said, "His name is Harry Rosser, and I know him quite well. He comes to the salon the odd time to get his hair cut. He never pays. Doesn't even leave a tip. Always says to charge it to Mr. Titman's account. Mr. Titman doesn't have an account. He is my landlord and has a stake in the salon, that's all. I never get paid for his wife's treatments, either."

"Did you ever ask Mr. Titman for money?"

"Only in the beginning. He just laughed and said he's giving me a deal on the rent and the percentage. I should be happy with that."

"Are you?"

"Of course not," she said vehemently. "The building could use some fixing and I figure the percentage is too high. Mr. Titman is not a nice man. He conveys that impression but he isn't."

She was correct. Mr. Titman had given me the impression of being a nice man. It occurred to me that his friendly demeanor and portrayal of a distressed husband may just have been a cover to hide his true nature. This wasn't the first time a client fooled me. I turned to Nelda. "Are you making a note of that?"

"I sure am, Mr. Canon," she said with her sweet voice. "That's what a secretary does."

I threw her an annoyed look. She always called me *Mister Canon* when she was pissed off. I guess I should have introduced her as my partner, but not as my secretary. My mistake. Sometimes I wonder, if making her my partner may not have been one of the smartest things I've done, but it was in many ways cheaper than having her as my employee. I couldn't afford to pay her a steady salary. As a partner she got paid when I did. And it is less trouble with the IRS. She's responsible for her income and her deductions.

Shrugging mentally, I didn't comment. So she was mad at me again. It never lasted long, but if it did I'd have to apologize.

"Is there anything else you may want to add?" I asked Brandon.

He gave a shake of his head. "That pretty much covers it all." He ran his fingers through his beard as if trying to bring some order into the wild curls. Then he dug around in his pocket and retrieved his handkerchief. After blowing his nose noisily, he shoved the handkerchief back into his pocket. "My brother was a good man. He didn't deserve to die such a horrible death. Alone in the middle of the night on a dark street corner. If his killer can be brought to justice that would bring closure. He deserves at least that."

Heaving his large body out of the couch, he held out his hand. "Thanks for doing this, Lews. You bring in that car of yours anytime and I'll get her in shape again. That's the least I can do."

I shook his hand, reminding myself to visit the bathroom as soon as he was gone and scrub my hands with soap and disinfectant. Usually, I'm not this sensitive, but I couldn't get the vision of all those germs living in Brandon's pocket out of my mind.

Shirley was struggling to escape the soft grip of those deep cushions. I tried not to stare at her naked thighs as her skirt moved up again. I couldn't help but notice their smoothness and nice shape. It wasn't hard to imagine the rest of her slim body. Suddenly I felt the strong desire to visit my lady friend Sonya.

Tearing my gaze away, I also rose to my feet. "Thanks for coming in," I said. "I'll be in touch."

Before they walked out, Brandon handed me a card. "My business card. Come by the shop and I'll look after you."

THREE

THE LOUNGE at The Dancing Leprechaun was packed at this time of night. Even though everyone these days complained about the economy, the lack of jobs, and how they struggled to make ends meet, they seemed to have enough money to go out to a restaurant for dinner or just have a drink at the bar.

The only reason I went there was Sonya McKinnon and the fact that the place was across from my office. I didn't have to use my car and if I had one too many drinks, which happened to be most of the time, I could always walk back to the office and sleep it off on the couch. The one with the soft cushions, but when you're drunk you can sleep anywhere. I usually wake up with a sore back. I promised myself a long time ago to replace that thing, but there never seemed to be any money left at the end of the month to buy another couch.

The music was blaring, as usual. One would expect soft Celtic music in a bar with the word *leprechaun* in its name, but that wasn't the case. They should have named the place *The Eardrum Buster*. It would have been much more appropriate. Most of the time I walked out of there with my ears ringing. Sometimes I stuffed pieces of tissue paper into my ears. It helped a little. How Sonya could stand working with that noise was beyond me. Actually, it was beyond me how anyone could spend more than ten minutes in there without getting a headache. But, according to Sonya, the music was only this loud in the evening when the young crowd came to dance.

I managed to find an empty stool by the bar. Sonya must have expected me, because she came over immediately when she saw me. Touching my hand in an intimate gesture, she said, "Hi, Lews. Haven't seen you for a few days. I've missed you. I was beginning to wonder if you were trying to avoid me."

"I would never do that," I told her. "You're the only person who can cheer me up."

She favored me with her most beautiful smile. She should have been a model instead of tending bar in a rundown nightclub. Of course, then I would never have gotten to know her. What famous model wants to waste her time with a guy like me? I'm not rich like Mr. Titman. "That's nice to hear," she said. "Why do you need cheering up?"

"I've started a new case and I've come into new information about another one. I'm afraid some of it may not be good."

"Well, I've got just the right recipe for cheering you up." She winked. "But I'm not getting off for another hour or so. Can I bring you something to tide you over?"

"Sure. The usual but make it a double. And then bring me a beer."

She patted my hand. "Coming up."

She went to get a bottle of Jack Daniels from the shelf. Watching her slender body move with the grace of a gazelle, I admired the shape of her buttocks. They filled out those tight slacks she wore quite nicely. I couldn't wait for her shift to end. After pouring a double into a tall shot glass she filled another glass from the beer tap and brought over both. "Enjoy. Now I'd better look after my other customers."

She moved away but not before she blew me a quick kiss.

"Your wife has a nice ass," a voice said beside me.

I turned to look at the speaker. He was short and fat with a round, friendly face. Giving me a broad grin, he lifted his glass. "Here's to nice asses."

"She isn't my wife," I told him. "But you're right. She does have a nice ass." I should have been annoyed by his remark, but somehow it didn't bother me. After all, Sonya wasn't my wife. If a guy wanted to admire her ass, why not? One thing was sure—she'd be going home with me and not with him.

"You two an item?"

"We go out sometimes."

"You should marry her," my new friend said.

"Why?"

He made stabbing motions with his finger in Sonya's direction. "A woman with a nice ass like that doesn't come along every day." He took a swig from his beer. "Yessirie, not every day. Hell, I've never had a woman with an ass like that. She's got a nice body, too." He gave me a sidelong glance. "You want another beer?"

"Thanks for the offer, but I haven't finished mine yet."

"That's okay. I can wait. I got nothing else to do anyway."

I don't always talk to every stranger at the bar, but somehow I felt like talking. Noticing the ring on his finger, I said, "Do you have a wife waiting for you at home?"

"I'm sure she's waiting." He chuckled into his glass. "She can't wait for me to come home to tell me what a loser I am."

"That's cruel. No wife should say that to her husband. Not good for a man's self-esteem. What do you do for a living?"

"I sell alarm systems." He peered at me out of bleary eyes. "Do you have an alarm system, Mr...?"

"It's Canon. Lews Canon. I can't afford one."

"Nonsense." He slapped his hand onto the counter top. "Nobody should be without an alarm system. Tell you what—I'll make you a good deal." He hiccupped, and grinned. "I can do that, you know, because I own the whole damn company." Then he took another swallow from his beer. Staring at me over the rim of the glass, he said, "There are plenty of criminals just waiting to break into people's homes. An alarm system is a must. A big, huge must." His words came out a bit slurred and I could tell he had already one too many glasses of beer. Perhaps even more than one. "I've been in the alarm business for nearly twenty years. *NWAS*. It stands for *No Worry Alarm Systems*. That's my company. *Burglars grab your stuff, we grab them*. That's our motto."

"Do you have an alarm in your home?" I asked.

"I live in an apartment." He chuckled as he seemed to think of something funny. "It's a huge apartment. I bought it to make my wife happy. Not that it helped any. My wife has a dog. One of those ugly ones with the punched-in face. That's our alarm system. You have a dog?"

I shook my head. "Never cared much for dogs. I'm more of a cat person."

"You have a cat?"

"No. I just like them."

He nodded solemnly. "I think I like cats, too. They're graceful and they don't bark. What was your name again?"

"Lews Canon." I finished the last of my beer and managed to catch Sonya's attention. I pointed at my empty glass. She nodded and held up her hand, fingers spread, which meant *give me five minutes*.

"Hey, your glass is empty," my neighbor said. "Time for another one."

"I already ordered."

"That one's on me; don't forget. You know, I like you. You seem like an upstanding guy. Good guys are like nice women—not easy to find, but when you find them you hang onto them." He stumbled over his words. Emptying his glass, he set it onto the counter. "Might as well order one for me. A man should never drink alone."

When Sonya came over with my beer, I said, "Bring another one for my friend here."

She gave me a strange look. "Your friend?" she asked.

"Yes." I grinned. "We haven't known each other for long. Actually, we just met."

She bent and put her lips to my ear. "Do you know who this guy is?" she whispered.

I shook my head. "Can't say I do," I said, keeping my voice low.

"His name is Benny Miller. He's the husband of Angela Steelwood."

That got my complete attention. "You wouldn't be talking about...?"

"The sister of Police Commissioner Steelwood? Yes, I'm talking about her."

"No kidding? *That* Angela Steelwood. Rumors are she has balls of steel. Pardon the pun."

I must have spoken louder than intended, because my so-called new friend said, "The rumors are completely true. She has the balls I'm supposed to have, according to her. Now you know why I spend my evenings at the bar getting drunk."

"Why don't you divorce her if you're so unhappy?" I asked.

"I would if it were that easy. She told me once if I ever tried anything funny, like leaving her, she'd cut off my penis and feed it to me. And I believe her. She's capable of doing exactly that." He reached for the glass Sonya had brought me. "She was married before, you know. Her ex-husband died under mysterious circumstances. Apparently, he slipped in the shower and hit his head against the corner of the tub. He died from head trauma. I think she murdered him. If I could only prove that I'd be free of her."

"Why do you believe your wife murdered her ex-husband?"

"Because she told me once after she had a few glasses of wine how easy it is to kill someone and getting away with it. Accidents in the home happen all the time."

"That's no proof that she actually killed someone. People say the stupidest things sometimes, especially after consuming too much alcohol."

"Not my wife. She's a cold and calculating bitch. I think she was giving me a warning. Did you know that we haven't had sex in five years and rarely before then?"

"I didn't know that." I chuckled. "Besides, it isn't really my business to know about your sex life. Not in your case, anyway."

"What do you mean by that remark? When is it your business?"

"Mostly never. Forget it."

He grabbed my arm. "No, no. I want to know."

"It may be important if you were a client, but you're not. You're a stranger."

"I thought I was your friend. Are you some kind of sex therapist or something? You could be one, you know. You have that look. Hey, you got one brown and one blue eye." He stared into my face.

"I'm a Private Investigator," I said, ignoring his remark about my eyes.

He reached for my glass of beer and drained it. Wiping his mouth with the back of his hand, he tried to focus his eyes on my face. "No shit? A private eye. I'll be..." He snickered. "Which eye do you use? The blue one or the brown one?" He dismissed his remark with the wave of his hand. "Just kidding. What do you investigate? People's sex lives?"

"I do if it's important to the case, but there are other reasons people hire me."

"Like what?"

"Missing relatives, cheating husbands or wives, finding deadbeat husbands, looking into murder cases, and other stuff like that."

"You said you investigate murders? Like old, unsolved murders?"

"That's right, but not too often." I had a feeling I suddenly knew where this was going and I wasn't wild about it. I wished I had that beer Miller drank. When I turned to Sonya to order one she was gone, busy serving other customers.

She must have sensed my desperation, for she turned to look in my direction. I lifted the empty glass and she nodded. Instead of coming over to get mine, she filled a new glass and brought it. Smiling, she put it in front of me and said, "I figured you'd need another one."

"How about me?" Miller slurred.

"Don't you think you had enough, Mr. Miller?" she asked. "I don't want you killing yourself when you drive home."

"Do you really care about my welfare?"

"Yes, I do. I care about all my customers." She smiled. "It's not good for business if they die after leaving here. Besides, repeat customers pay my salary."

Miller turned to me. "I like your woman. She's the only one who seems to worry about me. She's a jewel with a nice ass." He put his hand in front of his mouth. "Oops. I have a feeling I shouldn't have said that. It just came out. Forget I said that." He grinned foolishly.

"I don't mind." Sonya smiled. "I know it was supposed to be a compliment. A bit awkward and crude but still well-meant. Should I call you a taxi to take you home? You can always pick up your car in the morning."

"Maybe later. Right now I need to talk to Mister..." He looked at me. "What's your name again?"

"Canon," I told him.

"Right—Canon. The Dick. I'd like to hire you to investigate my wife. I want you to find out how she murdered her ex."

"That may be difficult to do. How long ago did this happen?"

"Twelve years ago. We've been married ten."

"Twelve years is a long time. It's considered a cold case, if it's a case at all. In addition, your wife is the sister of the Police Commissioner. It may be next to impossible to obtain any information at all."

"Don't you have any connections with the police department? I thought every PI does."

"I have. Sort of." I didn't tell him that I had been a cop for twelve years. Neither did he need to know that Steelwood and I never saw eye to eye. I didn't like him and he didn't like me. His father, Albert Steelwood, the Commissioner at the time, was one of the reasons I left the force. Not exactly voluntarily, I might add.

Miller pulled out his wallet and fished out a twenty. Handing it to me, he said, "I don't want you to do this for nothing. Here's a retainer. Whatever expenses you may incur, I'll pay for them and your time. I've got some money squirreled away in a secret bank account my wife knows nothing about. I'd rather give it to you instead of that bitch should she ever find out about that money. Because if she does, it will be gone, kaput, lost—to me, anyway."

Hesitating only for a moment, I took the twenty-dollar-bill and stuffed it into my pocket. I wasn't going to count the teeth in a gift horse's mouth. If he wanted to part with his money, that was fine by me. "I can't make any promises," I said. "Don't expect miracles."

"I won't. But maybe you can dig up some dirt on her. Something in her past that I can find useful. Anything. I want to nail that two-faced bitch against the cross in the church she's a member of. Pretends to be so religious, but I know better." He smashed his fist onto the countertop, barely missing my glass. "I was never good enough for her. She didn't even take my name when we got married. Wasn't good enough for her, either. A wife should take her husband's last name. That's just descent and respectful. They may do shit like that in those Arabian countries or in Quebec, up there in Canada, but this is America. Here, a woman is supposed to take her husband's last name." He looked at his watch. "I think I'd better head on home. The dragon will be waiting." He slid from his stool and stood in front of me, swaying. It was clear he wasn't in any shape to drive his car home.

"You're not driving, are you?" I asked.

"I came here with my car."

"You were sober then but not anymore. Let Sonya call you a cab, like she suggested. You'll thank her in the morning."

"Okay. You talked me into it. You're a good friend." He took his place again on his vacated stool. "While I'm waiting I'll have another beer."

"Not a good idea. I think you've had enough." I waved Sonya over and told her to call a taxi for Miller.

"Bring a beer for my friend," Miller said to Sonya. He threw five bucks onto the counter. "On me."

The cab came within five minutes. The driver helped Miller outside. Only when he was gone, I remembered he never gave me his address and phone number. Well, it didn't matter. I had his and his company name. I could easily track him down. After all, I was a detective. Finding people was part of my job.

I drank that beer Miller had paid for and then I had another one. By the time Sonya's shift was over I felt pretty good. In fact, I don't even remember when we left the Dancing Leprechaun.

Waking up in the morning, I found myself in Sonya's bed. I had a sour taste in my mouth and there must have been a bunch of construction workers with giant jackhammers in my head competing with each other who could hammer the loudest. I really should stop drinking. The next day was never a good day.

Sonya was already up. She must have heard me moaning when I slipped from the bed. "Good morning, Sleepyhead," she called from the open door. "Better get up. It's past nine o'clock."

"Shit!" I cursed. "Why didn't you wake me earlier?"

"I tried but you were out like a light, so I figured you need the sleep. What's your hurry, anyway?"

"I've got work to do."

"Like what?"

"Detective work. Did you forget what I do for a living?"

She laughed. "You call spying on people detective work? If you ask me, you're a Peeping Tom. Watching couples having sex in their car doesn't seem like honest work to me. But you know my feelings on that."

"Not all my cases involve cheating wives or husbands. It may interest you to know that I have a murder to investigate. Wouldn't you call that honest work?"

"Do you really believe you'll find anything on Angela Steelwood?"

She must have noticed the blank look on my face. "Don't tell me you forgot? You couldn't have been that drunk. Not at the time when you took on Mr. Miller as your client."

"I remember Mr. Miller," I said. "He gave me twenty bucks to investigate his wife." I touched my forehead to see if I had a fever or something. I must have been in some kind of haze when I promised Miller to look into his wife's past. She was the sister of Police Commissioner Allan Steelwood, for heaven's sake! A man who had no love for me. If he found out I was investigating his sister, he'd try his best to pull my license. Or worse, he'd send one of his mobster friends to have me assassinated.

"Well, I'm glad you remember." Her facial expression appeared worried. "You look tired."

"I'm fine, except for my head. Would you have an aspirin or something for my headache?" I asked.

"You'll find a bottle in the medicine cabinet. Go and wash up. I'll fix you breakfast. Do you have time for bacon and eggs?"

"I always have time for a hearty breakfast, especially if you're the one making it for me."

"You're sweet. Hurry up now and get ready. You don't want to eat cold eggs."

I found a bottle of pills and popped a couple. Then I brushed my teeth. This was not the first time I spent a night at Sonya's place and I had my own toothbrush. I don't know if that was of great significance, but somehow I always had the feeling Sonya took that as some kind of commitment.

After getting dressed, I went into the kitchen. Sonya had the table set already and she was just pouring the coffee when I sat down. The aroma of the brewing beans and the smell of bacon lifted my spirits considerably.

"Your eggs are in the oven," she said. "You'll have to get them yourself."

She took the place across from me. Sipping her coffee, she said, "You need a shave."

I rubbed my hand across the stubble on my chin. Even though I have read hair, it's still visible. "It'll have to wait until I get to the office," I said.

"You keep a razor at the office?"

"Sure do. I've spent many nights there on my couch."

"That old thing? You should throw it out and get something better."

"Some day when there is enough money."

She shook her head. "You never seem to have enough money. Have you ever thought about changing your career?"

"It has occurred to me, but I love what I do."

"You're lucky. Unfortunately, what people love doing doesn't always pay well. Artists are a good example. They love what they do, but there is a reason for the expression *Starving Artist*. Most don't make a living with their passion. For them it's just a hobby. They still have day-jobs."

"I'm not an artist. I'm an investigator. I deal with facts not fantasies." I took a sip from the coffee. It was still hot, and that's how I liked it.

"Eat your eggs before they get cold," Sonya said.

I grinned. "You can be such a mother sometimes."

"It's what you need. You'd never get a decent meal if I didn't cook you one." She gave me a thoughtful look. "Actually, you don't need a mother. What you need is a partner."

"I've got one." I knew what she meant and I also knew what was coming. I was surprised she used the word *partner*.

"I'm not talking about a business partner, and don't pretend you don't know what I mean. I'm talking about someone who takes care of you day and night."

"You mean a wife?"

"Well—yes. We don't have to get married if that's what scares you. At least move in with me. We could split the rent and you'd be closer to your office. How can you lose?"

I shoved a piece of bacon into my mouth to give me time thinking of a good answer. It didn't really matter how long I took to mull over her suggestion. It wasn't the first time she'd brought it up. I could never think of an appropriate comeback. Swallowing down the bacon, I stared into my coffee mug. "What other reason besides splitting the rent would you have to ask me to move in with you?" I asked for lack of something better to say.

"What other reason? How about because I love you, you big lug."

"Why?"

"I don't know. I just love you. Why do you need an explanation?"

When I looked up and into her deep-green eyes, I wondered for the umpteenth time what a beautiful woman like her saw in me. It's not that I'm disfigured or some ugly creature crawled out of some deep hole. In fact, I can safely say that I'm quite a handsome guy, if one overlooks my two different colored eyes, and possibly my carrot red hair, which, I think, looks rather good on me. I have a pleasant voice and all my own teeth. I've seen women turn their heads when they pass me. At least, I assume it was because of my good looks. Of course, there are plenty of other good-looking guys out there. Some of them have safer jobs and make tons more money than I'll ever make in my business.

"I still don't see what you find in me that you can't get from other men. Men with money. I'm sure there are plenty out there."

"Money? Is that what you think women look for in a man?"

"A smart woman does."

"Are you saying I'm not smart?"

"Of course you're smart. I would never get involved with a stupid woman." I grinned in an attempt to make light of a dumb remark. You never ever refer to a woman's intellect, even in jest. A smart man knows that. Perhaps that was one of the reasons I shied away from making a commitment. Maybe I was scared I couldn't cope with a woman's moods and always having to weigh every word I said. "That's why I'm wondering why a smart woman like you even shows an interest in an average guy like me."

"Same answer. I love you. Why do you question that, Lews? Accept it already. Maybe I love you because you're kind-hearted and I feel safe with you. You always have a friendly word for everyone you meet. You're a good listener, and..." she smiled, "a hunk in bed. Do you need any other reasons?"

"You make me sound like some kind of saint. I do have a few dark secrets, you know?"

"Like what?" She bent forward as if eager to hear what I had to tell her.

"Well, I snore when I lie on my back."

"I know. In fact, you snored quite a bit last night. What else?"

"I drink too much."

"I know that also. That's one of the reasons you spent the night here instead of driving home."

"I've cheated on my taxes."

"Who hasn't? Tell me something darker than that?"

"When I was eighteen I was secretly engaged to a seventeen-year-old girl. Her name was Nina Klinsky. We were going to run away together."

"So what happened?"

"Her dad found out. He threatened to kill me if I ever came near his daughter again. She was one of the reasons I joined the military shortly after that. I needed to forget about her."

"Wow! You never told me that before. However, nothing dark yet. Did you by any chance get her pregnant?"

"No."

"Did you have sex with her?"

"Yes. I guess we were lucky. I never used protection. Couldn't afford to buy rubbers. I needed all my money just to buy gas for my car."

"Now we're getting there. I have to say, though, neither of you was very smart. Having sex without protection is actually downright stupid."

"We were young and stupid."

"Tell me more."

"About what?"

"Your sex life with Nina Klinsky. Was she your first one?"

"No. My first time was with our neighbor, Mrs. Mahler. I was sixteen."

"Aha. This gets interesting. A married woman. Did her husband find out?"

"Fortunately not. He would have killed me for sure. He was a Marine away on maneuvers. She told me she was lonely." Images of her popped into my head and brought back some steamy memories. She taught me more than a young guy of sixteen had a right to know, things I'd never even heard of before. She showed me how to do it without protection.

Sonya must have seen it in my eyes. "Does she haunt you in your dreams sometimes?"

"I wouldn't exactly call it haunting." I gave her a lopsided grin. "There was nothing bad about my relationship with her."

"Except that she was a married, older woman. Any other secrets I need to know of?"

"Isn't that enough? As you can see, I'm not such a saintly guy after all."

She laughed softly. "It only tells me that you are human and not some cold-blooded, hard-eyed secret agent spying for a foreign country. I love you even more now." Her eyes studied my face. "Tell me something, Lews. And, please, don't give me an evasive answer. Do you love me?"

There was no dodging that question, and, by the look in her eyes, my answer was important to her.

"I do," I told her. It was the truth. I did love her, and she meant more to me than I was ready to admit. Any man would gladly move in with her without thinking about it. Hell, any smart man would marry her on the spot. Women like her were polished jewels in a box full of rocks. She was beautiful, smart, with a body like a Greek goddess. She was kind and a hard worker. She said what needed to be said without making it sound like a whine or unwanted criticism. And she knew when to keep her mouth shut and stop talking, even if she didn't have the last word in a conversation or argument. Actually, I can't remember a day where we actually quarreled over something stupid.

She was married before to a guy who treated her like dirt, beat her and forced her to have sex with other men while he watched. She was practically a slave. Fortunately, for her, he was killed in a car accident, or she may have ended up dead by his hand one day.

Perhaps, she did have a good reason to love me after all. I hate wife-beaters and violence against women at the best of times. I've seen too much of it in my business, as a cop and as a private investigator. Men who beat women and children should be put away for the rest of their lives, as far as I was concerned. They are nothing but cowards who take out their frustration on the weak ones, trying to prove how macho they are.

"That's all I wanted to hear," she said softly. "How's your head?"

"Much better." I looked at my watch. "I'm surprised Nelda hasn't called me yet, wondering where I am."

No sooner did I finish the sentence my cell phone rang. It was Nelda. "Where the hell are you?" She sounded irritated.

"Good morning to you, too, Sunshine," I said.

"Never mind trying to cheer me up. Have you looked outside?"

"Can't say I have."

"Well, it's raining. Are you planning to come in today? It's almost noon."

"Your watch must be fast. Mine says ten thirty."

"Close enough. Are you coming in?"

"What's the big emergency?"

"Mr. Titman is here. Wants to know if you found out something."

"Of course I haven't. Did you tell him these things take time?"

"You come in and tell him so yourself!"

The phone went dead. There were times when I couldn't help but have negative feelings toward Nelda. She was not the ray of sunshine I sometimes needed when I walked into my office. She could be downright miserable. Many times I had to remind myself why she was my partner. But then again, she did have some good qualities. She had a talent for finding out things and she was that voice of caution when I was too quick jumping into something that could prove fatal. And she was loyal and devoted to me, even if she didn't admit it. I've known her since she was a child. Her childhood was rough. Being larger than other girls her age, or, for that matter, any boys, had been her curse.

Her mother died when she was six and her father, a cop like me, never had much time for her. She grew up on the street, fighting and getting into trouble, but deep down, she wasn't a bad person. She had a strong feeling for what was wrong and what was right. Even though she ran with the wrong crowd for a while, she stayed away from drugs and alcohol. When she got out of jail, I asked her if she was interested in working for me. Being a felon with a criminal record, she didn't have much choice, but I think she was quite happy, because she accepted my offer eagerly. She always wanted to become a cop like her dad, but she lost that opportunity when she went to jail. Becoming a detective was the next best thing for her.

"Trouble in Paradise?" Sonya asked.

"Nothing I can't handle. I'd better get to the office, but I need a ride."

FOUR

MR. TITMAN SEEMED AGITATED when I walked in. "Your secretary tells me you haven't found out anything yet about..." he started, but I cut him off.

"Miss Pinetree is not my secretary. She is my partner. What she told you is true, Mr. Titman. She may or may not have mentioned that we have to be patient. Things didn't work out for me when I tried to follow you wife, things I didn't have any control over. My car broke down and I needed a tow truck. One of those bad breaks we sometimes get, but I'm still on it. Perhaps you can give me another location where I might pick up your wife's trail."

"Her trail? Julia isn't some kind of prey you are hunting, Canon. She's my wife." He gave me an almost angry stare. "If you can't handle it I may have to hire someone else."

"Mr. Titman, why this sudden change of heart? As I recall you nearly begged me to take your case and I fit you in. I may have lost another client because I decided to take *you* as my client."

Titman gave me a condescending smile. "I don't think you are overworked with too many cases, Canon. Look around. This place is a dump. A successful detective would be working in a different environment. At least get rid of that couch. A person could get lost in those soft cushions and never be found."

"I can't argue that," I said. "That couch is not my best advertiser. You're not the first one to notice that. Let me ask you a question: Why did you hire me if you have such a low opinion of me?"

"You were recommended. As to by whom? Well, let's say it was a mutual friend."

"I couldn't even guess who that would be. By the way, Mr. Titman, you haven't been quite truthful about yourself."

"I haven't? I have no idea what you are talking about."

"You told me that you are a broker."

"I *am* a broker. That wasn't a lie."

"Okay, I accept that, but I just found out that you are the owner of that beauty salon your wife visits. Also, you own the *Lucky Millionaire's Casino*. I always appreciate it if my clients give me as much information about themselves as is possible. It makes my job easier."

He chuckled. "I own many properties. There is no reason to list them all, because they have nothing to do with what I'm asking of you. You're supposed to investigate my wife not me. The fact that you found out these things assures me that you are a capable detective. I would have been disappointed had you not checked me out."

I didn't tell him how I came by the information. No need to change his assumption about me and my capabilities. "I'm glad that you have a positive opinion about me. You are wrong in one aspect though: It is important for me to know my clients. There may be a clue somewhere why things are happening. For instance, you suspect your wife of cheating. For me immediately the question *why is she cheating?* pops up. Is it something you are doing or not doing? Perhaps you are too busy with your investments to pay attention to your wife? You see where I'm going?"

"I see where you're going. I'm not an idiot."

I held up both hands in a defensive gesture. "I'm not implying you are. I just want you to understand why it is important for my clients to keep me informed about themselves or their activities."

"Well, I'm not prepared to do that, Canon." Titman rose from his chair. "My activities are of no importance here. Your job is to report to me my wife's activities not mine. That's what I'm paying you for. I expect results shortly, otherwise..." He stared out of the window for a moment. "Otherwise I will hire somebody else."

"I hope you won't do that, Mr. Titman. I'll try to find out something about your wife." I held out a hand but he ignored it. With one last look around my office, he shook his head and headed for the door. Before he walked out, he said, "Perhaps you should think about hiring a secretary, a beautiful, sexy one. It may help boost your business." He made a dismissing motion with his hand. "And get some descent furniture. I hate sitting on hard chairs."

"You could have used the couch," I suggested with a smirk.

He just snorted.

I stared at the closing door. When I turned to look at Nelda, who sat behind the desk like a wooden figure, I expected an angry reaction to Mr. Titman's remark. I wasn't disappointed.

If she would have been a robot, I'm sure her eyes would have been spewing laser beams. Hopefully not at me. "I'd like nothing better than to beat the crap out of that ugly, little dwarf," she shouted, rising to her feet. "Or better yet—rip his warty nose out of his face and shove it up his fat..."

"I don't need any details," I protested, interrupting her tirade. "Remember, he is our bread and butter right now."

"Too bad," she snapped. "I don't know what his wife sees in him. He doesn't deserve her."

I grinned. "What do you think she sees in him? He's her sugar daddy, that's what. Unless he's a pistol in bed." I shrugged. "One never knows."

Nelda made sounds with her mouth that would have made a proper lady blush. Perhaps even a sensitive man. "Just thinking about him and her that way makes me want to throw up. He's uncouth and has no feelings for anyone. It's not my fault that I don't look like a beauty queen. I have other qualities."

"Of course you have," I said soothingly. "Look, you are my partner. It's not every day that I make someone my partner. It means I saw something in you that didn't require you to be beautiful."

Her expression told me that I may have used the wrong words. "Then you agree with him that I'm ugly?" Those eyes made me cold all over. I was hoping she wouldn't draw that 45 she had strapped to her hip and use me for target practice. At least, it would be over fast, because I had seen her on the shooting range.

I lifted a hand in feeble protest, searching for the proper words. "Nelda, Nelda, you are too sensitive for your own good. You know I'm not a silver-tongued talker. Don't look for words that aren't there. I never said you're ugly and I would never say it."

Damn right. I wouldn't dare.

She let her shoulders slump. "I'm sorry, Lews. I didn't mean to get angry with you. You are right; I am sensitive about the way I look. I wish I weren't this ugly ogre, but I can't do anything about it. No amount of make-up can make me look like a Julia Titman." She showed me one hand. "Look at this paw. A bricklayer has smaller hands."

I didn't know how to respond to that. She did have huge hands. Of course, everything else on her was huge. "You have a beautiful voice," I said. "That counts for something."

Her chuckle told me it was safe to relax. "And you said you're not a silver-tongued talker, you devil. You could have fooled me." Sitting down, she put her elbows on the desk and rested her chin in her large hands. "What are we going to do now?"

I went over to the old couch and sank into it. "I don't know. Something will come up." Staring out of the window, I watched the raindrops hitting the glass and running down in little rivulets, hoping for inspiration. I hate rainy weather and I hate those commercials where people stand in the rain, laughing and waving their hands in the air, obviously enjoying getting wet. For me there is nothing more unpleasant than having cold water run down my collar. The only time I love rain is watching it from the inside of a dry, comfortable room.

Speaking of being comfortable—Titman was right, this damn couch needed to go. I inherited it when I rented this office. It came with the furniture, but it had outlived its usefulness. The only obstacle preventing me from buying a new couch was the lack of funds. "Maybe I can persuade Titman to advance some more money," I said into the silence.

"Good luck with that. First we'll have to come up with some useful information about what his wife is up to."

When the phone rang, Nelda reached for the receiver but changed her mind. "You answer it," she said. "It's Titman."

I wrestled with the cushion and managed to free myself from its death grip. "Canon here," I said into the phone.

"No need to identify yourself. I know it's you. I called you." Titman sounded irritated and condescending at the same time. "I've decided to give you another chance, Canon. My wife is a great supporter of the arts. In fact, there is one gallery she seems to have adopted. It is called *Angels and Lace Gallery*. You'll probably find her there tomorrow. I'll expect some answers." He hung up before I could ask for more information.

I shook my head. If he already knew where she'd be what did he need me for? He could drive there himself and check her out. Well, it didn't matter. All I needed to find out was the address of the place. At least I had another starting point. Not all was lost.

I checked my watch. It was close to noon. "You want to go for pizza?" I asked Nelda.

She gave me a puzzled look. "Are you asking me for some kind of a date or something?"

"Why would you say that?"

"You've never asked me to go for lunch with you before. What gives?"

I shrugged. "Nothing gives. Maybe I don't feel like eating alone today or maybe I just want to take you out for your birthday. You didn't think I'd forget, did you? I'm taking the rest of the day off. You should, too. My gift to you. Titman gave me a lead I'll follow tomorrow. If you have nothing else planned, you might want to accompany me to the Angels and Lace Gallery." I grinned. "A little exposure to a bit of art might do both of us some good."

"As long as it isn't some crazy modern art where one doesn't know what it is supposed to be, I have no problem."

Rubbing my hands, I said, "Okay then let's go and have a pizza and a beer. Tomorrow we'll start a new day."

———

The gallery was about half an hour's drive from my office. When we got there, I didn't see Julia's car anywhere, but that didn't necessarily mean she wasn't there. She might have parked her car in a parking lot somewhere and walked.

"I guess we'll go in and have a look around," I said to Nelda. Looking at that 45 on her hip, I added, "Better leave your weapon in the car. I don't think we'll be in any danger inside the gallery."

We were greeted by an older woman, who gave us a wide-mouthed smile from screaming-red painted lips when we walked in. "Welcome to my gallery," she said. "Have you been here before?"

I shook my head. "No, this is our first time."

"How have you heard about us?" She seemed eager for conversation. The place didn't look busy.

"Actually, we haven't. We were just driving by and decided to drop in." I gave her a friendly smile. "My niece and I are both art lovers. Who knows, we might just see something we like."

The woman giggled like a school girl. "Well, then, by all means, take a look around. If you have any questions, I'll be right here. By the way, my name is Chantelle. Enjoy."

"Thank you, Chantelle. Enjoy we will." The walls were covered with pictures of landscapes and people. Some were paintings and some were photographs. The photographs were the ones that caught my eye. There were quite a few featuring the same model.

"Isn't that Julia Titman?" Nelda whispered.

"No doubt, it is her." I had to admit who ever took the photographs had talent. Julia looked even more beautiful in the pictures than in real life. In most of them she was in various stages of undress, nude in many. Sometimes she was alone and sometimes she was with a male model. In fact, one didn't have to guess what the two were doing in some of the pictures.

"These are pornographic pictures," Nelda whispered again.

"It is art, my dear," I said, but I had to agree with her observation. I pulled out my little camera, which I carried with me at all times for occasions like this, and took a few snapshots, carefully shielding it with my body. I was sure Titman would be interested in these revealing photographs of his wife, especially the ones featuring her and a handsome man.

Chantelle must have been watching us, because she came over when she saw us staring at one particularly explicit picture. "A bit shocking, isn't it?" Her face was a little flushed when she looked at me. "Do you like it?"

"Who is the woman in the picture? She is most exquisite," I said, not commenting what she obviously was fishing for.

"That is Julia. She is our patron, that's why you see so many of her pictures in this gallery."

"Who is the male model?" Nelda asked.

"He is a hunk, isn't he? His name is George Cole. I don't know much about him. I've never met him personally."

"Are they involved with each other? I mean other than taking explicit pictures?"

"I'm not going to speculate on that. After all, Julia is a married woman." Chantelle lowered her voice. "It does appear that way, doesn't it?"

"Looking at these photographs, it certainly does. I mean one can practically see them thrashing about," Nelda commented.

I guess I wasn't the only one to notice that. "Perhaps they are just good actors."

Chantelle nodded with a big smile. "They probably are. Also, it's the genius of the photographer. He knows how to make a photograph come alive."

I had to admit, she was right. The photographer did have a knack for making a picture appealing. Of course, anyone could take a picture of a couple having sex. But there was something about the pictures that went beyond that first impression. Maybe it was the lighting or just the angle the way the couple was photographed. It might be a good idea to talk to him. He may have more information about Cole. "What's his name?"

"His name is Anton Bernard. He's a real artist. Not just as a photographer. He also paints. We have some pictures of his in the next room." She gave a little laugh. "Of course, for most of his paintings he uses Julia and George as his models."

"Would you by chance have his address?"

"Why?" She gave me a suspicious look.

"As I mentioned before, my niece and I are art lovers, not just of painted pictures. We also are interested in photographs." I made my chuckle sound as if I were embarrassed about what I was going to say.

"I'd like him to take a few pictures of my niece and me..." I coughed into my fist. "You know, just some fake pictures, of course. Strictly for our amusement and private use. You understand?"

Chantelle threw a quick and somewhat knowing look at Nelda before answering. "I think I do. Anton is very discreet; I can assure you of that."

"It's not what you think," Nelda said, giving me that icy stare.

Chantelle smiled knowingly. "I'm not thinking anything, my dear. Like I said, Anton isn't the kind of guy who judges people. He is a professional and takes his job seriously. And believe me, nothing shocks him anymore." She looked at me and winked. "I can be quite discreet also and nothing shocks me. I've seen it all." She chuckled. "Maybe even done it all. If you need a third person to...ah...assist, I could be persuaded."

"It's a tempting offer," I said.

"I think we can manage all by ourselves. Thank you very much," Nelda said sweetly, but she couldn't hide her annoyance. Neither could she hide those laser beams shooting from her eyes. "If you don't mind, we'll take that address now."

"Impatient, aren't you?" Chantelle said in an even sweeter voice.

Oh boy! Someone was unsheathing her claws. There was a tigress hidden inside that somewhat elderly but still lovely and soft-spoken exterior. A man could call himself lucky to light that smoldering fire and then trying to put it out again. However, I wasn't going to be that man. For sure not with Nelda around.

"We should be going," I said, using my best soothing voice. "Perhaps I'll drop in sometime and you and I can go for coffee."

"That would be nice." Chantelle gave Nelda a triumphant look. "I shall be keeping an eye out for you."

Women! Who understands them? I had no interest in either Nelda or Chantelle. Nelda was almost like a niece to me, and she was much too young anyway; and Chantelle? I wasn't interested in a relationship with another woman, as brief and passionate as it might turn out. I had Sonya. After all, I am a man of principles and integrity. At least, that's what I keep telling myself.

Chantelle walked to her desk by the front door and took out a little booklet. Then she wrote down something on a piece of paper. When she handed it to me, she smiled and winked again. "Don't keep me waiting too long," she almost whispered, trying to sound sexy. "I'll keep the fire burning."

"Sounds good," I said, keeping my voice also low. "Thanks for the info."

When we were outside, Nelda almost hissed, "What was that all about?"

"What?" I feigned ignorance.

"*I'll keep the fire burning*," she mimicked Chantelle. "That old bitch. She's lucky if she can even light a match, never mind getting a flame."

"She's not so old," I protested.

"She's ancient. At least fifty, if not older."

"Wow! If you think fifty is ancient, what does that make me?"

"Old."

"As you know I'm forty-one, little lady. In the prime of my life, but what would a twenty-one-year-old know about that?"

She laughed suddenly.

'What's so funny about all this?" I asked.

"The only time you call me 'little lady' is when I hit a nerve. You *do* feel old, don't you?"

"You know me so well." I sighed and put my arm around her shoulder, which was no easy thing to do, since she was an inch taller than me and bigger all around. "You know I love you like my own daughter, but sometimes you can be a little bitch."

She just chuckled. "I thought I was your niece and you want to do naughty things to me."

"Let the old bird think that. You and I will go and visit an artist."

It took us less than twenty minutes to find the place. Bernard lived in an older neighborhood. All the houses were two-story buildings with wooden siding and porches in front. Small windows suggested a third floor, but I've been in houses like that before and most of the third floors were nothing but attics full of old junk.

I didn't see Julia's car anywhere, so I decided it was safe to talk to Bernard, hoping he was home. I needed to find out more about George Cole, the male model.

When I rang the doorbell, an ancient chime inside the house

announced our presence, and moments later a tall, scrawny-looking guy opened the door. "Can I help you?"

Bernard looked like the typical artist. He was skinny and probably tipped the scales at no more than 140 pounds. Dirty-blond hair framed his narrow face with long, straggly strands, and his mustache and goatee needed a trim badly. He even wore a little beret on his head.

I had to suppress a chuckle when I realized he had spoken with a French accent.

"Hi, my name is Mark Conelli. I'm an investigator with Northbell Insurance. I'd like to ask you a few questions about George Cole. I understand he is one of your models."

"Who told you that?"

"That would be confidential information, but since she is the person displaying your pictures, there is no harm in telling you. It was Chantelle from the Angels and Lace Gallery who gave me the information. I hope I can rely on your digression not to tell her or anyone else that I mentioned her name. It could get me into trouble with my company." I hoped my smile was engaging. "She also mentioned Julia, the woman in the pictures with George."

"I see. Julia. Yes, she is one of my models. As is George." He motioned with his hand. "Please, come in. I don't want to discuss this outside." His eyes rolled upward. "Too many nosy neighbors, you understand."

"I know how that is," I said. "It seems they are everywhere."

He ushered us into what obviously was his studio. Partially used tubes of paint, easels with canvas stretched over frames, and a few finished and unfinished paintings leaning against one wall were clues enough. There were also cameras on tripods and lighting equipment. Actually, the room was a bit of a mess. A cot with a heap of blankets and cushions in one corner finished the décor.

I looked around and spied an unfinished painting featuring a woman dressed in a transparent flowing gown sitting on a unicorn. Even though the woman had ears like an elf and thin feelers coming out of her head, I recognized Julia's features. The muscular figure of a man wearing nothing but a thin loincloth leaning against a tree behind her was obviously George Cole.

"Even in a fantasy setting they make a handsome couple," I

commented. "Of course, it needs a talented artist like you to create that on a piece of boring canvas. Chantelle told me you are a gifted man; and I can see she was right."

"You are a connoisseur of the arts, Monsieur Conelli?"

I fluttered my fingers. "I don't know if I can call myself a connoisseur, but I certainly do enjoy looking at paintings. And your paintings are creations of beauty and utterly enjoyable. It almost makes me want to pick up my brushes and start painting again."

"You paint?"

"Not anymore. In college, that's all, but your paintings seem to draw out the artist in me. You are a true master."

"Thank you for the compliment, but Julia and George make it easy to create masterpieces." He rolled his eyes and sighed. "That George, he is such a sexy man, but he has only eyes for Julia. Too bad." He pointed to one of the easels. "I took the liberty to let my imagination run wild. Tell me, what you think."

I walked over to the painting. It wasn't quite finished. There on a rock beside a lake sat a satyr. His face was that of Bernard. Standing behind him, with his muscular arms around Bernard's chest, stood a human man. He was handsome and naked and he wore the face of Cole.

When I looked at Bernard, he shrugged and looked at the ceiling. "One can dream. I know this one is an impossible dream, but what can I say. I am in love—with a straight man. It happens."

"At least you are in love with someone, even if it's only a dream. Count yourself lucky. Some people never fall in love. To be in love is a good thing." I was babbling, not knowing what I should say. I fancy myself to be a tolerant guy, but I've never been overly excited about gays. For a guy to be in love with another guy? It somehow freaks me out visualizing what they do in the bedroom, but I would never openly say that. I don't hate gays and I don't condemn them. It's not their fault nature played a cruel joke. To be a man and not to like women? That is difficult to imagine for a straight guy, but then again, they probably think the same about us. To me sex is a private matter and nobody's business. Bernard's preferences were not my business.

"Do you have somebody you love, Monsieur?"

I nodded, thinking of Sonya. "I have someone. She's a lovely lady."

"That is good. You are lucky, also. So, what do you want to know about George?" He looked at me, curiosity obvious in his eyes.

"As I told you before, it is important that you keep our conversation private. What I'm about to tell you is confidential. Were you aware that Mr. Cole was married at one time?"

He shook his head. "No, I wasn't. That is a surprise to me."

"Well, he was, but he and his wife divorced a few years ago. He has a child, a little girl. Her name is Emma. Mr. Cole's aunt, Amelia Cole, was little Emma's godmother. She passed away just recently, and she left most of her considerable fortune to little Emma. However, there is one stipulation: She won't get her money until she turns twenty-one. Mr. Cole and his ex-wife are the trustees until then, but there is another problem. His aunt never liked his wife and she doesn't want her to get one penny. And her lawyer is quite sticky about that. He won't release the money until that obstacle has been cleared away. There may be an easy way to solve that problem. Can you tell me if Julia and Mr. Cole are—how should I put it delicately—are they having an intimate relationship?"

"You mean outside my studio?"

"That's what I mean. We saw the pictures in the gallery, and they looked quite realistic. Were they?"

He nodded, his lips forming the ghost of a smile. "Some things you cannot fake, Monsieur. Everything must look natural. I believe in pushing my subjects as far as they are willing to go. And Julia and George are willing subjects."

"Are they faking it or is there more to their relationship than just professional performance?"

Bernard stared at one of the pictures, but his eyes seemed unfocused. Then he sighed and nodded. "I'm afraid there is."

"That may be a good thing."

"Why?"

"Well, if we could prove that Mr. Cole and Julia have intentions of getting married, or at least live together, then she could be made the trustee instead of the ex-wife. Apparently, there is a clause like that in Amelia Cole's will."

Bernard scratched his head. "That may be difficult to achieve. You see, Julia is already married."

I gave him a, hopingly convincing, stunned look. "That is not good news. Tell me this—is she happy in her marriage? I mean, since she's intimate with Mr. Cole it might mean she is in an unhappy marriage, right? Perhaps there is a good chance she may want to divorce her husband. What do you think?"

He chuckled, but I didn't sense any humor in his apparent merry expression. "Her husband will never give her up. He'll kill her before that happens."

"Surely you're not serious. Would he really?"

"Yes, he would. Her husband is not a nice man. You don't want to tangle with him." He fell silent, stroking his goatee.

"You actually think that? You must have a reason to make such a statement."

"I have, but I already said too much." His gaze fell on Nelda who had been silent all this time and was apparently studying one of the pictures on the wall. "Your partner is very quiet," he said. Then he lowered his voice. "She scares me."

I laughed softly. "She only looks like that. She is really nothing more than an oversized puppy."

"Is she a real female or maybe, you know, half man, half woman?"

"I'm sure she's a woman," I whispered, "even though I've never seen her naked." Which was the truth, and I had no desire to change that status.

"Do you think she would model for me? I am fascinated by her. She may inspire me for my fantasy paintings."

"Why don't you ask her?" I suggested. "She is always open to new things and easy to work with. She may even pose nude for you. Then you can find out if she is a true woman."

Nelda turned to look in our direction. I was hoping she hadn't heard the last bit of our conversation. I waved her over. "Mr. Bernard wants to ask you something. I said you may be interested." Turning back to Bernard, I said, "Do you have a bathroom I could use?" I wasn't going to hang around for that one.

"Sure. Just down the hallway."

I headed in the indicated direction, giving Nelda a wink as I walked by her. "Be gentle with him," I whispered.

FIVE

WHEN I CAME BACK and joined them I couldn't believe my eyes. Nelda and Bernhard were both sitting on the floor, facing each other. Nelda was smiling happily, while Bernhard held his hands in front of her face, like two huge Ls, studying it intently.

"What's going on?" I asked.

"Anton is going to take pictures of me," Nelda announced. "Possibly even use me in one of his paintings."

"Why?"

"He thinks I have a strong face. And he loves my eyes."

Really? He's probably going to use them in a painting featuring demons and ogres.

"That's fantastic," I said. "There is a good chance you'll be displayed in one of the galleries. You may even become famous."

"No reason to get sarcastic." She threw me one of her scary looks, sending shivers of pure ice down my back.

"Perfect!" Bernard exclaimed. "This will be my masterpiece. You are a natural, mon chérie."

"I'm a natural," Nelda repeated with a triumphant smirk. "Merci beaucoup, Anton. You're a sweetheart yourself."

"I did not know you spoke French," Bernard said.

"Only bits and pieces I remember from school." Nelda laughed and slapped him on the shoulder. Bernard winced a little. "I like you, Anton. Too bad you don't like women."

"I may just make an exception with you," he said, joining her laughter. "But you must promise to be gentle with me and never to hit me. You are a strong woman. I have tender bones." He stood up and dusted off his pants. "I must get back to my work. Is there anything else I can help you with, Monsieur Conelli?"

"Actually, I had been hoping to find Julia and George here at your studio."

"They left about ten minutes before you came here," Bernard informed me. "They may have gone for a cup of coffee."

"Where? If you don't mind me asking."

"They usually go to the Café de la Mer. It is just around the corner."

I held out my hand. "Thank you so much, Mr. Bernard. You've been a great help. Like I said, this conversation stays between us, okay?"

"No problem. Glad I could help a little." I had expected a limp handshake; don't ask why, but he shook my hand with a surprisingly strong grip. Looking at Nelda, he said, "Whenever you're ready you come and visit me. I meant what I said."

When we were outside, Nelda walked without saying anything until we sat in the car. Then she turned to me and said, "If it was your glorious idea to suggest to Anton that he should use me as a model I'm not amused. Count yourself lucky things worked out between me and Anton, Mister! Did you want to be present when I took off my clothes?"

"Heaven forbid, no," I said, realizing at the same moment as those words left my mouth it was the wrong thing to say. Again. "I mean, it wouldn't bother me to see you naked."

"Why should you be bothered by my nude body?"

"Not really bothered. I may even enjoy seeing you without clothes. That didn't sound right, did it? What I want to say..."

"You're a dirty old man, Lews. A pervert. You're probably sitting in front of your computer at night looking at pictures of naked young girls."

Now it was my turn to react with indignation. "Young woman, you should know better than saying something like that. If you think that then you don't know me at all and I'm very disappointed. I do not surf the internet looking for dirty pictures or pictures of nude women, although if they pop up for some reason I don't look away. That doesn't make me a dirty old man. When I'm on the computer I search for information. Show some respect for your elders."

"Then you admit you're an old man?"

"I'm not an old man, neither am I a dirty old man. As I told you before, I'm a man in his prime."

"And I've told you many times that you should get married. Then you wouldn't have to look at pictures of young girls. Girls without clothes. Or women in a state of undress. I've seen you stare at the pictures you take with your high-power camera."

I threw up my hands. Literally. It is no easy thing in a car. "I give up. You win. You always have to have the last word. Typical woman. I'll have you know, I'm a healthy straight man and not too old to enjoy looking at naked women, but I don't make it a habit searching for them. To see you naked wouldn't bother me because you are like my own daughter. And no—I'm not a pervert. The pictures I take with my high-power camera are done in the course of doing my job as a detective and when I check them over it doesn't mean I'm drooling over them, but you should know that. If you don't then I'm extremely disappointed. Happy now?"

She punched me on the arm. Something she seemed to enjoy doing to people. "Don't take everything so seriously, Lews. I was only kidding." She smiled. "I'm almost choked up when you say you think of me as your daughter."

"Well, I do." I started the car. The motor sprang to life with a rumbling sound and kept on rumbling.

"You should get your muffler fixed," Nelda said.

"I need a new car, that's what I need," I said as I pulled out of my parking spot.

"What about that mechanic, the one you promised to look into his brother's murder?"

"Brandon Brandon? Well—yeah, he said he'd check out my car and fix it up. There hasn't been time to see him. Besides, I haven't even looked into the case. I'm not really sure where I should start."

"You shouldn't have promised him anything. The problem with you is you are too kind sometimes. People take advantage of that."

"Brandon doesn't look like the kind of guy who would take advantage of anyone. If anything, people may take advantage of him. He's a good guy. You can tell."

Nelda chuckled. "In your eyes, every man is a good guy and every woman is a helpless creature who needs your assistance."

"I find nothing wrong with that kind of attitude. I'm a positive thinker. For me the glass is always half full and not the other way around."

"That's just semantics, playing with words. There is nothing positive or negative about it. Full or empty, what's the difference? The liquid in a glass is still the same in the end." She made a sound of disgust with her mouth. "I hate stuff like that."

"Someday when you're as mature as I you will see the difference," I told her.

"I can hardly wait. By the way, I have to compliment you on that story about George Cole and his little girl Emma. The aunt was a nice touch. How do you come up with stories like that?"

"They just pop into my head."

"You missed your calling. You should have become a writer of romance stories instead of a detective. You might have become famous, made tons of money and be driving a BMW right now and not this beat-up jalopy."

"Right. All one has to do is write a book. It will be an instant bestseller and the money will start flowing. If it's that easy why don't you start writing?"

"I don't have the fertile imagination you seem to have." She leaned forward in her seat. "There is the Café de la Mer."

I saw the sign also. I also saw Julia's BMW parked right in front of the café. There was an open spot a few car-lengths behind her car and I pulled my old Cadillac into that spot. It would have been nice if it were another BMW. A brand new one, of course.

"What do we do now?" Nelda asked.

"You feel like a cup of coffee?"

She shrugged. "Sure. As long as you're paying."

"I always pay when I take a lady out for lunch or dinner."

"Wow! So now I'm a lady. That's a first. I hope you don't expect some kind of compensation later."

"Oh yes, I do. Don't think this is a free lunch, neither is it a social occasion. This is business and I expect your full cooperation with this case and with the investigation of Bart Brandon's unsolved murder."

"I knew you'd pull me into that one." She heaved a loud sigh. "I promise I'll help you with it. As if I had a choice."

I smirked. "There are always choices. You could quit the detective business."

"Sure, and what would I do then? Run away with the circus? I can see the headlines already *Come and see the ogre* or *Just recently captured: a real live female Big Foot.* Is that what you want for me?"

"Now you're talking nonsense. I don't think of you that way. You have an inner beauty that shines through that—that rough exterior, like a diamond in the rough. I see that in you."

"Oh, shut up and let's go for that cup of coffee. I hope you aren't trying to woo the women you date with such crap talk." She opened the door and promptly hit her head when she climbed out of the car. "Shit!" she cursed and slammed the door shut. "Such a big car and still not enough headroom."

I didn't comment. She was in a foul mood and nothing I could say would change that. *Maybe I should spring for a huge lunch instead of just a cup of coffee.* It was past lunchtime anyway and I could feel tiny pangs of hunger churning in my belly.

When we entered the café the aroma of cooking food intensified those pangs. I spotted our quarry sitting at a table near the rear of the café. We chose a table not far away from theirs. I was hoping to catch a few pieces of their conversation.

"I was thinking you might want to have a larger lunch," I said to Nelda after we sat down. "I will, even if you won't," I added hastily after looking into her eyes.

"This is a café. They won't offer much." She sounded almost civil.

"Well, we'll find out. It is called Café de la Mer, which means they may feature some kind of seafood. Do you like seafood?"

"Not particularly."

"Well, you order whatever you like." I was glad when the waitress brought the menu. Scanning it quickly, I noticed that they indeed featured seafood. I ordered grilled sea bass on a bed of rice. I love fish.

Nelda ordered poached chicken with fries.

While we waited for our food to arrive, I tried to listen in on Julia's conversation with Cole. I couldn't hear much, but I noticed that they were touching each other's hands quite often. They seemed to be deeply involved in some kind of discussion. Too bad I couldn't make out what that discussion was all about. At the table next to them sat four teenagers and their noisy conversations blocked out anything Julia and her consort were saying.

My fear was that we'd still be eating when they left the café. I had in mind to follow them to see what they were up to for the rest of the day.

I needed some evidence for Mr. Titman. A picture would be a good thing to have. Nelda sat across from me with her back to the couple.

I pulled out my little camera. "I'll take a picture of you," I said to Nelda.

"Why?"

"Because you look so cute today," I said while moving my chin back and forth in the direction of Julia's table.

Nelda pulled her brows together, which did nothing to help her appearance. She's not really picture material, especially not when she does that. "Are you okay? Seems like you're having some kind of fit." I think I detected actual concern in her voice.

"I'm not having a fit. I need a picture of—you know..." I whispered, shoving my chin forward again.

"What? Oh, right. I forgot we're not here for our pleasure. Just make sure I'm not in it. I hate having my picture taken. I never look good in any of them."

I managed to zoom in on the objects of our quest and snapped a few pictures. I even got one as they were holding hands. Then I took a picture of Nelda, just for the fun of it. She never noticed. If she did, she didn't say anything.

Our food arrived shortly after that and we began eating. My sea bass tasted quite nice and it looked like Nelda enjoyed her poached chicken. Unfortunately, Julia and Cole got up before we were finished with our meals.

"They're leaving," I whispered.

"I haven't finished my chicken," Nelda said, looking at my plate. "And you still have plenty left."

I did some quick calculation, trying to figure out how long it would take before we could leave the café so we could follow them. When I realized we'd never make it on time, I decided to stay and enjoy my meal, which, by the way, cost more than I had anticipated. These fancy cafés charge exuberant prices. Somehow, deep down I knew where they'd be heading. The way they'd been touching each other, it didn't take a genius to come up with the correct answer.

"Are we leaving?" Nelda asked, trying to swallow the huge piece of chicken she had stuffed into her mouth.

"No, we'll stay. I believe I know where they're going. Relax and don't choke on that chicken. I have no desire to perform the Heimlich maneuver on you."

"I wouldn't trust you anyway and I wouldn't want you pressing your body against my back with your arms around my chest. It seems indecent. Have you ever performed it on anyone?"

"No, but I've seen pictures."

"Wonderful. Now you see the reason I wouldn't trust you or rely on you. Speaking of pictures—don't you think the ones you took of them in here aren't enough evidence?"

I shrugged. "I have no idea what Titman wants. Perhaps he'd be happy with them, who knows? I don't even know what he's planning to do with whatever evidence I'll find. Is he going to divorce her? I doubt that. Where would he find another beautiful woman like Julia?"

"She's a cheater. I wouldn't put up with that. I'd kick her out."

"You're not a fifty-five-year-old short, fat man, who, according to my information, isn't even a nice guy."

"He's got money. There are plenty of brainless, beautiful women out there who will go for a guy like that." She did that thing with her eyebrows again. "Maybe he's well endowed."

"Of course! All women go for that. How could I not think of that?" I exclaimed, hitting my forehead with my flat hand. "Did you ever think he might genuinely love her? Besides, I'm puzzled. Why would you suddenly defend him? I thought you hated the man?"

"I'm not defending that ugly dwarf. I have no love for him, but I don't have any love for cheaters, either. Once you make a commitment, you stick to it, no matter what. If you don't like something, you bring it out into the open. You don't sneak behind somebody's back. It's not honest. If she's not happy with him, she should tell him why." She stabbed her fork angrily into the last piece of chicken. "That's just my humble opinion. I would never do that to anyone. Loyalty to me is most important."

"And that's what makes you the person I admire and love," I said, gently.

"Oh, stop being so dramatic and mushy. It worries me."

We finished our lunch and then we drove to the Silver Moon Motel. I had remembered Titman telling me about the phone call that made him suspicious. And I had a hunch we might find our couple there.

As expected, Julia's car was in the parking lot of the motel and I didn't need any more evidence about what she and her friend were up to. A woman and a man don't go to a motel during the day in the city they live to have a nice conversation or just to hold hands. I took a few more pictures and that was it. There was no need for us to follow them into their room to watch what they were doing.

———

I called Titman in the afternoon and told him I had something for him. He came by the office the next day. Searching for a place to plant his oversized butt, he frowned when he looked at the couch, then he chose the wooden chair to sit on. It wasn't comfortable, but at least a person didn't have to struggle to get up. Especially a short man with an overweight body like Titman. I had the fleeting thought it may have been a good idea to take away the chair. It would have been fun to watch him trying to escape the death grip of the couch cushions.

Before I let him look at the pictures, I asked, "Have you ever been to the Angels and Lace Gallery, Mr. Titman?"

Shaking his head, he said, "I'm not interested in art."

"Well, perhaps you should be. You might have found out all these things by yourself. You could have saved your money."

I showed him some of the pictures I had printed. First the

photographs from the gallery and then the pictures I took from Julia and Cole in the café. The one with Julia's car in front of the motel, with the name of the motel as background, I left for last.

He sat there staring at the pictures without making any comments, but I could see his jaw working. Then he finally said from between clenched teeth, "Who's that bastard?"

"His name is George Cole."

"I want to know more about him. Find out!"

"What are you going to do once you have the information?"

His expression was cold. "None of your business, Canon. Just get me the info."

"We can't jump to any conclusions here. Appearances may be deceiving. They may just be discussing a project they are working on."

He snorted loudly. "I can imagine what project they were working on. It doesn't take a genius to figure that one out. Look at this picture!" His pudgy finger stabbed one of the pictures I had taken in the gallery. The one with Cole and Julia embracing each other in a position that couldn't have been more than obvious showing what they were doing. "Even in our first year of marriage she never did this with me. And the expression of ecstasy on her face? I never got that from her." His growl sounded like the rumbling of an enraged tiger.

"Expressions can be faked, Mr. Titman," I said, trying to defend his wife but not believing it myself. "She's probably a good actress."

"Oh, yes, that she is. She's fooled me until now, but that is finished. The curtain is coming down." His face suddenly hardened as if he had made some kind of decision. "You know what? I'll give you a hundred grand if you make this Cole disappear when you find him."

It came a bit as a shock to hear what he just said. "Are you asking me to kill him?"

He grimaced. "You're a smart guy, Canon. You figure it out."

"Hold it, Mr. Titman. I don't kill people. Not for any kind of money. If that's what you're planning to do, all bets are off. Our contract ends now. I won't be party to murder."

Looking at me with a thoughtful expression, he said, "Forget I asked. It was the anger talking. Just get me the information about Cole."

"How can I be sure you won't kill him after I get what you want?"

"I don't kill people, either. It's too messy to clean it up afterwards."

He handed me an envelope. "Here, to make the deal a little sweeter. And don't drag your feet."

I took the envelope, hoping it was a check with a worthwhile amount. I could surely use that money. "I'll send you a final bill once we're done," I said.

"Fine. Just get me what I need to know." He got up and walked out. No handshake, no goodbye. He certainly didn't act the way he did when I first met him. He still looked like an owl with his dark-rimmed glasses, but somehow his eyes didn't have that watery appearance anymore. Now they seemed to belong to some kind of predatory animal. Even his pear-shaped nose didn't look so comical in his pudgy face.

I removed the check from the envelope Titman gave me, thinking of Bart Brandon and wondering if Titman could have had something to do with his murder. I remembered Shirley telling me the name of one of the two men who, according to her husband, murdered an unknown man behind Titman's casino. It seemed at least one of them, Harry Rosser, was somehow involved with Titman. Why else would he get free haircuts at Shirley's salon?

At that moment, Nelda walked through the door. "Seems I missed our benefactor," she said.

"You mean Titman?"

"I saw that ugly dwarf driving away in his huge, fancy car. He didn't look happy."

"He wasn't."

"Can't blame him. I guess you showed him evidence of his wife's infidelity?"

"He wants us to find out more about Cole. In fact, he asked me to kill him."

She stared at me. "He did what?"

"He wants me to assassinate Cole."

"I hope you didn't say you would. I want nothing to do with that."

"Come on, Nelda. You know better than even suggest I did that. By the way, he offered one hundred thousand bucks if I did the job."

"Wow! That's a lot of money. It would come in handy."

It was my turn to look bewildered. "You don't really...?" I didn't finish the sentence, because she lifted a hand to stop me.

"Never," she said. "You are not that kind of a man. Did he at least give you more money?"

I waved the check. "Five hundred bucks."

"Better than nothing. We need it. I guess we'd better dig up some dirt on Cole so we can milk Titman for more of his dough."

"There is someone else I'd like to get more information on. A guy by the name of Harry Rosser. He seems to work for Titman. You remember Shirley Brandon telling us about him and his possible involvement in the murder her late husband witnessed?"

"Shirley Brandon? Yes, I remember her. How can I forget a non-paying client? I also couldn't help but notice how you checked out her naked thighs when she struggled with the couch."

Ignoring her obvious attempt to needle me, I said, "I'm not doing it just for her. I'm doing it for her son and her brother-in-law who helped me out when I needed help. He didn't charge me anything. I'm only paying it forward. A twelve-year-old boy reminded me of that principle. It was his murdered father's philosophy. Nothing wrong with that."

"I believe in an eye for an eye. You do me wrong I do you wrong. In fact, I'll do you worse." She pulled her eyebrows together and closed one eye. Mentally, I moved her open eye into the middle of her forehead and held that picture in my mind. Maybe she was some kind of ogre in human disguise. It was a bit scary thinking of her that way.

"They actually have a name for that," I said. "*Revenge.*"

"Well, that's what I believe in."

I studied her for a moment. "Do you sleep okay at night?" I asked.

"Why shouldn't I?"

"Revenge is never a good thing. It feeds negative energy. Doing something nice for someone is a positive thing. It creates happy feelings. You should try it sometimes."

She walked over to her desk and sank into her chair. "If somebody does something nice for me I'll do something nice for them—eventually. When I was in jail, one of the guards used to bring me cigarettes. She was always courteous and friendly to me. Treated me like a human being. I haven't forgotten. Someday I'll look her up and thank her."

"Cigarettes? I didn't know you smoked."

"I don't. I traded them for stuff with other inmates." She powered up her computer. "I'll do a search for Cole. You know, it might be a good idea to look into Julia Titman's history, also. I'm sure she's on some of the social media, her being a former fashion model and such."

"You do that. I'm not into this internet thing. What do people write about?"

"You'd be surprised what you can find out. People like to brag and talk about what they're up to. They even talk about their romances. It is possible she mentions Cole somewhere. It's worth a try."

"Okay. While you're doing this research, I'll drive down to my old precinct to see some former friends of mine. Maybe I can persuade one of them to look into Bart Brandon's file."

"I didn't know you still had friends in the force?"

"There might still be a couple who remember me with fondness." I gave her a sour grin. "I ruffled a few feathers before I left. Some of my *old* friends probably still carry a grudge. I know the Commissioner does."

"Since you mention the Commissioner—are you going to investigate his sister?"

"Angela Steelwood? Damn right I am. I have to do something to earn the twenty bucks her husband gave me as a retainer."

"Do you think it's wise?"

"No, it isn't, but I've never backed away from a challenge."

"Good luck, then. And—be careful, Lews. Okay?"

I put my hand over my heart. "I'm touched. You seem worried about me."

"I'm always worried about you. Sometimes you do stupid things. Actually, most of the time."

"When did you grow up and become so mature? You're talking to the man who saved you from getting into more trouble, remember?"

"How can I forget? You mention it at every opportunity."

"Only when needed. May I point out that I'm twice your age. According to you I'm an old man. I'm allowed to do stupid things."

She gave me one of her condescending smiles. "In that case, I'm also allowed to be a little stupid sometimes."

"How do you figure?"

"Because you're trying to convince me that you are still a young man, in your prime, as you put it. That means I'm just a little girl, a gentle baby."

I nearly choked on that one. She was taller and more massive than I, and I couldn't help myself to remind her of that. My mouth has a mind of its own sometimes. "You're a big girl, and not just physically. Hardly a gentle baby. Men are afraid of you. No baby can achieve such a feat. Remember, you just turned twenty-one. You're an adult now."

Her laser-eyes drilled a couple of holes right through my head, but she didn't comment on what I so delicately had implied. Perhaps she was becoming a bit more mature and mellow after all. One could only hope. "That was barely a couple of days ago. I don't feel any older."

"Birthdays are like that. You don't even know when they catch up with you. Bang! One day you realize you are not a teenager anymore and responsible for your actions." I walked toward the door. "Well, I'd better get going. I'll stop for a bit of lunch at the donut shop across the street from the precinct. I should find at least one of my old acquaintances there."

"You're not taking a large gamble trying to find a cop by going to a donut shop. Perhaps I should accompany you there to protect you from some of your old friends?"

My expression must have betrayed me, because she held up a hand, like a traffic cop trying to stop traffic. "Just kidding. We wouldn't want to make it a habit going out for lunch together. People might talk."

She knew how to twist a knife in a wound. "Now you're making me feel bad. I'd take you along, but there is no sense both of us going there. I need you here to do some digging."

"I know. Don't feel bad. I'll pick up a hamburger later. I don't mind eating alone. You just go on now and do your job. Good luck."

SIX

THEY WERE THERE, as expected. All four of them. Sitting at one of the tables in the back, drinking coffee and eating donuts. And laughing. Actually, there were five, but I didn't know the one sitting by the window.

I felt a pang of nostalgia. That used to be my spot.

John Pallitser saw me first. I never liked him and the feeling was mutual. When he spotted me walking toward their table, a huge grin spread across his scarred, ugly face. It didn't make him any handsomer.

"If it isn't The Loose Cannon," he said. "You have some guts to show your face in here."

I wasn't surprised by his reaction. It seemed the years hadn't changed him. Still the loudmouth. The other three turned around. There was Jerry Golden, Frank Kabinsky, and Noel Cunningham. Kabinsky had grown a mustache. Golden and Cunningham still looked the same, a little older, of course, and Golden was nearly bald now.

"Lews," Kabinsky called out, obviously surprised to see me in here. I hadn't seen or spoken to any of them since I left the force in 2010.

"Hey, Frank," I said, suddenly feeling guilty for not looking him up during all these years. He and I had been partners for nearly three years.

He shook my hand and gave me a hard look. "Time has left its mark on you," he said. "Everything alright?"

I nodded. "Can't complain." Then I shook Cunningham's hand and then Golden's. From close Golden looked old, and I figured he must be near retirement by now. "You lost some of your hair," I said, giving him a friendly smile.

He ran his hand across his skull. "I should get a wig. It would make me look younger."

I looked across the table at John Pallitser. "How's it going, Pallitser? Still beating up defenseless old men?"

"That old guy pulled a knife on me."

"They never did find that knife."

"Yeah, yeah, rub it in. I still say there was a knife. Besides, I've been cleared. Funny, you should bring that up, Canon." He pulled his mouth into a sneer. "You of all people. A guy who snitches on his own partner."

"I was never a snitch and you know it. Those were trumped-up charges to get me kicked off the force. Besides, Meloni got what he deserved." I tried to keep the bitterness out of my voice but succeeded only partially.

"That's water under the bridge, Lews," Kabinsky said, obviously trying to smooth out things before they went too far. He had always been the voice of reason. "No need to open old wounds. We all know you got the rotten end of the stick. Say, what brings you here after all this time? I mean, it's been seven years. I heard you have your own agency now."

"Since 2012. Canon Detective Agency."

"Things are going good?"

I shrugged. "Can't complain. Trying to keep a low profile."

"How do you get clients then?"

"They find me. Word of mouth." I smiled. "If you're good word gets around."

"You ever lick that alcohol problem of yours?" Pallitser pulled his fat lips into another sneer.

"I never had one. Not one I couldn't handle, anyway."

"Rumor has it your wife left you for your attorney." He just wouldn't leave things alone, and I had no idea how he found out. I was ready to smash my fist into his ugly mug, but he was a cop and I only a civilian. I wouldn't stand a chance in court.

"I guess you got it right."

"You probably spent more time with a bottle than with her." He laughed. "Or maybe your attorney gave her what she needed, a good..."

"Why don't you shut up, Pallitser!" Kabinsky told him, sharply. "I'm sure Canon didn't come here to talk about the past and his personal love-life." He looked at me. "By the way, that tall guy across from me is Edward Chang. He got transferred to our precinct a couple of years back—from San Francisco."

I gave Chang a polite nod. "I hope you never regretted coming here. Must have been quite a change."

He chuckled. "Except for the weather things are the same. There are as many murders here as back home."

"You're in Homicide then?"

"I'm Kabinsky's partner."

"He's a good guy. Best partner one could ever have."

"I gather you and him were partners?"

"For three years, until they split us up. Much of what I know I learned from him."

"Don't be so modest." Kabinsky laughed. "You had your share of fresh ideas. We made a good team, you and I, that's for sure. You always had my back. I never forgot that. A shame they partnered you with Meloni. Things would have been different if they hadn't done that to you."

I shrugged. "Like you said—water under the bridge. Who knew Meloni was dirty?"

"There were rumors," Cunningham, who had been quiet till now, said. "Apparently, the Feds had him under surveillance."

"Who told you that?" Kabinsky gave Cunningham a surprised look. "You never mentioned anything before."

"Because nobody ever asked." Cunningham sounded defensive. "Besides, I wasn't going to get involved. I had enough troubles of my own."

"I remember somebody tried to bring you up on charges of brutality. That kid you caught robbing an old lady," Jerry said.

"That little son-of-a-bitch kicked me in the balls. He deserved everything I gave him," Cunningham growled. "I believe he's the reason I couldn't have any more kids."

Pallitser laughed. "Maybe he did you a favor. You already had five."

"So what? I love children; so does my wife. I was hoping for a son. What can a guy do with five daughters? All they ever want is new clothes."

"I know what you're saying," Kabinsky said, grinning. "I got three girls myself." He looked at me still standing by the table. "Why don't you pull up a chair and join us, Lews?"

"Maybe another time. I just wondered if I could swing by the precinct later on and talk to you in private. I'm working a murder case. The husband of one of my clients got murdered last year. Perhaps I could have a look into the file, get some insight."

"You're not a cop anymore, Canon," Pallitser said. "Those are police files and not meant for the public."

"There's no harm in me looking at them," I told him. "I'm not some schmuck off the street, Pallitser. I used to be a cop. That should mean something. I can keep a secret if I have to." My eyes searched out Kabinsky again. "What do you say, Frank?"

"Sure, come by later. I should be in the office at around four."

"Thanks, Frank. I appreciate it." I touched the shield of my baseball cap. "It was good talking to you guys. A pleasure to meet you, Chang. Keep an eye on my old pal Kabinsky for me. He's getting on in years."

Chang laughed. "He can still run pretty good."

I walked away, wondering what they'd be talking about after I was gone. Probably about me, speculating if I had really been a dirty cop. They might even talk about the raw deal I got from ex-Commissioner Albert Steelwood. He retired four years after I left the force. Now his son, Allan Steelwood, sat in his chair, and he was as crooked as his father.

I should have had a donut and a coffee, but for some reason it hadn't felt right to sit with my ex-colleagues. Too much time had passed and the connection I had with them was nothing but a flimsy thread now.

So I went to a diner down the street for lunch. Even though I was a bit of a loner and functioned quite well without other people surrounding me, I wouldn't have minded some company. Food somehow always tastes better when you can point out to another person how much you're enjoying it.

After spending an hour in the diner, I drove to the police station. It was a bit strange and almost eerie walking into my old precinct. Sort of like coming home, but somebody else sat at the desk that had been mine, and it took only a moment for that nostalgic feeling to disappear. Kabinsky was already at his desk. None of the other detectives I knew had returned.

"So what's on your mind?" Kabinsky asked when I pulled up a chair to sit down across from him.

"Like I said, I wouldn't mind looking at one of last year's murder cases. The guy's name is Bart Benny Brandon."

"Bart Benny Brandon," Kabinsky repeated. "Well, let's have a look." He did something on his computer. "Here we are. There isn't much here. It says he was thirty-three years old. It happened near a bus stop shortly after midnight. He was stabbed. There are two witnesses— no, not witnesses. A couple of nurses found him and called it in. That's really all there is."

Kabinsky looked up. "It says it was probably a robbery gone wrong."

"His family doesn't believe it was robbery. Even though whoever stabbed him took his money, they didn't take his watch, his ring, and a golden cross he had around his neck. They believe he was murdered."

"It doesn't mention any of those items here."

"That's because whoever investigated the death didn't think it was important." I bent forward. "Does it mention in the report that the man was black?"

Kabinsky shook his head. "No, it doesn't, but that's really irrelevant."

"His brother thinks it is relevant. In his words *who cares about another dead nigger!* He feels if Bart had been white his death would not have been shrugged off as a plain robbery. There would have been an investigation."

"That's quite some accusation." Kabinsky looked straight at me. "Do *you* believe that, Lews?"

"Does it matter what I believe? You and I both know racism isn't dead. Who was the investigating officer?"

"Pallitser."

I gave a little grunt. "Well, I'm not surprised."

"Why would you say that?"

"Remember the old man he beat up?"

"The one with the knife?"

"That one. He was black."

"That proves nothing." Kabinsky shook his head. "Your assessment of Pallitser may be tainted. It is well-known that you never liked him. What did he ever do to you?"

I sighed. Sometimes one has to forget about certain things that happened in the past and move on, and some things are best forgotten, but events have a way of popping up when you least expect it. "It's not what he did to me. I never told anyone. When I was a rooky cop back in 1999 I partnered for a short time with Pallitser."

Kabinsky raised one bushy eyebrow. "I never knew."

"Not many do. We were both street cops, walking the beat in a bad neighborhood. One evening we came upon a couple of guys who were beating up another guy. When I tried to interfere, Pallitser stopped me with the words *probably just some unsatisfied customers teaching their dealer a lesson. It happens all the time.* The guys doing the beating were white; the guy they beat was black."

"Perhaps he was right. You said it yourself, you were a rooky. It is possible Pallitser knew the guy. It wouldn't be the first time we turned a blind eye. We both did."

"I know we did, but it doesn't make it right. Similar incidents happened more than once with Pallitser. At that time I figured that's just the way things were done. You taught me different, Frank."

"Well, most of us try to do the right thing. Pallitser has his faults, but he isn't a bad guy. I'm sure of one thing, he can't be bought. By the way, he's in Internal Affairs now."

"Good for him. Some guys have all the luck. Find anything?"

"Not yet." Kabinsky stared silently at the monitor screen. "What makes you believe this Brandon guy was targeted to be murdered?" he asked after a long pause.

"Because he witnessed a murder a week before his own death."

"What murder?"

"He saw a couple of men stab another man and then throw him into a dumpster. It happened in the back lane behind the Lucky Millionaire's Casino. Perhaps you can find a record of that murder?"

Kabinsky let his fingers move across his keyboard. "You say it happened a week before Brandon's death?"

"That's what his family told me."

"I found something here. Another unsolved murder. They discovered the mangled corpse of a man in a landfill. He has never been identified. They figured he was from out of state, possibly some vagrant." Kabinsky lifted his head to look at me. "There is nothing in here about a body in a dumpster."

"How do you think that body got into the landfill?"

"Did this Brandon fill out a police report about the incident he witnessed?"

"He didn't. According to his wife, he was told by his boss not to say anything. His boss didn't want the bad publicity."

Kabinsky scratched his head. "I have to admit there is something fishy about this whole thing. Who is his boss?"

"Frederick Titman. He owns the Lucky Millionaire's Casino. Do me a favor. Check if you have anything on this Titman?"

"I don't have to do any checking. I know him. Rumor has it he is involved with the Ramiro Family. So far we haven't been able to prove anything."

"If memory serves me right, the Ramiro Family is responsible for the distribution of most of the drugs in this city."

He nodded. "You are correct. They also control a large number of the downtown prostitutes and their pimps. This Family is well organized and has a bunch of cops in its pocket, with connections to powerful politicians. You may be entering dangerous territory here, Lews. I advise extreme caution."

"Thanks for the advice. The problem is I made a promise to Brandon's widow. She needs to know the truth about her husband's death."

"It will be difficult to find out the truth. It's been a year and the case is closed. There were no witnesses. According to the report, the two nurses who found him didn't see anything. I'm afraid you're following a cold trail."

"That's because Pallitser botched the investigation. He should have done more." I felt angry inside. It seemed my investigation into Bart Brandon's murder had come to a halt even before it really began. "Do you have the names of the two nurses?"

"I do, but they claim when they came upon the victim he was already dead. They didn't see it happening." Kabinsky's expression was serious. "I'm sorry, Lews. I can't give you any more information because there isn't any. Perhaps Pallitser could have done some more digging, but there wasn't much to go by. It was late at night and there were no witnesses. Leave it be."

"One more thing, Frank. Do you have a file on Angela Steelwood?"

He gave me an astonished look. "Are you talking about Commissioner Steelwood's sister?"

"The very same. Why? Is that a problem?"

"Are you kidding me, Lews? It is a huge problem. I start snooping around in his sister's file and it will raise a red flag. He'll be all over me in no time. I can't risk it. You of all people should know better than that. I'm too close to retirement." He didn't look happy, but I wasn't going to be scared off.

"In other words, there is a file on her," I pushed.

"I didn't say that. And if there were a file, it would probably be locked. Besides, why would you think she is in the police computer?"

"Just a hunch."

His expression was one of open curiosity. "What's your interest in her, anyway?"

"It may be nothing. Just some drunken guy talking possible nonsense. The incident I'm interested in happened in 2005, my first year in Homicide. I seem to remember a report I came across that caught my eye, but I didn't think much of it at the time. I'm not sure, but I believe Angela Steelwood's name popped up in that report."

"What kind of report was it?" Something in his voice made me wonder.

"An accident report about Angela's husband." There was no reason I shouldn't tell him.

"We don't have to search for that report. I remember it well," Kabinsky said softly. "I was the investigating officer. Apparently, Angela's husband slipped in the bathtub and hit his head. He was unconscious when I got there. They took him to the hospital by ambulance. He died there. I had no cause to doubt her testimony."

"Did you actually investigate it?"

Shaking his head, he said, "I was taken off the case."

"Why?"

"Commissioner Steelwood took over. He told me he would handle it."

"He was her father. There should have been a conflict of interest." If I had any doubts about this, they were disbursed now. Why would the Police Commissioner get involved? Just because Angela was his daughter? I seriously doubted that. If it would have been an open and shut case there would have been no reason for him to take over the case. "You didn't question the Commissioner's involvement?"

"No. Angela's husband didn't die under suspicious circumstances. He slipped, hit his head, and died. It happens all the time. It was an unfortunate accident. And the Commissioner's interest? It was his daughter we're talking about. I would have done the same if she were my daughter." He was defending his position, but I could see something else in his eyes. "Why bring this up now, Lews?"

"You may or may not know that Angela married again. I met her husband." I looked around to see if anyone else was near, but nobody paid us any attention, mainly because most of the cops present didn't know me. I saw nothing but new faces. Even so, I spoke with a low voice. "What I'm telling you stays between us, okay? Her husband suspects that she murdered her first husband and now he may be her next victim."

"Does he have reason to believe that?"

"Maybe. Apparently, she told him how easy it is to kill someone and getting away with it. According to her, accidents in the home happen all the time."

"Sometimes people talk stupid. Why doesn't he go to the police with his suspicion?"

I laughed. "Frank, are you hearing yourself? She is Allan Steelwood's sister. Nobody would believe him, and it would put his life in even greater danger. Allan Steelwood is more dangerous and ruthless than his father ever was."

"You believe this man?"

"I didn't at first, but now, after talking to you, I'm not so sure."

"So what are you going to do?"

"I don't know—yet, but I'm a firm believer in karma. We are responsible for our actions and have to atone for our sins somehow; sometimes it takes a while for it to happen, but eventually it does. The Universe works that way. When you least expect it, your deeds of the past will pop up and demand payment. Some people call certain events coincidence, others call it twist of fate, and some will say everything happens for a reason. I'm one of those people. I met her husband in a bar; apparently, by chance. Perhaps it was fate." I rose from my chair. "We'll see what happens. Take care, Frank. We'll have to get together for coffee. Talk about old times."

He didn't laugh when he looked at me and said, "I had no idea you were into this deep stuff, Lews, and you've become so serious. All the time we knew each other, you were this cool guy, a bit on the crazy side, even unpredictable, at times." His lips formed a tiny smile. "They called you *The Loose Cannon*; not without reason and not just because of your name. You're not that guy anymore. What happened?"

"Time happened, old friend. And maybe the fact that I got branded, railroaded, and blackmailed to make me quit the force. Possibly also because my wife left me for another man and took me for everything I owned. Things like that have a tendency to change a man." I wasn't bitter, not much anyway, not anymore, but it was difficult to stay calm when talking about someone you loved and assumed they loved you back, just to find out it wasn't so.

"I'm sorry to hear that about your wife." He paused, seemingly searching for the right words. "Some things we can't control. Life is like that. I lost mine a couple of years ago."

"I didn't know, Frank."

"No, you wouldn't. She died of cancer. It happened quite suddenly."

Now I was lost for words. "Theresa was a good woman." I said. "At least you still have your daughters."

"Yes, I still have them. Rosalie, my oldest, is twenty-five now, married and has already a couple of kids. Two boys." He smiled. "One is four and the other one two. The oldest wants to become a policeman like his grandfather."

"I hope you'll talk him out of it." I reached across the desk to shake his hand. "Sorry about your wife. Perhaps we can keep in touch."

He nodded and shook my hand. "I'd like that. You and I, we made a good team. Too bad things turned out the way they did. I hope things work out for you. By the way, how are you doing? Is there a woman in your life?"

"I have a lady-friend. Her name is Sonya. She's a bartender at the Dancing Leprechaun." I chuckled. "The place is across the street from my office. So if I feel like a beer I don't have far to go."

"I'm happy to hear you haven't turned into a monk. A man needs a good woman. Well, you take care and good luck."

"Thanks. Be seeing you."

He was right. We had been a good team, almost friends, but that was in the past. We were two different people now. Time did that to us. Time and that son-of-a-bitch Albert Steelwood. I promised myself to nail his daughter's hide to the wall and not shed a tear.

When I got back to my office, Nelda was still there. "How did it go?" she asked.

"As expected," I replied.

"Was it successful? Did you find anything?"

I shrugged. "Depends how you look at it. Maybe it's what I didn't find."

"What do you mean?"

"Sometimes the clue is so obvious that you don't see it because it is hidden in what you don't see."

"Are you talking in riddles now? What you just said sounds like so much gibberish."

"Maybe gibberish to you, little girl, but it's pretty clear to me."

She shook her head and gave me one of her looks. "Have you been drinking again? Or are you trying to impress me by pretending to be this wise man of mystery?"

"Neither. By the way, what did *you* find out?"

"Probably more than you."

"Let's hear it."

"Not much on Cole. Actually, nothing. It is different with Julia. She is active on social media, but she doesn't mention Cole anywhere.

However, I found out something that may be of great interest to you, may even blow your mind a little."

"She's a man in disguise?" Sometimes I do say stupid things. Why? Don't even ask.

She shot me a quick glare. "You never stop, do you?"

I just grinned and shrugged. "Sorry. Go on."

"Well, as you know, Julia used to be a model. She went under the name Julia Brenner. It was her mother's maiden name, but here comes the clincher: Guess who her mother is married to?"

I spread my hands, indicating I had no idea. "Hit me with that one."

"Aneta Brenner is married to a man you hate. His name is Albert Steelwood."

"What? The former Police Commissioner?" There was a sudden desire in me to sit down. I fell into the couch, instantly regretting it. As I fought with the cushions, I said, "That makes her Allan and Angela Steelwood's sister. Tell me you're kidding me."

"I wish I were. Actually, she is their half-sister. Aneta is Albert Steelwood's second wife."

I tried to sit up but surrendered to the cushions. Struggling in their merciless grip like a wolf in a trap, I groaned, "Why am I surprised? It seems the Universe is run by some cruel joker. This means Mr. Titman is our present Police Commissioner's brother-in-law and our ex-commissioner's son-in-law."

"I thought you'd like it."

"What are the chances? Titman told me I was recommended by a mutual friend. Now I can guess who this friend was."

"Commissioner Steelwood. I wonder why he would recommend you. I thought he hates you."

"He recommended me because he hates me. Somehow I have a feeling Mr. Titman is going to spell trouble for us. We'd better be on guard. Remember, he asked me to kill Cole? Perhaps that was a trap." My gut was suddenly churning, and it wasn't just because I was hungry.

Nelda's eyes studied me silently. "You know," she said after a while, "it might be a good idea to drop that other case."

"You mean the murder of Shirley Brandon's husband?"

84

She shook her head. "No. I'm talking about Benny Miller, the husband of Commissioner Steelwood's sister Angela."

"Why?"

"This whole thing is beginning to turn out weird. I don't like weird things."

"I have to admit it is weird, but look at it another way. Since all these people seem to be connected, it may make our job of investigating them even a bit easier."

"How do you figure that?"

"Well, by digging deeper into Titman's background, I may dig up some stuff involving our Commissioner. Since they are related by marriage, the Commissioner might be inclined to close his eyes a little when it comes to Titman's affairs. By the way, our suspicions about Titman were correct. He is in bed with some very bad people. In fact, he is a bad guy himself. As far as Angela Steelwood is concerned, the Commissioner may have had his hand in covering up for her."

"How does the murder of that Brandon guy fit into this?"

"Bart Brandon was an employee of the Lucky Millionaire's Casino, a place owned by Mr. Frederick Titman. Don't you find that coincidental?"

"I find it creepy," she said.

"Creepy or not, those are the facts. As I told my ex-partner Frank Kabinsky this afternoon, the Universe sometimes works in mysterious ways." I changed the tone of my voice and made it sound hollow. "There are more things in heaven and earth, Horatio, than are dreamt of in your philosophy," I quoted. "What seems impossible suddenly happens. Everything is connected somehow. We don't always see it. Most of us are blind. We stumble through life without noticing what happens all around us. You just have to open your eyes."

"Oh, just stop with this crazy talk already. You're making my skin crawl." She was almost angry. "My eyes are wide open. All I can see is trouble ahead. Whatever happened to those simple cases where you go on a stakeout, take pictures of cheating wives, present them to their husbands, and we're done?"

I tried to calm her down. "We have a case like that, except it turned into something not so simple. Let's stay calm and not panic. We did our job with Julia and gave Mr. Titman the information he wanted. What he does with that is out of our hands. We won't worry about Cole. That's not our job anymore. Let Titman do his own digging. Now we'll move onto the next case."

"Which is?"

"Finding Brad Brandon's murderer."

"Which may bring us right back to Mr. Titman. Wonderful. And who is this Horatio, anyway?"

"Who?"

"You mentioned some guy named Horatio in your stupid talk. Who is he?"

"Oh that? I just quoted something from Shakespeare's Hamlet."

"In other words, showing off your superior knowledge to an uneducated person like me. You never quit."

"Oh, for heaven's sake, Nelda, will you ever stop this? Don't always be so sensitive about things. My intentions are never to make you feel dumb or uneducated. What about Harry Rosser? Did you do a search for him?"

"I did. Nothing."

I sighed. "I may have to talk to Kabinsky again. I'm sure the guy is in the police files. By the way, I only had a light lunch and I feel like eating a steak tonight. Want to come with me for supper?"

"I had a hamburger, but thanks. Besides, I'm going to the gym tonight."

"Oh, I forgot. Your martial arts club." I shrugged. "Well, I asked."

"You did and I'm wondering why. Did you have a fall or something? Or some kind of stroke? It happens with people your age, you know."

"I will repeat this again: I'm only forty-one and I feel fine. You're the closest thing I have to a family and I realized I've been neglecting you. I just thought we should spend more time together."

"We are together every day in the office." She gave her head a slight shake. Watching me trying to escape the death grip of the cushions, she said, "You need some help with that, old man?" Without waiting for my answer, she came, grabbed my hand and pulled me up.

"I would have managed," I said. "By the way, you are quite strong."

"Sure, you would have managed, but when. You should go to the gym once in a while and work out before you get too weak."

SEVEN

IN THE MORNING, I got a call from the Seven Saints Hospital. The caller asked me if I knew a Benny Miller. When I told her I did, she said, "Mr. Miller was checked in yesterday morning. He is in intensive care right now. He asked us to contact you."

"Why is he in the hospital?" I asked.

"He had an apparent heart attack. That's all I can tell you."

"A heart attack?" I said, wondering why he asked I be contacted. "Thank you for calling." I hung up. In a way, it didn't come as a great surprise to hear that Miller had a heart attack. After all, he had been overweight and he seemed to have an alcohol problem, which made him a good candidate for getting a heart attack. But why he would ask them to get in touch with me made me wonder. I decided to pay him a visit.

He was awake when I walked into the room. When he saw me, he gave me a feeble smile. "I'm glad you came, Mr. Canon. I'd offer you something to drink, but the nurses refuse to stock the bar." His voice sounded weak and a bit hoarse.

"Glad to see you can still make jokes," I said. Looking around the room, I found a chair and pulled it closer to the bed. Then I turned on the recorder I carried in my pocket. "They tell me you had a heart attack, Mr. Miller."

"So it seems," he said, struggling with the words. "Fortunately, only a small one. They did all kinds of tests and Doctor Cooper told me he found high amounts of Chromium and Zinc in my blood and urine."

"And that's unusual?"

"People take Chromium to regulate their blood sugar. Some men take Zinc to prevent prostate cancer, but it is also taken for other reasons. Chromium and Zinc are metals and some people are allergic to metals. I am one of them. I don't take those supplements, not anymore. When I did take them I got heart palpations."

"Then how do you explain them in your bloodstream?"

"My wife has a whole cabinet full of vitamins. She must have slipped them into my food without my knowledge."

"Why would she do that?" I knew what he was going to say but asked anyway. For the record.

"Because she wants to kill me. I told you that once already when I hired you."

"Yes, you mentioned it. Tell me, why do you think your wife wants to kill you?"

"Why? She has many reasons." He coughed and closed his eyes for a moment. Then he whispered, "Five million reasons."

"I don't understand." I guessed what he meant, but I wanted him to say it.

"She took out a life insurance policy on me in the amount of five million dollars. I am worth much more dead than alive. Does that sound like a good reason to want me dead?"

"A five million dollar life insurance is a good reason to murder someone, I guess." I repeated the number to leave no doubt. "I fail to understand, though, why you believe your wife wants to murder you, Mr. Miller. Could there be another reason besides the life insurance?"

"Because the bitch hates me. I never told anyone, but she hates men in general. She's a butch, that's what she is. We haven't had sex in years. She never liked it. Did I tell you that she murdered her ex-husband?"

"Yes, you did. That's why you hired me in the first place—to investigate her ex-husband's murder, remember?"

"Right, I remember. Are you gonna marry that waitress with the nice ass?" He tried to chuckle but managed only a cough.

I switched off the recorder. I would have to edit out that last sentence. "Do you remember her ex-husband's last name?"

"Moonglow. Herman Moonglow. I remember it because it is a strange name."

"Herman Moonglow," I repeated. "I shouldn't have any problem remembering that one. Listen, I hope you get better soon. I'll look into your wife's background, I promise."

He lifted a hand with his thumb up. "Good man. I have faith in you."

After leaving his room, I decided to talk to Doctor Cooper. The nurse told me he was busy but he would see me as soon as he was able to. I waited nearly an hour until she told me to go into his office.

"My name is Lews Canon," I introduced myself. "I'd like to talk to you about Mr. Benny Miller."

"Are you one of his relatives?" Dr. Cooper asked.

"No, I'm a Private Investigator. Mr. Miller hired me to look into his case."

"His case? What case?"

"He believes his wife wants to kill him."

Dr. Cooper gave me a surprised look. "He believes that? That's a serious charge. Are you certain he isn't just imagining it? It happens when people have a traumatic experience, like a heart attack. It's not unusual for them to become paranoid and get all kinds of crazy ideas. Did he give you a valid reason?"

"He did and I'm inclined to believe him. I need to ask you for a favor. Angela Steelwood, that's Mr. Miller's wife, was married before. Her ex-husband died in 2005 of an apparent heart attack after slipping in the shower. His name was Herman Moonglow. There is a good chance he was sent here, because your hospital is the nearest. Do you think you could check it out?"

"I'm not so sure, Mr. Canon. I can't just give out information about our patients to anyone, you must understand that."

"I do understand. That information is confidential. I have the same policy about my clients. But sometimes certain circumstances override policies like that. Mr. Miller is bringing up serious charges against his wife. Don't you think it is our responsibility to investigate such charges? He told me about the Chromium and Zinc in his blood. He doesn't take vitamin supplements. Can you explain how they got into his system?"

"No, I can't."

"Well, Mr. Miller claims his wife may have fed them to him in his food. Apparently, she's into vitamins, so his assumption is not farfetched. Mr. Miller was lucky. He lived after suffering an apparent heart attack, but Mrs. Miller ex-husband wasn't so lucky. Don't you think it's a strange coincidence that both of her husbands would have a heart attack?"

He shrugged. "Not really. It happens all the time."

I leaned across his desk and looked him straight in the eyes. "Dr. Cooper, I used to be a cop and I still have friends on the force. It would be easy for me to convince one of them to obtain a court order. I would like to avoid that, because it may not reflect favorably on your hospital. So let's do both of us a favor and go the easy route. I promise, I won't reveal anything you tell me to the wrong people. After all, I am a licensed investigator and do have my principles. I don't blab to everyone on the street about my cases."

"I don't know," he said, hesitating, but I could see he was ready to capitulate. All he needed was another gentle push.

"You would not want to be responsible should Mr. Miller be right and he dies after the next attempt on his life. So follow your conscience and take a look. Please, Dr. Cooper. A man's life may be at stake here."

"All right." He spread both hands. "You convinced me. But not a word to anyone, please. I can't afford to have this come out. I do have a responsibility to this hospital's reputation and to our investors."

"Yes, the investors. We must make certain they don't get annoyed. Don't worry. I can keep secrets."

It didn't take him long to find the name of Herman Moonglow in the files. He had indeed been admitted to the Seven Saints Hospital in 2005. Cause of death was listed as heart attack.

"Did the coroner do an autopsy?" I asked.

He nodded. "Yes, but there is more here in the report." He looked up. His expression was grave. "There were high amounts of iron, magnesium, and calcium in his blood and urine. The attending physician left a note that Mr. Moonglow regained consciousness briefly after being admitted. He complained of being dizzy. Apparently, that's why he slipped in the shower in the first place."

"Dizzy?" I asked.

"Large doses of the supplements mentioned may cause dizziness, among other disorders."

"I guess there is no way you could print out that report?"

He shook his head. "Sorry, I can't do that. I'm already violating hospital policy by showing you this." He stared at the screen. "What are you going to do with what you've learned?"

"I will go ahead with my investigation of Mrs. Steelwood." When I saw his face going dark, I assured him, "Your name will not come up, Dr. Cooper. I'll keep my promise. I'm grateful for your assistance. You may just have helped save a man's life."

Kabinsky was at his desk when I walked into the precinct. When he saw me, he grinned and said, "We have to stop meeting like this, Lews. Twice in a row? People may get the wrong idea." He became serious when he looked into my face. "Something wrong?"

I sank into the chair that was still in front of his desk. "I just came from the hospital. One of my clients is there. He had a heart attack. Apparently, induced by high amounts of some vitamins he's consumed, given to him by his wife without his knowledge."

"Who is he?"

"His name is Benny Miller. He's the husband of Angela Steelwood."

Kabinsky ran a broad hand across his forehead. His face looked strained when he stared at me. "What do you want from me, Lews?"

I pulled my little recorder from my pocket. "I want you to listen to this." I switched it on but stopped it before it came to the part about Sonya's ass.

"Is he pressing charges?" Kabinsky asked in a quiet voice.

"Not yet. He wants me to investigate his wife and find proof of his accusation. I have good reason to believe now that she murdered her ex-husband twelve years ago. I managed to read his chart. He also had high levels of toxic substances in his blood."

"I wish you wouldn't drag me into this, Lews."

"You were the investigating officer in that case. Like it or not, you are involved."

"I can't just open a case that's twelve years old. Not without just cause. Steelwood will have my head. I can't go up against him. You must understand, Lews. Come on, give me a break." This was not at all like him. The Kabinsky I remembered was not this pleading, almost pathetic old man crouching in his chair.

I rose. "I understand, Frank. I wanted you to hear this, that's all." I put my recorder back into my pocket. "I'll keep this in case it is needed at some time in the future."

"I'm sorry, Lews. I really am. You have no idea what the atmosphere is like these days."

I felt my mouth pulling down. "You forget I experienced some of that atmosphere when I left. By the way, Commissioner Steelwood and Frederick Titman have more in common than you think. Check out Julia Titman, Frederick's wife. She used to be a fashion model and went by the name Julia Brenner." I tipped the shield of my cap. "Be seeing you, Frank."

The need for a drink prompted me to drop in at the Dancing Leprechaun. Sonya wasn't there. Her shift didn't start until five. It didn't matter. I sat down at one of the tables in the corner and ordered a sandwich and a beer. They didn't serve much else. The place was empty at this time of day and it was quiet. This was a nightclub and the action didn't start until evening. That's when all the young people dropped in to wind down from a hectic day.

I usually try to avoid noisy places like that. If it weren't for Sonya, I don't think the Dancing Leprechaun would be on my list of places to visit. Perhaps Nelda was right and I was getting old.

My thoughts drifted to Kabinsky. I couldn't really blame him for being afraid to get involved in this affair. Allan Steelwood was a dangerous man and not to be crossed, as had been his father before him. Digging into his sister's past might reveal things about him, things he might want to keep hidden.

My ex-partner Steven Meloni popped unbidden into my mind. He had been a dirty cop; as dirty as they come. After I exposed Meloni for being involved in dealing drugs, taking bribes, and giving false testimony in a murder case, he went to jail. Even his father, who was a judge, couldn't save his hide. Meloni and Allan Steelwood were friends, and I knew Steelwood had been involved also, and I was ready to prove it. However, his father, Commissioner Alex Steelwood, pulled some strings and any evidence I thought I had suddenly disappeared, along with one of the witnesses of the murder Meloni and I had been investigating.

I had implicated a couple of other cops, but I lost in the end. Sometimes it is best to close your eyes and look the other way. You can never win a fight against people like the Commissioner. His position gave him a great advantage. He had connections to other corrupt people in places of power, even to organized crime. I had seen Alex Steelwood in the company of crime boss Enrico Ramiro, head of the Ramiro Family, a known criminal organization.

Allan Steelwood, our present Commissioner, was as dirty as his father. I suspected him to be behind the disappearance of the main witness in my murder case, but I couldn't prove it.

The only reward I received for being a good cop was to be forced to resign. Steelwood had literally given me an ultimatum—to resign or to be charged with the beating death of a drunken panhandler.

It was a trumped-up charge, but one I could not fight and hope to win. I had come across the unconscious body of a vagrant. He had been beaten badly. I tried to wake him up by slapping him a few times. As luck wants it, a passerby got the whole thing on his cell-phone. He claimed I was the one who beat the man, who later died from his injuries.

I finished my sandwich and ordered another beer and another after that. By the time Sonya started her shift I was feeling good and had no cares in the world.

"I think you should go home," she said.

I gave her a happy grin. "I'm at home right here and I feel fine. How about bringing me another beer?"

"You are drunk. I'm not giving you another beer or anything else. Come on, I'll take you to my place. You are in no shape to drive home to yours." She grabbed my arm and I stumbled beside her to the back door where her car was parked.

Even in my drunken stupor I could tell she was angry with me, because she didn't say anything until we were inside her suite. "You should cut down on your alcohol consumption, Lews," she scolded me.

"I know, but sometimes I need a few beers to calm down my

nerves," I told her. "You don't know the crap I'm dealing with right now."

"What you need right now is a cup of coffee to clear your head."

I sat down on the couch and watched her brew me a cup. She had one of those machines that brews only one cup at a time. It didn't take long until she put the cup in front of me. "Drink this and then lie down and sleep it off. Take the couch. I have no time to make up the bed for you. I have to get back to work."

She threw a blanket onto the couch and rushed out again. I sat there, sipping my coffee and feeling like an idiot. Sonya was right. I should stop with these drinking binges. When I was done with my coffee, I went to the washroom, took a shower, and after that I flopped down on the couch.

I must have fallen asleep immediately, because the next thing I became aware of was a hand shaking my shoulder. I opened my eyes and saw Sonya's face above me. She looked tired. "You want to join me in my bed?" she asked. "I need a warm body to cling to and a pair of strong arms to hold me."

"What time is it?"

"It's two o'clock."

"In the afternoon?"

"No, in the morning. It's still dark outside. Now—come to bed."

I was suddenly wide awake and my head was not feeling too badly. Once we lay in bed, she snuggled close and I held her tight. We made love and the world was suddenly a happy place again. Amazing what the affection of a woman can do to a man's disposition.

When we sat at the breakfast table, she looked at me and smiled. I smiled back and she reached across the table and touched my hand. "I love you, you know."

"I know," I said.

"How about you? Do you love me?"

"Of course I do. What other reason would I have to hang out with you?"

"The sex," she said, her eyes studying my face.

"Don't be silly. If I wanted strictly sex I could go and visit a hooker."

"A hooker costs money. I give it to you for free."

"You enjoy it, don't you? Well, I enjoy it, too. I enjoy the sex and I enjoy the love you give me. I wouldn't have it any other way. Sex without love is not what I seek."

"You could have it more often if you'd move in with me," she said coyly.

"Please, don't start that again. You know my feelings on that one. Let's just keep our relationship the way it is. Who knows, someday we may take it to the next level but not yet." I looked at my watch. "I'd better get going. Can you drive me? I suddenly remembered how I got here last night. My car is back at the office, and it's a long walk."

"No problem. I'd like to do some shopping anyway."

Nelda was already in the office when Sonya dropped me off. She sat behind her desk and was reading the newspaper. She didn't say anything when I walked in; she just shoved the paper at me. A small article circled with a red pen caught my eye immediately.

The headline of the article read *Decorated war hero murdered.*

As I read on a cold shiver ran down my spine.

The body of a man, identified as George Cole, was found last night near his residence. Police suspect he was killed during a robbery. Cole...

I looked up to see Nelda watching me.

"It's our fault," she said with a quiet voice.

"Perhaps in a small way it is, but it is possible his death has nothing to do with the case." I felt suddenly cold inside. There was a good chance I was wrong. It was just too much of a coincidence that Cole should wind up dead only two days after I gave his name to Titman.

"I'm sure Titman had Cole murdered. He looked quite angry when I saw him drive away last time he was here. Like a man ready to kill someone."

"Just because he was angry doesn't mean he did commit murder. Let's face it he just received news about his wife's infidelity. Any man would be angry and ready to kill his rival." I don't know why I defended Titman. Maybe I didn't want to accept that it was our doing a man had been murdered.

"He offered you money to get rid of Cole. Did you forget?"

"No, I haven't, but I was hoping it was all said in the heat of the moment." The words came out of my mouth, but I didn't believe them myself.

"I guess we can stop trying to dig up information on Cole," Nelda said. "We should have asked for more money from Titman."

"I haven't given him the final bill yet," I said. "I think I'll take a ride down to his office."

Nelda shook her head in disbelief. "You must be crazy. Do you really think he'll pay you more money? He got what he wanted. He doesn't need us anymore. In fact, now we are a liability."

"At least I can confront him and let him know that we are on to him. That fat, little bastard surely fooled me. I don't like to be made a fool of," I said angrily.

"Why don't you take your gun and shoot that ugly dwarf," Nelda suggested. "Nobody would miss him."

"Would you visit me in jail?" I asked. "Besides, he's probably surrounded by bodyguards who would frisk me if I took a gun along. We missed our chance when he was in our office and more vulnerable."

"You could always strangle him."

I chuckled. "I wouldn't get my hands around his fat neck." A serious thought popped into my mind. "I hope he doesn't hurt Julia."

"She's his wife and he probably loves her, despite her being unfaithful. He'll never find another woman like her. And don't forget she's the sister of the Police Commissioner."

"That might be a deterrent not to harm her, but she's only the half-sister, being the daughter of Albert Steelwood's second wife, and not exactly the Commissioner's favorite. As for loving her? If Titman's mad enough he won't let that hold him back, either. Men like him can buy plenty of good-looking women. I've seen uglier men with gorgeous women. Enough money buys pretty much anything."

"No man can buy my sexual favors," she said.

"Not every man pays a woman to have sex with him."

"We should find out who did it," Nelda said.

"Let the police handle it. It's out of our hands. There would be no money in it, anyway. Aren't you the one who said we can't afford pro-bono jobs?"

"I did say that, didn't I? I just feel so crappy about this whole thing."

"So do I, but there is nothing we can do about it now." I needed to change the subject. "How did your martial arts class go yesterday?"

She shrugged. "Fine. In fact, I'm still pumped up and feel like beating the crap out of somebody, especially after reading the newspaper this morning."

"As long as you don't take your anger out on me," I said.

"It wouldn't be a bad idea for you to join a martial arts class. You'll never know when you need the skills."

"I hate violence. I had enough of it to last me a lifetime after spending those weeks in Bosnia in 1995. Why do you think I never carry a gun?"

"I wondered about that. What about when you were a cop? You carried a gun then, didn't you?"

"Yes, I did. With reluctance, I might add."

"Didn't you ever have to use it? I mean you were a cop for twelve years. You must have had occasions to draw your gun."

"Quite a few, but I drew it only when absolutely necessary."

"You ever shoot anyone?"

"As a cop?"

"Yes. And if yes was it a killing shot?"

Her icy blue eyes drilled holes right into my brain and I felt like a prisoner who was being interrogated. She had a way of drawing even information that was buried deep from a person's memories; memories best left buried.

"Yes," I said, not happy about it as forgotten memories rose to the surface like bad seeds in a jar.

"What happened? Or don't you want to talk about it?"

"Too late now. This happened in my second year as a homicide detective. I shot a guy who was in the process of robbing a bank. He shot at me first but missed. I didn't miss. Even though I'm not fond of guns doesn't mean I can't hit my target, but most of the time I drew my gun only for show, to intimidate."

"Was he the only one you shot?"

"No, he wasn't. Can we drop the subject?"

"I never shot anyone, but..." She patted the 45 on her hip. "This goes wherever I go. It deters people from messing with me."

Oh, Nelda. If you only knew. You don't need a gun to keep people from messing with you. One look into your face and eyes is enough. You'd cause the devil to run back to hell, screaming.

I thought it but didn't say it. As I said, I hate violence. No need to get her aroused, especially since she had announced only moments ago she felt like beating up somebody. I wasn't going to be her punching bag. Of course, I knew she'd never do that. Those were just my own stupid thoughts. She respected me too much, and, in many ways I respected and loved her exactly the same.

"You should at least practice self-defense," she said, stubbornly refusing to change the subject.

"I was trained in self-defense when I was in the army. I'm out of practice and, I guess, getting back into it wouldn't hurt, but so far I haven't needed it."

"Not yet but one never knows. By the way, I forgot to tell you. Yesterday, these two guys dropped in. They said they were from NWAS and they had orders to install a few cameras in our office. Courtesy of Mr. Miller."

"And did they?"

"Did they what?"

"Install cameras?" I looked around the office and actually saw something that hadn't been there before. It was like a small bubble in one of the corners near the ceiling.

"Yes, they did. I see you've spotted one. We have three. They are connected to my computer."

"Why yours?"

"Because I suggested it to them. I'm in the office more often than you and therefore use the computer more often. On top of that, I know more about computers than you. Does that make sense to you?"

"I guess so. Should I feel safer now being in the office with cameras watching and recording my every move?"

"They can be shut off but they suggested to leave them running at all times to minimize the chance of them being off when they're needed. I have no problem with them. Why should you? Are you doing things in here when I'm not around that nobody else should know of?" She gave me a little smirk.

"Don't be silly. What would I be doing? I don't even curse when I'm alone. You know better than that."

She laughed. "You must be the only guy I know of who doesn't swear. Hell, I know some women who use swear words all the time."

"Good for them. What can I say in my defense? I just don't believe a man or woman needs to use profane language to let people know how tough they are. I never heard you talk like that."

"Sometimes I do. Mostly when I'm with people who also do it. It seems people expect me to curse. I don't look exactly like a dainty lady, so why should I behave like one, right?"

"I don't expect you to curse. In fact, I hope you never do around me. I'd be disappointed."

"I won't." Her face had smoothed out and she didn't look so scary anymore. Her smile was almost gentle. "You are so different from most men I run across. And you certainly don't fit the image people have of a detective. You don't cuss, you don't carry a gun, you don't smoke, you don't wear dark sunglasses. Hell, you don't even wear a decent hat."

"What do you consider a decent hat? I'm wearing a baseball cap."

"That's exactly what I mean. Who ever heard of a detective wearing a baseball cap?" She threw up her hands. "You're just a weird guy. Even your eyes aren't normal. You should cover them up with dark glasses. I wouldn't be surprised if you scared potential customers away when they look into your eyes."

I sighed. "Well, like you said—I don't fit into a mold. I am Lews Bullseye Canon." I grinned. "One of a kind. And I like it like that."

"What was my dad like?" she asked suddenly.

Her question came out of the blue, unexpected. "Your dad? He was a special kind of guy and my best friend. No, he was more than a friend. He was like an older brother to me. A good cop, I might add. By the way, he didn't care much for cursing, either."

"Did you know each other long?"

"Since 1993. I was seventeen. I had just bought my car—a 1983 VW and I wanted to see how fast it would go. I was stopped by a young cop and he asked where I was going in such a hurry. I told him I was late for my baseball practice. It was a lie. He knew it was and he gave me a lecture about the dangers of speeding and a warning. No ticket. Then he wanted to know the name of the team I played with and when we'd be playing. I didn't have to make up that one, because I actually was a baseball player. He came to watch me; perhaps just to see if I had spoken the truth. As it turned out he was also into baseball. That cop was your dad. Somehow he took a liking to me. We became good friends and I was best man at his wedding. That was in 1994, a month before I joined the military. He's the reason I became a cop when my tour of duty was finished."

"You never told me any of that. I don't remember much about him. He never seemed to have any time for me. That's all I remember." She sounded bitter. I knew exactly how she felt.

"Not because he didn't care. He cared a lot about you, but being a cop isn't an easy life. You spend much of your time chasing criminals; you work irregular hours and never seem to have time for your family. It was even harder for him after your mom passed away. Being a single parent is a tough job."

"Yeah, my mom. I don't remember her at all. I was only six when she died."

"She was a beautiful woman and a lot of fun. Your dad loved her deeply. She was still so young. Only twenty-eight. Her death was a huge blow to him. It changed him."

"He never talked about her. How did she die?"

"She was hit by a drunk driver." I remembered the day when Kevin called me and told me about the accident. It was one of those days that etches itself into one's memory and stays there forever.

"Perhaps someday you can tell me more about my parents. I really would like to understand my own roots a bit better." She stared at her computer screen. "My dream was to become a cop like my father so I could spend more time with him, but I screwed that up with my own stupidity."

"We all make mistakes in our lives and they do carry consequences. I've made plenty of mistakes in my life. Some things we can't change, but we can make the best of it. You made a mistake and you paid for it. But that is behind you. You must look toward the future. You're still young." I smiled. "Who knows—someday you may inherit all this." I made a sweeping motion with my arm. "Isn't that something to look forward to?"

"You're joking, aren't you?" She shook her head in apparent disgust, but she was smiling. "Listen, Lews, I appreciate what you did for me. I really do, but I can't see myself doing this for the rest of my life. There has to be something better out there for me."

"I'm sure there is, but in the meantime let's concentrate on right now." I was suddenly reminded again what we read in the paper. "Too bad about Cole. I didn't know the man, but he didn't deserve to be murdered for having an affair with another man's wife. Julia is as guilty as he is."

"Do you really think Julia is safe?"

"I hope so. I don't think Titman would be so stupid and murder his own wife."

She gave me a thoughtful look, which was a bit scary in itself. "You know, we are already condemning Titman. I have no love for the man, as you are aware, but what if he had nothing to do with Cole's death? What if Cole is just the victim of a robbery?"

"No." I waved off her concern. "He's guilty; I'm sure of that. It would be too much of a coincidence, but how can we prove it?"

"My question is do we *have* to prove it?"

"We don't. Titman hired us to bring him evidence of his wife's infidelity. We did that. What he did with that information is not our concern." I didn't believe that, but deep down I knew I was right. The death of George Cole was a police matter. There was nothing we could or should do about it. Nobody could hold us responsible for Cole's murder.

"It may be our moral obligation to look into it." She was too stubborn to give it up, and I couldn't even blame her.

"Let it go," I said. "For now, anyway."

"Okay. Like you said, *for now*."

EIGHT

A FEW DAYS after Cole's death I received a call from someone I didn't expect—Julia Titman.

"Who gave you my name and number?" I asked.

"My hairdresser Shirley Brandon."

"What can I do for you, Mrs. Titman?"

"I'd rather not say it on the phone. Can I come and see you?"

"How about one hour from now?"

She was in my office an hour later. Appearing tired and even somewhat disheveled, she didn't look as glamorous as in the pictures on the walls in the gallery, but she was still a beautiful woman. She was one of those women blessed with a natural beauty that left her looking good even in the morning without a ton of makeup.

She sat on the wooden chair, legs crossed, studying me out of gray-green eyes. "Can I trust you, Mr. Canon?" she finally asked.

I spread my hands. "I'm like a priest, Mrs. Titman. Whatever you tell me will stay a secret with me."

She actually smiled a little. "I'm not here for a confession, Mr. Canon."

I smiled back. "I didn't think so; after all, I'm a detective not a priest. What did you want to tell me?"

"I believe my husband murdered a good friend of mine." She said it bluntly.

"Who is this man your husband allegedly murdered?" I pretended ignorance.

"His name is George Cole."

"The man who was found stabbed to death a few days ago?" I asked.

"You read about it? Did you read the whole article?"

I nodded. "I did. Apparently, he was the victim of a robbery."

"That's what the police say. He wasn't robbed. He was murdered and my husband is behind it. In fact, I fear for my own life." Her eyes were large and her face flushed. I realized she tried to stay calm, but she couldn't hide her anger and frustration.

"Why would you assume that, Mrs. Titman?" I couldn't tell her that I knew the answer to that question already. I could not let her know that her husband hired me to spy on her and that I was most likely responsible for Cole's murder.

"Because George Cole was not just a friend, he was my lover. My husband must have somehow found out. Do you know who my husband is?"

I couldn't carry on with the charade. She needed to know part of the truth, even if only for my own piece of mind.

"I know who your husband is, Mrs. Titman. I also know who you are. You are the former fashion model Julia Brenner. You are Police Commissioner Alan Steelwood's sister. Why come to me with your suspicion? Why not go to the police?"

She sat silent for a moment. "I don't think you understand, Mr. Canon. I can't go to the police, because my brother is deeply involved with my husband and the people he is associated with. My brother wouldn't blink an eye if something happened to me. He despises and hates me."

"Why?"

"Because he never accepted my mother as his stepmother. Neither did my sister. I was always the intruder into their happy family. The half-sister who should never have been born. I tried to break away from them when I changed my name to Brenner, my mother's maiden name, but it didn't work. My brother sold me to Frederick Titman—my husband." She spoke loud and seemed near hysteria. I suddenly did feel like a priest.

"Sold? I don't think I understand."

"I don't know the details, but I know that my husband had some hold over my brother and to appease him, my brother made a deal with him. I was the bargaining chip."

"I wasn't aware they did stuff like that in this country." I had to say something.

She laughed. "You can't be that ignorant not to know the things that go on beneath this veneer of civilization that covers the so-called free world, Mr. Canon. You are a detective and you must have come across a lot of ugliness in your career. You wouldn't believe the things I've witnessed in the five years I've been married to a monster. Yes, don't look so shocked. My husband is not the nice quiet man he portrays. He is a monster, a man with no conscience. He thrives on the sufferings of others. That and power and money."

"You are right. I've seen plenty of ugliness, but that is the world we live in, Mrs. Titman. I don't know what you want from me."

"I want you to kill my husband. I have money. Whatever it costs." Her beautiful face had undergone a sudden change. Her eyes seemed almost to glow and her expression made her look ugly.

I was a bit shocked hearing her say that but not surprised. I held up my hands as if I wanted to ward off a demon. "I don't know where you got the notion that I am an assassin. I don't kill people, no matter how much money I'm offered. I'm an investigator, and that's all. I consider myself a man of integrity."

"It's not a matter of integrity. It's a matter of justice, but I guess I got the wrong information about you. I thought you believed in justice."

"Why would you say that? Who else did you talk to besides Shirley Brandon?"

"John Pallitser."

That made me sit up straight. "John Pallitser? Then you did go to the cops!"

"I didn't. I overheard my brother and my husband mentioning his name once. And I got the impression that he was not one of their favorites. According to my brother, John Pallitser is a loudmouth and a racist but much too honest to be of any use. So I figured the feeling may be mutual."

"Well, your brother got it right about the loudmouth and racist, but I'm not sure about Pallitser's honesty. He and I never got along and I have to admit that I don't like him and he never liked me. I wonder why he would give you my name."

"He said you were a loose cannon, a man with a temper and unpredictable. By the way, he said the same thing about his relationship with you."

"Did you tell him you want your husband assassinated?"

"Mr. Canon, give me some credit. He's a cop. All I said was I wish my husband were dead or in jail, to which he replied he may just have the guy who could help me out. He said you were down on your luck and probably in need of money."

That made me chuckle. "That's the impression I gave him? Wow! I'm touched by his concern for my welfare. Why would he think I would kill someone in cold blood for money?"

"He didn't say that. I just figured that's what he implied. The rest was my idea." She looked at me with pleading eyes. "I really do need your help, Mr. Canon. If nothing else, find out how George died. I know my husband didn't do the stabbing, but I'm quite positive he hired the men who did. Find them for me." She opened her purse and pulled out a check book. "I am willing to pay you. Will a thousand dollars be enough to get you started?"

I hesitated, but the sight of that check made my heart beat a little faster. I'd be a fool to turn down money we needed badly. And since Nelda seemed to insist we do something, we might as well do it and get paid. It may ease our conscience and fatten our bank account a little. "Thousand dollars will be fine," I said, giving in to the voice of Nelda inside my head.

"Thank you, Mr. Canon." She retrieved a pen from her purse and filled out the check. Slipping off the chair, she handed me the check. "I hope to hear from you."

When she was gone, I stared at the closed door. Strange, how things have a way of being twisted around. It was kind of ironic. First her husband hired me to follow her and now she hired me to investigate him. Fate surly had a strange and almost sadistic sense of humor. If one could find any humor in it.

Miller called me a couple of days after Julia's visit.

"Mr. Canon, I just wanted to tell you I'm being released from the hospital. I won't be going home. I'll be renting a small apartment not far from my company. I won't even need a car to get to work, except when I'm on the road."

"That's great. Let me know when you're settled in and give me your address in case I want to get in touch with you."

"No problem. By the way, did they install those cameras in your office?"

"They did. Thank you, but I'm still not sure if they are necessary."

He chuckled into the phone. "Necessary or not, but they should give you a certain feeling of security. At least, if somebody breaks into your office you'll be able to identify the thieves."

It was my turn to chuckle. "Why would anyone break into my office? We have nothing worth stealing, except for an uncomfortable couch, a couple of worn desks. Stuff like that. All old and not worth anything."

"You have a computer?"

"Yes, two of them, but even they are ancient."

"It's not the computers, it's the information you have on them. Are you doing your banking on your computer?"

"Banking? Don't make me laugh, Mr. Miller. We don't have enough transactions to make it worthwhile."

"Don't shrug this off, Mr. Canon. If you have a computer, you will have personal information on it. Most people don't realize how much information thieves can gain from their computer or disregarded hard drive. And you have info on your clients, remember that. I gotta go. I'll get in touch with you again soon."

I was happy to hear Miller was okay again. I pondered what he had said about information. He was right, there would be information about my clients, but I'm still not really living in the twenty-first century. I still keep most of my files the old-fashioned way—in a filing cabinet. I know Nelda transfers some of the info into her computer. I prefer to look at paper.

I called Kabinsky in the afternoon and asked him how the

investigation into Cole's murder was going. He told me not much progress had been made as far as he knew. According to the investigating officer, Cole's death was not considered to be murder. Sure, they treated it as a homicide, but it was pretty clear it happened during a robbery.

"Maybe he wanted to be a hero and fought back," Kabinsky said. "He got killed during the struggle. That's all there is to it."

"You have any suspects?" I asked, somewhat annoyed with the way he treated Cole's death so callously.

"None yet. You want the truth? I don't believe they'll find any. It's one of those cases that will never be solved. What's your interest in the case anyway?"

"Cole was Julia Titman's lover."

There was a pause as Kabinsky digested the news. At least that's what I assumed he did. Then he said, "Are you implying anything with that?"

"I believe Titman had Cole murdered."

"Why would you think that and what's your obsession with Titman anyway?"

"It's not an obsession. I never told you, but Titman hired me to check up on his wife. He suspected she was unfaithful. I'm the one who told him about Cole. He was furious and offered me one hundred thousand dollars to kill Cole. When I told him I wouldn't do it, he said he didn't actually mean it, but I know he did, especially since Cole ended up dead a couple days later. Julia Titman also believes her husband is behind Cole's murder." I left out that she offered me money to kill her husband. "In fact, she is scared for her life."

There was another pause. "And you know that how?"

"This is just between you and me, Frank. She hired me to find proof her husband had Cole murdered. I'd appreciate it if you informed me about anything that may come across your desk concerning the death of George Cole."

"Lews, you're asking me to share confidential information with an outsider. It could get me into trouble. You're not a cop anymore."

"I'm asking as a friend. I would never divulge my source, you should know."

"Sorry, I can't take the chance. Things have changed these last few years. You have no idea. I wish you wouldn't involve me in your cases. First you want me to look into Angela Steelwood's file, accusing her of murder, and now it's Titman, a known mobster, who also happens to be the Commissioner's brother-in-law? I have no valid reason to do any of those things. I'm not going to jeopardize my job and my pension."

"I would never ask that of you, but don't worry, I'll manage. If for some reason you have something you might want to share I'd be grateful. You can call me in the office, my cell or at my lady-friend's place." After I gave him Sonya's number, I wondered if it had been such a good idea. "Don't call there unless it is really important and don't put her number into your computer. Should I find out any additional information, I'll let you know. Take care, Frank." I hung up with questions popping into my mind. What was he afraid of? Losing his pension? Why?

It seemed I was on my own. I had to find another way to get information on Titman.

What better way to do that than to visit the lion in his den.

I had never been to the Lucky Millionaire's Casino and I needed to look it up in the phonebook. When I got there, I saw they had valet parking so I parked my car on the street a block away and walked back. The place was fancy and screamed of great wealth. There was a sign over the huge glass doors that read: *Enter at your own risk. Only those who are willing to take a chance should pass through these doors.*

Well, I was willing to take a chance but not with my money. As soon as I walked into the vestibule a girl with flaming red lips, wearing a huge smile and not much else came up to me and pressed a glass into my hand. "Welcome and good luck, sir," she beamed.

"Thanks, Gorgeous," I said for lack of anything else to say, feeling like an idiot as soon as the words left my mouth. *What do they say these days to the girls in places like this?*

As I wound my way through the maze of walkways between the slot machines, I stopped once in a while to look at the rotating numbers and swirling colors on the screens. One thing was immediately clear to me: these were not the machines where you played with pennies or nickels, or even quarters. I saw numbers that made my head spin.

Then there were the tables where dealers dressed in dark suits dealt cards to men who oozed money and power. Girls who were practically nude cheered them on and fed them drinks. I felt out of my element. This was a world as foreign to me as a jewelry store would be to a monkey. I did not belong here and I had no desire to ever want to.

I had no idea where I would find Titman, so I decided to ask. Figuring he would probably have his office on the second floor, I climbed the plush covered treads of the fancy staircase. When I spotted a couple of burly guys in suits, I headed for the door they were guarding.

One of them put his hand on my chest and stopped me in my tracks. "Where are you headed in such a hurry?" His other hand hovered chest-high close to his open coat. I could see the bulge of a holster.

"I'm looking for Mr. Titman," I said.

"Do you have an appointment?"

"No, but he'll see me."

"Mr. Titman is busy and he doesn't see anybody without an appointment. Now—beat it!"

He was a big guy, but I've never been intimidated by guys like him. You know the old cliché: the bigger they are the harder they fall. However, I had no intentions starting a fight, but I wasn't going to retreat like a scolded puppy with its tail tucked between its legs.

I'm five eleven, which made me as tall as he. So I stared into his eyes and said, "They call me *The Loose Cannon* and there is a reason for it. You may have a gun tucked away inside your jacket and you feel confident. I'm a martial arts expert. I bet I could hit your face with my flat palm and push the bone splinter of your nose up into your brain, killing you instantly, before you can reach that gun of yours. Are you willing to take that bet?"

"Hey," the other guard said sharply, "are you forgetting about me, tough guy? You may be able to kill Tony, but I'll put a bullet into your brain before he hits the floor. Are you willing to also bet on that? So why don't you behave like a normal person and walk away. Go and play roulette or something and get that anger out of your system. I'm not going to ask you twice."

I turned with a slow and deliberate motion and favored him with a glaring look. I had practiced it many times and I hoped it looked as good and intimidating as it did in the mirror. "I'm not angry. In fact, I'm as cool as an Eskimo in his igloo. And that makes me dangerous. Obviously, you have no idea who I am. But I feel generous. I will overlook your feeble attempt at trying to stop me from seeing Mr. Titman. Be a good boy and tell him Lews Canon wants to talk to him. I don't need an appointment for Mr. Titman. If you don't follow my request your job here as doorman, as glorious as it may be, will be in jeopardy; I promise you that."

"No need to get so huffy and puffy about it. We get all types of nuts wanting to talk to Mr. Titman."

I had to give the man credit. He had balls. "Well, I'm not some nut. I am Lews Canon. You'd be wise to imprint my name into your brain. I'll be the man responsible for getting you fired from your cushy job if you don't let me through."

"Okay, okay." He stepped aside. "You can walk in, but I have to announce you first."

"You do that, my friend. It's Canon. Lews Canon. Can you remember that? On second thought, don't bother. I'll announce myself." Before he could protest, I brushed by him and opened the door.

Titman sat behind a huge desk. Much too huge for a short man like him, but it was probably there to impress people. The large window behind him added to the effect he obviously was trying to achieve. His body was silhouetted against the bright light falling through the window, making him appear larger than he actually was.

He lifted his head to see who dared to enter his kingdom without being announced. When he saw me, he looked surprised for a quick moment, but then his face smoothed out. I noticed he didn't wear his large, dark-rimmed glasses. In fact, he didn't wear any glasses. They had made him look like an owl, now he looked like a fox that had eaten too many chickens.

"How did you get in here, Canon?" He spoke sharply. It was obvious he was annoyed at somebody, mostly at me.

"Through the door," I said, walking up to his desk.

"What do you want?"

"You never paid me everything for the job I did. I want another thousand dollars."

At first, he just glared at me, and then he broke into a smile. It wasn't a friendly smile. "You have some nerve coming into my office unannounced and demanding money. If you're trying to shake me down, you picked the wrong man." His eyes were tiny slits now. "I paid you more than I should have, Canon. We're done. If you were smart, you would have taken my other offer. Let me give you some friendly advice. Forget we ever saw each other. I never hired you. Do you understand?"

I leaned onto the desk. "I understand you completely, Titman. Do you think I'm a moron? I know who and what you are. Don't try to intimidate me with this fancy office, with your two idiot guards out there, and the people you associate with. In reality you're nothing but a two-bit hustler, a crook, and a murderer. I know you're behind Cole's murder and I'm going to prove it."

His face didn't betray his thoughts, but you didn't have to be a genius to figure out what he was thinking. Then he chuckled and clapped his hands. "Nice speech, Canon. Did you rehearse it in front of the mirror? You know, I don't have to try to intimidate anyone, including you. People who know me are afraid of me. And they have reason to be."

"They may have, but I'm not afraid of you."

"Perhaps you should be. You're not very smart waltzing in here, accusing me of murder and threatening to expose me. I could make you disappear and nobody would ever find you, but I am hoping it won't come to that. In a way I underestimated you."

"Most people do. I leave that impression with people, so don't feel bad. What makes you think you underestimated me?"

"I hired you to investigate my wife, nothing else. That's what I paid you for. I was told I could depend on that. You were never supposed to stick your nose into my personal life."

"You never did tell me who recommended me."

"I guess there is no harm in telling you. It was Police Commissioner Steelwood. As you can see, you come highly recommended." He laughed when he said that, making it sound like some kind of joke.

"Why would Steelwood recommend me to you? He hates my guts."

"That's precisely why. In his words: Canon is an alcoholic and a bumbling idiot, who couldn't find his grandmother if she were lost. I counted on that. I figured you could handle a simple job like finding my wife's lover and not bother with anything else."

I chuckled grimly. "I'm happy to hear the Commissioner has such a low opinion of me. It will come as a great surprise when I put an end to his and your career."

"Spare me your theatrics, Canon. And don't try to be a hero. You think you know me, but you don't. You have no idea who you are trying to mess with. So drop it. Stop looking into my affairs or the affairs of my associates. You'll stay healthy much longer that way. Am I clear?"

"Oh, yes, you make it clear, but let me tell you, you fat little prick. You feel safe here inside these walls, and you think you are protected by your friends. Don't be so sure. I could end your miserable life right now and nobody could stop me."

Suddenly he had a gun in his hand and aimed it at me. "If anyone died right now it would be you, but I don't feel like having my carpet cleaned. So get the hell out of my sight, you stupid moron, before I change my mind!"

If I would have had a gun, I might have shot him right there, but my gun was safely stashed away inside a wooden box in my suite. And with good reason.

All I could do was shake my head in apparent disgust. I even managed a smile. "I guess you win this round, but don't worry, I'll keep in touch. Keep looking over your shoulder or check your fancy limousine before you get in. I may just be sitting in the backseat waiting for you." I tipped the rim of my baseball cap with one finger. "You take care now, Mr. Titman. Enjoy each day, because your days may be numbered."

He rose out of his chair and I realized again how short he was. He must have been sitting on a fat cushion. Waving his gun, he shouted after me, "How dare you threatening me in my own office? I'll put a bullet into your brain if you're not gone in five seconds, you piece of shit!"

I didn't look back, hoping he could control his rage long enough to let me leave his office alive. Closing the door behind me, I breathed a sigh of relief. That had been close. Maybe I had gone a little over the top playing my role as this macho, fearless superhero. I had certainly drawn his real persona out of him and he had shown me his true colors.

This man was dangerous and a man had to be stupid to awaken his wrath.

And I was that man. Perhaps Titman had taken the bait and he would come after me. I was counting on it. However, I played a dangerous game and it could backfire if I weren't careful. From now on I had to be on guard at all times. I was the one who needed to look over his shoulder, not Titman. There was nothing I could do to him.

"See you around," I said to the two guards as I walked away.

This called for a drink to calm down my nerves, so I headed for The Dancing Leprechaun. Sonya wasn't there. It was her night off. I sat by the bar for a while, but I only had one Scotch and a couple of beers before I headed home. I could have gone to Sonya's place, but I needed to be alone to do some thinking.

NINE

WHEN I GOT to my office the next morning, Nelda was already there.

The place was a mess. Some angry person had taken a knife to the cushions on the couch; there were pieces of plastic and Styrofoam everywhere, but that wasn't the worst of it. Both of our monitors had been smashed into tiny pieces and the files from the filing cabinet were spread across the whole floor.

"What the hell happened here?" was all I could say.

"Somebody broke in," Nelda said, brightly.

"I need to sit down," I said, looking around, but even the wooden chair had been busted into small chunks; good only for firewood. Nelda pointed to my chair behind the desk. "They didn't break that one."

I moved behind my desk and sank down. My gaze fell onto the computer console under the desk. It was still in one piece. Nelda saw my look and said, "They weren't too smart. They broke the monitors but left the towers intact. Our information is still safe on the hard drives."

"Who could have done this?" I asked.

"We can find out easily," Nelda said. "Did you forget we have cameras?"

"I did, but now that you mention it I remember. You said the recordings are on your computer. How can we check that now without a monitor?"

"We'll have to buy new ones. There is a bright side—it's cheaper than buying a whole new computer. I have to go to the bank anyway and deposit the check you gave me. The one from Julia Titman. There is a computer recycling store across the street from the bank. I'll go there." She grabbed her purse and headed for the door. Before she walked out, she said, "Maybe you could gather the files and put them into their folders and back into the cabinet while I'm gone. You can also check which ones are missing. Obviously, they were looking for something."

There was nothing else to do anyway, so I got busy with the files. It didn't take me long to discover which files were missing and it didn't come as a huge surprise.

Titman's folder was missing, along with all his files, like the picture of Julia and other information. But that was okay. We still had everything on Nelda's computer. I hoped.

She came back just as I finished putting the last folders into the filing cabinet. She carried two boxes. "They gave me a better deal if I bought two. We need them anyway."

It didn't take her long to hook up her new monitor. The pictures from the cameras were amazingly clear. They showed two guys entering the office. One of them was tall and wiry looking, while the other one was big and heavyset. The only problem was both men wore balaclavas. "Too bad, there is no way we can identify these guys," Nelda commented as we went through the pictures.

The big guy was smashing the monitors with a crowbar, while his partner pulled the files out of the cabinet. It was the big guy who slashed the cushions with a long-bladed knife.

"There is more. One of the cameras taped it all as a nice video. We'll be able to watch how things went down in moving pictures."

There wasn't really anything new to see. The same stuff the other two cameras snapped in still pictures was caught in motion, with one exception—now we had sound. The tall guy spoke with a deep voice, while the big one had a surprisingly high voice for a man his size. It was almost comical to hear him talk. Unfortunately, they never mentioned any names.

Then we did get a break. The big guy removed his balaclava to wipe his face. His head and face were clearly displayed. He was bald with a prominent nose.

Nelda copied everything onto a couple of flash drives. Handing them to me, she said, "You should keep at least one of them in a safe place."

I nodded. "I think I know exactly where I will keep it."

I told her about my visit to Titman. She didn't approve at all. "That was a stupid thing you did, Lews. First of all, you should have told me about it before you went, and second of all it was a stupid thing to do. Things could have gone terribly wrong. You could be dead."

"That's only one thing," I said, smartly.

"Sure, try to be funny now. What did you actually learn?"

"Not much, I admit. But I'm convinced now that Titman ordered the murder of Cole. And I have a strong suspicion he is behind this break-in. The fact that his files are missing leaves no doubts. Why would they take those files and none of the others?"

"Because those two guys aren't the smartest?" Nelda suggested. "If it were me doing the break-in I would have smashed the consoles; I would have taken all the files, and I would have burned down the place."

"I'm sure glad you weren't involved in this," I said. "We'd be looking at charred remains now."

"What will you do with these pictures?" she asked.

"I'll go down to visit my old friend Kabinsky and show them to him. That's what I'm going to do."

I called him on his cell phone. I could tell he wasn't happy to hear my voice.

"Somebody trashed my office last night. I want to file an official report and then I want you to look at some pictures. When will you be at the precinct?"

"Not until after lunch."

"Good. I'll meet you at about three o'clock." I hung up before he could object or make excuses. Then I drove to Mama's Big Ones and had a hamburger and fries. They make the best burgers at Mama's. Fat, juicy and thick patties, with bacon, cheese, and all the trimmings. The fries are homemade and the portions huge. Someday they may kill me, but in the meantime I enjoyed them.

Kabinsky was friendly enough when I walked into his office, but something about his demeanor made me wonder. He took down my report, even though he said it wasn't really his job. "I'm in Homicide, which means I investigate murders not break-ins."

"You can give the report to the proper department, Frank. I want to show you some pictures. Maybe you'll recognize at least one of the guys." He put the flash drive I gave him into his computer. I watched his face as he looked at the pictures and the video, but he didn't give me an indication that he recognized the guy with the big nose or the tall one with the deep voice.

"They took Titman's files," I informed him.

"That doesn't mean Titman hired these guys," he said. "Maybe they're just a couple of hoodlums who grabbed that file to mislead you; purely coincidence they took that one. Anything else missing?"

"Not that I know of. I didn't go through all the other files. It would take too much time."

"Well, perhaps you should take the time. They may have taken only the pages containing the information they were seeking."

"The video doesn't show anything like that."

He looked at me. "Take my advice, Lews. Forget about this. Like you said, you lost nothing except for an old couch and a couple of monitors. Let it go at that. For your own sake. Nothing is gained by stirring up more trouble."

"Did you forget about Cole? He's dead. Somebody murdered him."

"He is the victim of a robbery. The case is closed."

"Just like Bart Brandon was the victim of a robbery, right? You remember I asked you about that case, don't you? Just bear with me and do me another favor. See if you can find anything in the police files about these two clowns who broke into my office."

Kabinsky lifted his shoulders and heaved a deep sigh, signaling his annoyance." I don't have much to go on. All we have is the face of one guy." However, he did a search. It didn't take long before he found a picture that matched the face of the big man. His bulb-nose was prominent, especially in contrast to his small ears. There was a picture of him standing with bare arms and they were covered with tattoos.

"His name is Jeremy Nightingale. He's had a couple of assault charges against him, but they didn't stick. Three years ago he was investigated involving a murder case. His lawyer got him off on a technicality. The case was thrown out of court."

"Who was his lawyer?"

"Heimi Rosenthal."

That caused me to chuckle. "Rosenthal? How the hell can a small-time crook afford a high-priced lawyer like Rosenthal?"

"Beats me. Maybe he won in the lotteries. It happens."

"Fat chance. He wouldn't have to break into other people's businesses."

"Maybe it's his hobby. According to your own report he didn't take anything of value. The only thing he and his partner did was tear your place apart." Kabinsky leaned back in his chair. "I don't know what to tell you except what I already suggested. If you want us to arrest this Nightingale, you'll have to press charges. He'll be out on bail in twenty-four hours. Then there will be a court case, who knows when, though. You'll have to hire a lawyer. It'll cost. Is it really worth your trouble?"

"Maybe it would be. By the way, I have a strong feeling this guy works for Titman. More than ever now I'm sure Titman is behind this."

"You have no valid proof of his involvement, Lews."

"Remember I told you that Titman offered me money to kill Cole? I didn't do it, but Cole ends up dead anyway. Strange coincidence, isn't it?"

He stroked his mustache. "It appears that way, but how can you prove any of this?"

"Well, I can't. Everything is circumstantial and assumption. I have no concrete evidence that Nightingale and his accomplice were hired by Titman to break into my office. Nothing that would hold up in court, anyway. However, I have pictures that put them at the scene of the break-in. In fact, the pictures clearly identify Nightingale. That can't be denied."

I was frustrated, but I could also see his frustration. "We're always coming back to the same thing, Lews. They took nothing of value. We can charge Nightingale and, hopefully his accomplice, only with break and enter with the intention to steal, but they stole nothing except one file. That's all. It's a misdemeanor at best. We don't have the manpower to waste on petty crimes."

"No, I guess not. That will never change." I rose. "Sorry about wasting your time. Perhaps something will come up. Something I can use. You take care now."

I wasn't happy when I drove away. I decided to drop in at the office before I went home. Nelda had cleaned up everything. She even hooked up my new monitor. At first, I thought I should look through the files to see what else might be missing, but then I decided not to bother. I was just about to leave when the phone rang.

It was Benny Miller. "Listen Canon, I want to drop something off at your office. Will you be there for a while?"

"Actually I was ready to leave. Can it wait till morning?"

"It could, but I'd like you to see it now. There is also something I want to tell you. It can't be done over the phone." He gave a small chuckle. "Phone might be bugged. I'm a bit paranoid these days."

"Okay, I'll wait for you."

He came within the hour. When he walked through the door, he looked around the office and said, "Did a tornado hit this place?"

"We're redecorating." When he gave me a strange look, I said, "Somebody decided to pay us a visit and smash up some stuff. I think they didn't like the couch."

"From what I can see I have to say I don't blame them." He smiled. "How did it work out with the cameras?"

"Great. We got pictures."

"That's good news. There should be no problem finding the culprits. Did you go to the cops?"

"I did, but I can't expect any help there." I looked at the little bundle of cloth he carried in his hand. "What do you have for me?"

He walked over to my desk, laid the bundle onto the top, and then he opened the bundle. Inside the piece of cloth was a plastic bag and inside the bag a gun. "I'm not taking it out," he said. "I don't want to destroy any prints."

"Whose gun is it?"

"It belongs to my wife."

"I'm sure you have a good reason to bring me your wife's gun."

"You bet I have. I never told this to anyone, but I know she murdered a woman. Shot her to death. This is the gun she used."

I looked at him a bit closer, wondering if he had been drinking. "When did this happen and who is the woman she shot?"

He was looking for a chair, spied Nelda's behind her desk and went to it and sat down. Wiping his flat hand across his balding head, he said, "It's hot in here. Don't you have an air conditioner?"

"Supposedly we have one, but it doesn't work and our landlord is too cheap to get it fixed. Anyway, you haven't answered my question."

"Oh, right. This happened about two years ago. The woman she shot and killed was Mildred Stone. She was also a candidate for the position of president for the Preservation of Heritage Buildings Society. My wife wanted to make sure she got the job." He pulled out a handkerchief and wiped his forehead. "How can you stand this heat?"

"I don't spend much time in the office. I drive around a lot." I didn't go into detail about not having an air conditioner in my car, either. "You say it happened two years ago. Did you go to the police with this?"

"No."

"Why not?"

He laughed. "I didn't have a death wish. We're talking about a woman who is active in the community, a woman with connections, and a woman who happens to be the police chief's sister. What would my chances have been?"

I saw his point. "Not very good." I reached for the plastic bag and pulled it closer. "You are sure she did it and this is the gun she used?"

"One hundred percent. You see, Mildred Stone was the one with the best chance to get the position. A few days before the vote my wife said to me *I want that job. The only way I'll get it is with that bitch out of the way. Something needs to be done.* Well, she did something about it. The night it happened she came home and demanded I have sex with her. She was like a nymphomaniac, couldn't get enough of me. I must admit it was the best sex I ever had in my life. The next morning it was in the papers about Mildred Stone's murder. She had been shot."

I had to smirk a little. "Why would you assume your wife was the murderer just because she demanded sex from you? You lived a man's dream."

"It wasn't like her. We hadn't had sex for a long time. Remember, I told you she's a lesbian. I guess, killing that woman really turned her on and she didn't care who she had sex with. I was the next best thing."

"Any other indicators she was the one who shot Mildred Stone?"

"During the heat of having sex with me she exclaimed *what I did tonight was exhilarating and such a turn-on. Such a thrill and what a high!* I didn't know what she meant until I read the papers in the morning."

I pondered what he told me. His reasoning was logical and made sense. "What do you want me to do with the gun?"

"Keep it in a safe place. Perhaps if *you* took it to the cops, they might look into it."

"I'm afraid I don't have much pull with the police department, but it's worth a try. I'll put the gun into our safe for now and then I'll decide what I'm going to do with it and the information you gave me," I told him. "Who knows, something may develop."

"Good." He heaved a sigh of relief. "Just to know she doesn't have this gun any longer makes me feel a little safer. At least she won't shoot me with it."

I didn't have the heart to tell him that she could always hire someone to do the job for her or buy another gun. I didn't want to be responsible for giving him a real heart attack; one that may just be fatal this time.

"By the way," he said and retrieved his wallet. "I wanted to give you this." He handed me a small envelope. "It's a check for $500.00. I think you can use it."

I took the envelope but said, "You already had those cameras installed in my office. I haven't had a chance to thank you for that."

He dismissed it by shaking his head. "Having those cameras didn't stop those guys from breaking in, did it? What you need is a real alarm system. It may not prevent thieves from breaking in, either, but there is a good chance it may scare them away."

"Maybe if I get into more money and better furniture it may warrant such an installation, but not now. I really can't afford it."

"We can probably work something out." He got up and held out his hand. "Thank you, Mr. Canon. I'll see you again."

I went home and had a few shot glasses of Scotch and drank a couple of beers. Then I crawled into bed and dreamed about Angela Steelwood. She was wearing nothing but knee-high boots. Waving a gun in my face, she demanded I have sex with her. While we had sex, she changed into a short, fat man with Titman's face. I woke up sweating and my heart pounding. I made myself a promise to lay off the booze for a while.

In the morning, things didn't seem so bad. I called Kabinsky. "Listen, Frank, I have new information about a two-year-old murder. There is a good chance Angela Steelwood may have murdered a woman by the name of Mildred Stone. Can you look into the case?"

He didn't sound happy. "I asked you about your obsession with Titman. Now it seems the Commissioner's sister is your target. As I told you before, I truly wish you wouldn't involve me in your crusade, Lews."

"You're a homicide detective, aren't you, Frank?"

"I investigate current murders not cold files, especially not ones that involve the Commissioner or his sister. Take my advice, don't pursue this. Nothing good will come out of it. It isn't healthy."

"Too bad you feel that way, Frank. I remember when you thought differently."

"That was then. Things and people change."

I hung up without commenting on it. I was disappointed and asked myself again *what is he scared of?*

I drove to the store and did a bit of grocery shopping. I took my time, because there was nothing else to do at the moment. It was shortly after noon when hunger pangs attacked my belly, prompting me to go and have something to eat, but I changed my mind when I started the Cadillac. Something must have happened to the muffler, because it rumbled like an old oil drum rolling down a cobblestone street. So I decided to visit Brandon Brandon to get it fixed.

As I headed for Brandon's garage, thinking how nice it would be to have a CD player in my car, I heard the sound of sirens. Looking in the rearview mirror, I saw a police car with blinking lights close behind me.

I didn't remember seeing that car before, but I hadn't been paying much attention to the traffic.

Then I noticed the flashing headlights.

I guess that's for me. Wonder what I did wrong now.

Pulling over I stopped the car, rolled down the window and waited for the cop. Watching him in the side mirror, I saw how he adjusted his gun belt.

"Can I help you with something?" I asked him when he stood beside my car, his hand on his gun.

"Registration and driver's license," he said with a bored voice.

I opened my glove compartment and retrieved the registration. Then I fished my driver's license out of my wallet. Handing both documents to him, I asked, "What is this all about?"

He seemed to study the registration and my license for a while. Then he looked at me and said, "You have a noisy muffler, Mr. Canon."

I gave him a friendly smile. "I know. It must have just happened. This morning everything was still quiet. In fact, I'm on my way now to have it repaired."

"Do you know the speed limit on this street?"

"I believe it's thirty." I wasn't quite sure but figured it wouldn't be lower than that.

"Well, then you were speeding. I clocked you at fifty."

Oh boy, I could see where this was going. "Listen," I said, keeping my voice calm and speaking in a confidential tone. "I was a cop for twelve years. Sometimes we were asked to fill a certain quota of tickets and some of us got a bit overzealous. Are you certain I was speeding?"

He looked at me coldly. "When I say you were speeding then you were speeding. Step out of the car, please."

"Officer, mistakes happen. I'm one hundred percent certain I wasn't speeding. In fact you should probably give me a ticket for driving too slow."

"I will not repeat myself. Step out of the car—now!" He had his gun halfway drawn from its holster.

It looked like this guy meant business. Shrugging, I opened the car door and slid out.

"Giving you a lip?" a voice said. Then I saw another cop coming toward us.

"This guy is trying to be a smartass," the first one replied.

I looked at the other cop. He was big and had a mean face. Somehow, I had a feeling this wasn't going to turn out well.

"I'm not trying to be anything," I said defensively, eyeing the newcomer. "I was just explaining to your partner here that mistakes sometimes happen. Besides, I wasn't speeding."

"Sure you weren't," the second cop said. "Nobody ever speeds. Against the car and spread your legs!"

I complied with his wishes and let him frisk me.

"He's clean," the one who did the frisking said. He sounded surprised.

"I don't carry a gun," I explained. Then I tried again. "Listen, you're making a mistake. I have friends in the force. This may not look good on your record."

"Are you threatening us?"

"I wouldn't dream of it. I can see you two are a couple of straight-shooting cops, but I'm sticking with my story. I did not speed." This day was not going as planned. I didn't need a speeding ticket, especially not from a couple of idiots who were trying to make points.

One of them punched me in the ribs, hard. I made a *whoof* sound and tried to turn around, but a hand pressing into my back kept me pinned against the car.

"We're taking you in," the first cop said. "Don't resist!"

"You're arresting me?" I asked while trying to get some air into my lungs. "You must be kidding. On what charge?"

He punched me again. "Threatening an officer of the law and for resisting."

"I did neither, Officer." I was losing my patience but tried to keep a cool head. Nothing was gained by actually resisting and giving them more reasons to arrest me.

The next blow into my back made me mad. I twisted around and grabbed the fist that was heading for another painful collision with my ribs. "I don't know what game you morons are playing, but I've had enough." I had my teeth clenched and my words came out with an angry hiss.

The second cop stepped back and aimed his gun at me. "Now you've resisted and attacked an officer of the law," he said with a smirk on his face. "One more threatening move and I'll blow your head off! I may do that anyway for calling us morons."

I relaxed, shut my mouth, and let the first one cuff me. Then they pushed me toward their cruiser car and shoved me into the back.

They took me to another precinct, and I realized these two had deliberately targeted me. I knew this day was not going to be added to my list of wonderful days that happened to me. They hustled me past the front desk and down a corridor. After taking off my cuffs they pushed me into a darkened cell.

Looking around, I found a bench in the back and headed for it. I sat down and tried to take a few deep breaths to calm my nerves but gave up with the deep breathing because of the pain in my back and ribs.

There was something going on here that I didn't like. Why would they take me to a different precinct? Why did they arrest me in the first place? Certainly not for speeding or a noisy muffler. I remembered my car and realized it was still running. I never shut off the motor. Hopefully, I had at least closed the door.

Groping around in my pocket, I found my cell phone. The cop had missed it when he frisked me. Perhaps because I carried it in the pocket of my pants. Searching in my jacket pocket I found Brandon's card and dialed his number. He answered it after the fourth ring.

"Lews Canon here," I said, keeping my voice low.

"Hey, Lews Bullseye Canon. I wondered when you'd..."

"Listen," I said urgently, interrupting him, "I don't have much time. I'm sort of indisposed at the moment."

"Indisposed? What exactly does that mean?"

"No time to explain. I had to leave my car in a hurry. I think it's still running, too. It's somewhere on Humboldt Street, near the Museum. Can you go and pick it up? Take it to your shop. It needs a muffler, and fix whatever else needs fixing." I could hear voices coming down the corridor. "And hurry. I hope the car is still there."

I didn't wait for his reply. My newly found friends were coming back for me. I shoved the phone back into my pocket just in time.

They opened my cell door and told me to come out.

"Are you going to beat me up some more?" I couldn't help myself from saying it.

"Just move and shut up!"

They took me through a door and down another corridor. Shortly after that I found myself in an interrogation room. There was a table and a chair on each side of the table.

"Make yourself comfortable," the big one said, smirking. Then they both left the room.

I sat down, wondering what was coming next.

TEN

WHEN THE DOOR OPENED AGAIN, a couple of other cops walked in.

I stared at the tall one. He looked older. Eight years older, to be exact. Actually, he was only one year younger than me, which made him forty.

"Hello Canon," he said. "What a surprise!"

"Steven Meloni. Why do I have this idea that I'm the only one who is surprised? You knew I was here," I said. "I thought you were in jail."

"I've been out of jail for five years now."

"I have a feeling having a judge for a father had something to do with it. Too bad for you he couldn't help you when you were sent to jail for being a crooked cop."

His handsome face turned ugly. "Look who's talking. You weren't exactly on the up and up."

"I never took bribe money and I never got involved with the mob. Your mistake was to give false testimony on the case we worked on. A murderer is walking free because of you. By the way, how did you manage to get your job back as a police officer?"

"My record is clean. I got exonerated."

I couldn't help but chuckle. "I guess your daddy the judge pulled a few strings, right?"

"I made a few mistakes, I admit, and I paid my debt, but that's enough about me. Let's talk about you. It seems you're still sticking your nose where it doesn't belong."

"What can I say? I'm a PI. It's my business."

"Well, it looks like you screwed up this time. You should have listened to the advice your old buddy Kabinsky gave you. He's seen the light. Don't expect much help from him." He smirked. "Don't look so shocked. Your old friend is protecting his own hide these days. That's what you should have done, but no, you had to be the knight in shining armor. Look where it got you."

"I have a clear conscience, Meloni, and I sleep well at night."

"Enough chit-chat, Meloni," the other cop spoke up. "Let's get the job done."

Meloni grinned. "Take it easy, McLean. You'll get your chance. I'm just exchanging stories with an old friend. Did you know that Canon and I were partners?"

"I had no idea and, frankly, it doesn't interest me. Go, put the cuffs on him!"

"Okay, okay." Meloni lifted both hands. "He's not going anywhere." He came around the table, dangling a pair of handcuffs in his hand. "Hands behind your back, Canon, but you know the drill."

Reluctantly, I let him put the cuffs on my wrists, immediately experiencing a feeling of helplessness. "What am I charged with?" I asked.

Meloni shook his head from side to side, making a frown. "I don't really know, but it doesn't matter. What matters is that you are here. You know, I've dreamed about an opportunity like this while I sat in jail. I was ready to kill you."

"And now?"

"That desire is still there, but don't worry, I won't kill you—not yet anyway."

"But you will, eventually, right?"

"Stop jabbering, Meloni," McLean said. He grabbed the edge of the table and pulled it away from me. Then he came around and kicked me in the chest with his foot. My chair fell backwards from the force of the kick. And I with it.

Meloni pulled me and the chair up again. Then he punched me in the stomach with his fist so hard I thought my breakfast would decide to leave me.

I glared at both of them, feeling the rage building up inside me. Much good it did me. Only in the movies the hero jumps up and uses his feet to beat his torturers unconscious and to free himself. I felt helpless because there was nothing I could do.

"If you would tell me what you want from me, perhaps I could tell you," I managed to get out between spasms of pain.

With an ugly laugh, Meloni stood wide-legged in front of me. "Actually, there is nothing you have that you can give us. We're only a couple of messengers."

"Don't keep me in suspense and give me the message already," I said.

"Okay, here it is." This time he hit me against the side of the head. I had seen it coming but couldn't move my head fast enough out of the way. His balled fist connected painfully with my cheekbone. Grinding my teeth, I tried to block out the immediate pain. Another punch against my jaw and lips made me cry out from the pain and the anger rising up inside me.

"Not in the face," McLean warned him, sharply. "It's not supposed to be obvious."

"We can always say he stumbled and knocked his head against the doorjamb," Meloni said with a sneer.

"Let me have a go at him," McLean said. "Come on and hold the chair."

After Meloni moved behind me and got a hold of the chair, McLean kicked me in the chest again with his foot. It was clear to me he was fond of doing that, but then he smashed his fist into my ribcage —twice. I wasn't aware of any cracking noises, but I could have sworn I felt something give away. Bruised ribs would be the mildest result of that punch.

He used me for a punching bag for a while, and then Meloni took over again. I was beyond feeling pain by then and just sat slumped over in my chair, letting it happen, mind and body numb.

Eventually, they stopped. I don't remember them leaving, but suddenly I was alone. Somebody came into the room and removed my handcuffs. Then they led me back into a holding cell. It could have been the one I had been in before. I didn't care, and it didn't matter. I fell onto the floor and lay there, half conscious, aware only of excruciating pain. I don't know if I passed out, but when I heard a voice, I opened my eyes and saw someone bending over me. It was a woman's face and I thought it was Sonya, but then I saw the uniform and realized it was just another cop.

"Can you sit up?" she asked.

I tried and actually succeeded, but I was ready to fall back again because of the sudden pounding in my head.

"That's some nasty cut on your cheek and it's all swollen. So are your lips. What happened to you?" she asked.

I tried to laugh but gave it up when it came out like a Neanderthal's attempt at communication.

"Take it easy," she said. "I'll have someone look at that. You don't want to get an infection. You must be in pain. Do you want something for it?"

I nodded.

She left and came back a few minutes later. "Here, take this." She pushed a pill between my swollen lips and then she held a glass against my mouth. "It should make you feel better soon."

I swallowed the pill and took a sip from the glass. "More water," I said, my voice sounding like the love-call of a frog. I took the glass from her with shaking fingers and drained it.

"What are you in for?" she asked.

"Apparently speeding," I managed to say.

"Did you have an accident?"

I wanted to laugh but gave it up when my lips refused to cooperate. So I just shook my head.

"What's your name?"

"Lews Canon." I looked for my wallet, found it and removed my driver's license. Giving it to her, I said, "I was never formally booked."

She studied my license for a moment, and then she said, "Hang on a minute." She left me alone again. I managed to get to my feet and stumble to the bench, where I sat down. The painkiller hadn't kicked in yet and I felt as if I had fallen into a pit and fought a pride of mean lions. When I touched my ribs, I wished I hadn't done that.

The female cop came back and handed me my license. "There is no record of your arrival at the front desk. Who brought you in?"

I shook my head. "Don't know. Two cops in uniform. They never identified themselves. However, I was worked over by Meloni and McLean."

"Worked over? Are you saying they gave you this swollen cheek and bleeding lips?"

This time my chuckle came out nicely. "That and more. I think I have some broken ribs."

"Shit!" she cursed. "Let's have a look." She helped me take off my jacket and peel off my shirt. When she saw my exposed upper body, she said it again, "Shit! Who did you say did this to you?"

"Meloni and McLean. Two fine officers of the law."

"I know everyone in this precinct, but I don't recall a Meloni or McLean. Are you sure they were cops?"

"They actually never told me. They didn't wear any uniforms. They wore suites. I assume they were detectives."

Shaking her head, she insisted, "They're not from this precinct, but I'll find out." She touched my chest gently and when I winced, she said, "Sorry. This doesn't look good. What did they use on you?"

"Feet and fists."

"You want me to call a doctor?"

"No, I just want to get home."

"Do you need transportation?"

"Yes, but I'll call my partner. She can pick me up." I don't know how my smile looked when I said, "I've had enough of cop cars for a while."

"Before you can leave I have to check and see if I can find a reason to hold you. You said you were brought in for speeding?"

"That's the reason the cops that arrested me gave me, but that was only an excuse. I wasn't speeding. All I had was a noisy muffler and I was on my way to have that fixed."

"Where is your car now?"

"Hopefully in the repair shop. I managed to call my mechanic and tell him to pick up my car."

"Good. Now give me a moment." She turned to leave, but I stopped her.

"Before you go, which precinct is this?"

"The Twenty-third."

While I waited for her return, I put my shirt and jacket back on, with some difficulty, but I managed. Then I fumbled for my cell phone in my pocket. I was happy to discover it was still there and in one piece. I had Nelda on speed dial, and I was hoping she would answer her phone, something I couldn't always rely on, but she answered on the second ring.

"What's up?" she asked.

"Not much, except I need you to pick me up."

"Your voice sounds strange. Are you drunk?"

I managed a chuckle. "I wish I were."

"Where are you?"

"In Jail. Don't ask for details, just come and pick me up. I'm at the Twenty-third Precinct."

"Can you repeat that? I can barely understand you."

"The Twenty-third Precinct," I repeated, trying to formulate the words carefully, even though my lips didn't want to play ball.

"Okay. I'll be there within the hour."

I leaned back against the wall, taking shallow breaths. The pain had slowly subsided but wasn't gone. I would have a few unpleasant days ahead of me and I wasn't looking forward to that. I touched my lip and it felt like a huge balloon, the way someone must feel after getting a double dose of Botox. There was blood on my finger.

The female cop came back again. "You are free to go. We have nothing on you."

"What about Meloni and McLean?"

"As I told you, I don't know them. Neither does the Desk Sergeant, but we'll do some checking. Is somebody picking you up?"

"Yes. She should be here in a bit."

"Good. Now, come out and sit in more comfortable surroundings until then. That's the least we can do for you." She smiled. "Unless sitting among cops makes you uncomfortable."

"It won't," I assured her. I followed her out of the cell, down the corridor and into the room with the desks. None of the other cops paid us any attention. I looked around if I could recognize the two who had brought me in, but none of the faces looked familiar.

After I sat down, my new cop friend said, "I noticed you perusing the room. Did you recognize anyone?"

Shaking my head, I said, "No. Of course, that means nothing. They could be sitting in their cruiser and watching for speeders or..." I let out a chuckle, "...drivers with a noisy muffler."

There was also a good chance they weren't from this precinct, and a slight chance they weren't even cops, but I didn't voice my suspicions.

"This is a mystery," she said. "It's never happened before. Not as far as I know, anyway."

"Do you mind if I ask your name?"

"Sorry, I should have introduced myself. I'm Sharon. Detective Sharon Masters."

"Pleased to meet you, Detective Masters."

"Call me Sharon."

"Okay, Sharon. I'm Lews." I decided to tell her more. It couldn't hurt. "You asked me before if I'd be uncomfortable among cops and I said no. In fact, sitting here brings back many memories." I had to laugh when I saw her expression, mostly inside, though, because stretching my bruised lips was too painful. "Not the kind you may be thinking of. I used to be a cop."

Her face smoothed out but she seemed interested. "Really? How long ago was that?"

"I left the force in 2010."

"Why?"

"Long story and not pleasant. One of the two cops who beat me, Meloni, used to be my partner."

She tilted her head and pursed her mouth. "Why do I have a feeling there was bad blood between you two?"

"Your feeling is dead on. He was as dirty as they come and he was sent to jail because of me."

"If he was in jail, how could he become a cop again?"

"Judge Nathan Meloni is his father."

"That would explain it. It seems to me this beating you received was some kind of revenge, payback."

"That is probably true but only part of a much larger story. By the way, I'm a PI. I'm the owner of *Canon Detective Agency*." I reached into my inside pocket and pulled out one of my cards. It was a bit crumpled but still legible. Giving it to her, I said, "It seems I have stepped on some important people's toes with my latest case and this is their way of warning me."

"Who are you investigating?"

I hesitated, wondering if I could confide in her. I didn't really know anything about her, except that she seemed concerned about my welfare. I decided to trust my gut. "A mobster by the name of Frederick Titman."

"I know who he is and I'm not sure I want to hear more. He's bad news. I don't know why you want to mess with him."

"Not by choice. I have a client who hired me to do so." I didn't tell her who and didn't mention Commissioner Steelwood. Like I said, I knew nothing about her. Sometimes it's best not to reveal too much.

"I think your ride just arrived," Sharon said.

I turned my head to look toward the front desk and saw Nelda talking to the Desk Sergeant. "Yes, that's her." Getting to my feet brought on a small wave of pain, but I refrained from moaning. "I'd like to say it was nice meeting you, Sharon," I said, trying to smile. "Perhaps under different circumstances it might have been, but thank you for your concern and kindness. I appreciate it. It helps to make my memories of Precinct Twenty-three more positive."

"I wish they'd be nothing but positive. We have good and dedicated people working here. Perhaps someday you'll come back for a visit. We could go for coffee." Her smile was encouraging and I was glad Nelda didn't witness it. I didn't need any comments from her. "Here is my card if you want to get in touch with me," she said.

Nelda had spotted me and came over. "You look like hell," she said as a greeting. "Did you have an accident?"

My attempt at a grin failed. "I ran into somebody's fist. I'll explain everything later. Just get me home."

"It might be a good idea to have a doctor look at that cut on his cheek," Sharon said to Nelda. "He may need stitches."

"I'll look after him," Nelda assured her.

Once we were in the car, she asked, "Where is your car? Did somebody steal it?"

"I don't think I ever have to worry about that. No car thief wants that piece of junk. It should be in Brandon's garage."

"Should be? I don't understand."

"Then let me tell you everything about the exciting day I had." I proceeded to give her a detailed account of what took place. She didn't interrupt me. One of her positive traits—she knew how to listen without making comments suggesting what she would have done under those circumstances. Once something happened, no amount of good advice can change it.

When I finished talking, she asked, "How are you feeling? Are you in a lot of pain? You want me to take you to the hospital?"

"I took a painkiller and it helps a little. No hospital. Drop me off at Sonya's place."

"Are you sure? Because of all that crusted blood on your face it's difficult to tell how badly you're injured, but your face is swollen and it looks like your eye is closing up. And I don't even want to mention your lips. You'd better put some ice on everything—and soon. You're unrecognizable. The way you look would horrify most animal lovers and make even a nun run away from you." She threw me a sidelong glance. "I don't think there's much doubt about who's behind this assault on you."

"I know. My good old friend the Commissioner, but most likely Titman put him up to it."

"What are you going to do about it?"

"Carry on with my investigation, what else? I'm going to Internal Affairs and file a complaint against Meloni and that McLean."

"Good luck. It'll be your word against theirs. And you don't have many friends in the police force, remember?"

"I'm aware of that. I'm still counting on Kabinsky, though, but I may even be wrong about him." I remembered Meloni saying something about Kabinsky having seen the light. I wondered what he meant. Looking at my watch, I discovered it was almost five and it suddenly occurred to me I hadn't eaten since breakfast. "Do you have plans for supper?" I asked.

Nelda gave me a puzzled look. "Are you asking me out again?"

"Can't I do that? Can't I ask my partner to have supper with me without getting the third degree?"

"Of course you can, and I'm not giving you any third degree. To answer your question: no, I have no plans. I never make plans for going out to eat. Usually, I cook supper at home."

"Just for yourself? Wouldn't it be easier to go out?"

"I like cooking and I like trying out new recipes. Is that so odd? After all, I am a woman and women are known to cook. Does that sound old-fashioned to you?"

"Oh, no, not at all," I was quick to reply. "It's just that some of you modern young women feel it may be beneath you to learn how to cook. Women want to do the same things men are doing or not doing. Whatever. They don't seem to realize that men have to do certain jobs and women do certain jobs—out of tradition. Of course, I've heard of couples where the men actually do most of the cooking. Not that there is anything wrong with that..."

"Perhaps you should stop talking while you're ahead. Now you're just rambling nonsense. The worst or perhaps good thing is I can only understand bits and pieces because of your busted lips. How often did they hit you on the head?"

"Why?"

"I think you should have your head examined after all. You may have a concussion, and that cut on your cheek looks nasty even under all that crusted blood. You will need to get that stitched together or you'll end up with an ugly scar. I'm taking you to a doctor friend of mine. He won't ask any questions."

I was going to argue, but I knew it would have been useless. So I let her take me to her doctor friend. I was hoping he was an actual doctor and not some guy who had learned his trade from the internet or from practicing on dogs.

When we stopped in front of an old house, my fears were amplified, but I had decided to trust Nelda. She helped me out of the car and I leaned on her when we walked across a path of broken tiles toward the dark entrance. The weathered front door didn't inspire any confidence into a good outcome of my adventure, either.

Nelda banged her fist against the door and a couple of minutes later it swung open to reveal a dark vestibule. The tall, frail-looking man who stood in the open doorway could have been an escapee from a Frankenstein or Vampire movie. "Yes?" He asked with a rusty voice while peering at us from behind huge glasses. His eyes were magnified by the thick lenses, lending him the look of a giant lemur.

"Hi, Dr. Jhamir. I'm Nelda Pinetree. Remember me?"

He scrutinized her for a moment with his lemur-eyes. Then his dour face lit up and he actually smiled. "Ah, yes, the kickboxer. Have you been injured again?" I had almost expected some kind of foreign accent, but except for his rusty voice he sounded quite normal.

Nelda chuckled softly. "Not me but my friend here needs a bit of medical attention."

The good doctor looked at me and nodded. "I can see that. Please, come in."

We stepped through the door into the vestibule. The door closed behind us and Dr. Jhamir threw a thick bolt to lock it. I guess he didn't trust a regular lock. We followed him through another door, down a short corridor and then we descended a set of stairs into the basement.

I expected some dark dungeon, but I was surprised as we entered a brightly lit room. It looked exactly like a regular doctor's office.

"Have a seat and let me look at that," Dr. Jhamir told me.

I took one of the two chairs, happy to be sitting. I was suddenly aware again of the tight pain on the side of my head and my chest.

"First we'll have to clean that," the doctor said. He went to a cupboard and removed a bottle and some swabs. It stung when he applied the swab to my cheek and lips, but what's a little more pain when your whole upper body seems on fire?

He must have noticed when I winced. "Does it hurt?" he asked.

"A little," I said.

"Do you need a painkiller?"

I shrugged and felt sorry immediately. Before I could answer, he said, "I think you do." Getting another bottle from his cupboard, he shook out a pill and handed it to me. "Here. Swallow this." Then he poured some water into a glass from a pitcher he had standing on a desk. "Better drink some water also."

He waited until I had emptied the glass. Then he said, "I'll have to use a local anesthetic before I stitch you up. I hope that's okay with you?"

"Whatever you have to do," I said, not caring what he did at this point.

"That's quite some nasty split," he said while he did the sewing. "Good thing you came. It may not have healed well. By the way, the stitches will dissolve in time. Leave the wound covered for three days and then have someone look at it again to make sure there is no infection. Also, it may be a little late for that already, but it wouldn't hurt to put some ice on your cheek to bring the swelling down. There isn't much I can do about your swollen lips."

"Can you give him a quick check if everything is okay with his head?" Nelda asked. "He may have a concussion or something."

Dr. Jhamir looked into my eyes, and then he moved his finger slowly back and forth in front of me. I followed that finger, noticing how knobby his fingers were.

Arthritis, I thought. He's probably retired. He does look pretty old.

"He's fine," he said. "Anything else you want me to check?"

"I may have a couple of broken ribs," I volunteered.

"Are you in a lot of pain?"

"The pill you gave me helps."

"Take off your jacket and shirt and we'll see. I can't give you an x-ray. I don't have the equipment."

His lined face didn't show much emotion when he saw my bruised upper body, but I could have sworn his eyes grew a little larger behind those thick glasses; if that was indeed possible. He probed my chest with his knobby fingers and mumbled something to himself when I flinched.

"What's the verdict, Doc?" I asked when he straightened out.

"You're lucky. No broken ribs but they're badly bruised."

"What can you do?"

"Not much. Keep on taking painkillers and take shallow breaths. The human body is a wonderful machine and you'll heal." His dry lips formed a little smile. "Eventually. When you get home, don't take a hot bath. Just wash your body with a cold cloth. Some cold compresses may also help." He looked at Nelda. "It might be easier if someone assisted with the washing."

She smiled. "I'll take good care of him."

"That's good." He nodded and watched as she helped me put on my shirt.

"Thank you very much, Doc," I said. "How much do we owe you?"

He made a dismissing motion. "I'm not doing this for money. It's my way of paying something forward."

"This is the second time in the last couple of weeks I heard somebody tell me that," I said.

"Perhaps there is a message in that somewhere." He held out his hand. "You take care of yourself, friend of the kickboxer." He chuckled. "Take my advice. Stay away from situations like the one that caused your injuries. Next time you may actually have broken ribs. They are much more serious."

"I'll keep it in mind. Thanks again."

Before we walked out of the door, he handed me a pill. "Take this before you go to bed tonight. It'll help you sleep and speed up the healing."

When we were back in Nelda's car, I asked, "Who is this guy? He seems to know his stuff, but is he a real doctor?"

"He is, except he's not practicing anymore, not legally, anyway."

"What do you mean by not legally? I assumed he was retired."

"He is retired, or maybe I should say sort of retired. He actually lost his license a few years ago—for malpractice."

"Oh, I see. In other words what he's doing is not legal? How did you get to know him?"

She shrugged. "In jail."

"He worked in the jail you were in?"

"Not as a doctor. He was a jailbird, like me."

"Wow. This is getting better and better." If it wouldn't have hurt so much I would have laughed, but I gave it up on the first try. "You know you have to be careful socializing with known felons, especially with ones like the good Doctor who are still involved in illegal activities."

It was her turn to laugh. "Who's to know? Unless you'll blab it all over the place. Dr. Jhamir is a good person and always willing to help others without asking anything in return. He got a bad break, that's all."

I leaned back into the seat. "I guess it happens. I shouldn't be so quick to judge him, since I don't know any details about why he lost his license and it isn't really my business."

"No, it isn't," she said. "And I'm not going to enlighten you. I don't want you to freak out."

"Freak out?" I was surprised to hear her say that. "I never freak out. Besides, now you've made me curious."

"Forget it. It isn't important. By the way, where do you want me to drop you off?"

"Not at my place. I need some tender love and care. Take me to Sonya's."

"Did you forget she's working at this time of night? Tell you what, I'll take you to my place and I'll cook you a nice supper. Do you like Spaghetti and meatballs?"

"Sure I do, but I don't care much for those tomato sauces."

"Well, then you're in luck, because neither do I. I'll make you some delicious, spicy meat gravy." She grinned. "It'll be out of a can, though. I even have a cold beer in the fridge."

"Sounds good to me. Now, step on it and let's get home. You drive like an old woman."

"At least I won't be picked up for speeding like some people I know."

ELEVEN

THE PILL DR. JHAMIR had given me to take before I went to bed must have been really strong, because it nearly knocked me out and I slept quite well on Nelda's couch. When I woke up in the morning, the pain was kicking in again, but it wasn't as severe as the day before and I could actually breathe without wanting to scream with every breath I took. I swallowed a couple of painkillers and then I had breakfast.

Nelda made bacon and eggs with hash browns, and after a cup of coffee I felt nearly human again. "So what do you want to do today?" she asked me after breakfast.

"I think I'll take the day off," I said. "I'll have to call Brandon about my car, and then I want to talk to Sonya and ask if it's okay to spend a few days at her place."

"You can crash here again tonight if it's not convenient for her. I don't mind." Nelda smiled. "It's actually quite nice to take care of somebody and cook for another person. I never did anything like that for my dad. There was never an opportunity and it saddens me."

"We'll see. I appreciate the offer."

I called Brandon. When I announced myself, he said, "If you're wondering about your car I can tell you it's here. You're lucky nobody stole it, but then again—who would want to steal it? Why did you leave it running with the door wide open?"

"It's a long story. I got picked up by the cops for speeding. They didn't give me a chance to shut off my car. Were you able to work on it?"

"You need a new muffler, but you probably know that. Even a guy who doesn't know anything about cars can't miss something like that. Then I'd like to give your engine a bit of a tune-up. It needs it."

"You go ahead and do what you must. Just don't run up an exuberant bill, okay. I'll trust your judgment. I am laid up for a couple of days so you have some time to work on the car. Call me when you're done."

"Will do."

After talking with Brandon, I debated if I should phone Sonya. I didn't want to worry her needlessly, but she deserved to know about my incident, and I did want to spend a few days with her. I needed some cuddling.

She was still home when I called. I told her a little about my ordeal but didn't go into details. She'd find out soon enough.

"I'm here until four. Come by now and we can still talk a little."

Nelda drove me to Sonya's place. Since it was not too far from our office, she decided to stay in the office and do some paperwork.

Sonya was shocked when she looked at my chest and my back. "Why did they do this to you?"

"Because somebody didn't like me snooping in their affairs."

"I told you many times you should give up this detective business and look for an honest job. Anything is better than this and nothing is worth getting beaten up over. Next time they may kill you."

"I'm not easy to kill," I joked.

"You're not invincible, Mister Tough Guy." She touched my chest with gentle fingers. "Does it hurt?"

"A little but it'll pass. With your magic fingers it will get better in no time. When you're gone I'll take a shower. I feel a bit grimy."

"Don't make the water hot," she advised. "It's better to have it on the cool side."

"You're the second person who tells me that."

Pulling her eyebrows into a mock frown, she said, "I hope it wasn't another woman. Did she see you like this? I mean without a shirt?"

"No woman. A *he* and he was a doctor."

"That's good. That means you've been to a doctor. How are the ribs? Any broken?"

"Just bruised."

She gave me a kiss on the cheek, the good one. "Go take your shower, and then rest. Doctor's orders. I'll be back shortly after midnight." She smiled. "If you feel up to it maybe I can make you feel really good with my special therapy session. Apparently, pleasure speeds up healing and it'll make you forget the pain for a while."

"I have a better idea, you stay home and we can start the therapy right now," I said with a grin. At least I thought I was grinning. My lips still felt as if I had been to a dentist.

Sonya laughed. "Maybe you should stop trying to smile until the swelling on your cheek has gone done and your lips are back to normal. You look like a zombie right now, and I don't make love to zombies." She threw me a kiss. "I gotta go. See you later." Before she walked out of the door, she said, "There is meatloaf in the fridge and leftover mashed potatoes. You can heat everything in the microwave."

"Any beer in the fridge?"

"There are a few bottles. Don't drink them all."

———

I spent the next few days resting in Sonya's apartment. I didn't do much besides watching TV and drinking beer. On the third day I went for a walk to my office to check up on things. Sonya offered to drive me but I declined her offer. "It's only about half an hour walk and it'll do me good to get some fresh air."

Nelda wasn't there. I hadn't spoken to her since she dropped me off at Sonya's. There was a message from Brandon on the answering machine telling me to come down to his shop and pick up my car. I remembered I hadn't given him Sonya's phone number. He didn't have my cell number, either. It's not on my calling card, for various reasons.

I called Brandon and told him I'd be picking up the car in a couple of days. I still needed the rest to recuperate.

Then I called Detective Sharon Masters at the Twenty-third Precinct.

"Hi, Sharon. This is Lews Canon. How are you?"

I think she was surprised about my call. "I'm good. Hi, Lews. I meant to call you. How is your face and how are the ribs?"

"They're fine." I laughed into the phone. "You sound like someone calling a restaurant inquiring about their ribs."

"I guess you must be feeling okay if you can joke about it. By the way, I did some digging. I can't find anything on a Peter McLean or Steven Meloni. Sorry."

"Thanks you for that information. How about those two cops who brought me in?"

"Nothing, either. I have no idea who they were. We'll probably never find them."

"They may not even be cops," I said, voicing something I had already suspected before.

"I never thought of that." She paused. "Is there anything else you wanted to tell me?"

"No, not really. I just wanted to find out if there was any news."

"None other than what I told you."

"Good then. I'll let you go. You're probably busy. Perhaps I'll talk to you again."

She chuckled. "Keep in touch, Lews. I'd like to know how this plays out. I hope you get better soon."

It seems I had made another friend in the police force. It wouldn't hurt to develop that relationship, but I needed to be careful. This new friend was a woman, and a good-looking one at that. It could easily turn into more than just casual friendship. I didn't need to complicate my life any more than it already was. I had Sonya and she was enough woman for me.

The next day I felt quite good and I figured I should pick up my car. I called Nelda. We had lunch together and then we drove to Brandon's shop. She dropped me off with the words, "I'll be driving to Anton's place. He said he wants to take a few pictures. There is nothing else I can do at the office right now."

I watched her drive away with some misgivings. I hoped Anton Bernard wasn't just playing with her. She was not the most attractive medium to inspire an artist. But that was just my opinion. I was not an artist and I had to admit I could be wrong.

"Good luck," I said to nobody in particular and walked into Brandon's garage.

The swelling on my face had gone down, but I still had a small bandage covering the sewed-up split on my cheek. My lips still hurt a little when I smiled, even though the cuts were almost healed.

Brandon peered at me and asked, "You have an accident?"

"No, just a run-in with an old friend."

"Must have been some old friend. I hope he looks as bad as you."

"He will if I ever get the chance," I said, grimly. "You said my car was ready."

"Yep. Got you a new muffler and tailpipe. Tuned her up, installed new sparkplugs, changed the air filter, oil filter and the oil. She runs pretty good. By the way, I replaced the oil pan. It was leaking. No more just adding oil. Make sure you do your oil and filter changes from now on." He grinned. "The body of that old lady needs a lot of makeup to look young again, a complete makeover, actually, like those over-the-hill movie stars, and you know how much good that does them. In the end they're still old. Even a new motor wouldn't make much difference with this one."

I sighed. "I guess I need a newer car. How much do I owe you?"

"Don't worry about that. I hired you to look into my dead brother's case. Consider this a retainer. Anything new?"

"I'm afraid not much. I've talked to one of the cops I know, but he seems to be reluctant to do anything about it. It doesn't look promising, but you never know. Now that I put it out there, something may develop. I've handled stranger cases."

I left the garage, enjoying the relative silence of my new muffler. Even the motor seemed to run smoother; it almost purred like a happy cat. I felt guilty for not being able to show any results for Brandon. I decided to pay Kabinsky another visit and tell him about my encounter with Meloni.

The last time I saw Kabinsky he had not been happy to see me again and I did not call him about my impending visit, figuring he may just find some excuse and leave his office to avoid me. When I got to the precinct, he was in. There was some actual concern on his face when he looked at me and said, "What did you run into?"

"Not what. Who. I met an old friend. Meloni."

"Meloni? He did this to you?"

"He and some guy by the name of McLean." I watched his face but he didn't react to the name. "They took me into one of the interrogation rooms at the Twenty-third Precinct and worked me over."

"I don't understand. Why would they do that?"

With a shrug, I sat down in the chair in front of his desk. "Why? Meloni's motive was probably payback. McLean was just a hired hand. They both were. Somebody hired them to deliver a warning and make sure I understood."

Kabinsky's eyes were serious. "I told you to listen to my advice, Lews."

I gave him a grim smile. "Strange, Meloni said the same thing. You should know me better than that, Frank. I don't react well to threats and intimidations. Now more than ever will I continue with my investigation. Somebody doesn't want me to dig, which means I'm onto something. By the way, I had no reason to assume Meloni and McLean weren't cops."

"Did they say they were cops?"

"No, they didn't have to. Why do you think most cops can be spotted a mile away? Because they just act differently than civilians."

"Are you telling me Meloni is a cop again after having spent time in jail?" Kabinsky asked, obviously not believing what I told him.

"Did you forget his father is a judge? However, I might be wrong. I never saw any badges."

"If Meloni is a cop again he should be in the files." Kabinsky began typing on his keyboard. Shaking his head, he said, "I can't find anything."

"How about McLean?" I suggested.

"Nothing either. Are you sure his name is McLean?"

"That's what it sounded like."

"Let me try different ways to spell the name." He did, and suddenly his face lit up. "I found something here. Here is a guy by the name of Peter Mekleen. He's a member of the SWAT team."

"Do you have a picture?" I got up and walked around the desk to look at the computer screen. I recognized him immediately, even though he wore a black uniform. "Yeah, that's him."

"Is it possible Meloni is also a member of that same SWAT team?"

He shook his head again. "His name doesn't come up. Sorry."

"Well, at least we have one of them. This Mekleen needs to be questioned. I'm not going to let it rest." A sudden thought popped into my mind. "It's possible Meloni changed his name also."

"It's possible." Kabinsky frowned, giving me a look that almost screamed desperation. "I wish you would not pursue this, Lews. Next time you may not walk away with just a beating. You said it yourself, somebody hired them."

That made me chuckle. "Like I said, I'm not going to be intimidated. I will find out who is behind it and somebody will pay one way or another. Did you look deeper into Frederick Titman's files? There must be something that ties him to a crime somewhere. How about his connection with the Ramiro Family?"

"Lews, don't ask me that. I'm pleading with you, forget all this. Take your losses and move on. For your own sake."

I got up and looked down at him. "I can't, Frank. I'm sorry."

"So am I," he said, his face expressionless. "So am I."

I looked at my watch and noted it was just after three. I had a sudden idea. "You told me Pallitser is in Internal Affairs now. Do you by any chance have his number?"

"I do. Why?"

"I want to discuss something with him. Do you mind giving me his number?"

He seemed reluctant but he gave it to me. "Take care, Frank," I said, suddenly thinking of something. "By the way, Meloni mentioned you. Are you sure you haven't run into him somewhere?"

"I'm sure, Lews. Why would I keep that a secret?"

"I don't know. You tell me, Frank."

"Are you insinuating something, Lews?"

"Nothing, just wondering," I said, and walked out. Once I sat in my car I called Pallitser. He seemed surprised to hear my voice. When I told him that I wanted to talk to him, he agreed. "I'll be in the office for another hour."

It took me only twenty minutes to reach the office of Internal Affairs. When I walked in, Pallitser sat behind his desk and watched me walking toward him with visible anticipation.

I pulled up a chair and sat down. "I see you're moving up in the world," I said.

He didn't comment other than saying, "What is it you want, Canon?"

"Well," I said, "you and I have never been great friends, Pallitser. You're a racist and a bigot, but basically you're a good cop and you believe in justice. I know you can't be bought, unless you also have changed."

"Great speech, Canon, but it won't make me like you any better. You didn't come here to tell me what a great guy I am." His eyes were cool, but I could tell by the way he cocked his head that he was curious about my visit.

"I want you to investigate Commissioner Steelwood. I believe he is involved with the mob."

He was clearly taken aback by what I'd said. "You must be kidding me. Commissioner Steelwood? I can't just start investigating him without a good reason."

"You'll find a reason. But first I'd like you to check out a member of the SWAT team. His name is Peter Mekleen."

"What is your connection with him?"

"He and my ex-partner Steven Meloni used me as a punching bag a few days ago. Call Detective Sharon Masters at the Twenty-third Precinct. She will confirm that I was there, but she doesn't know that Mekleen is a member of a SWAT team. Kabinsky found him for me in the databank. Once I have more information I may just press charges against him and Meloni. By the way, somebody hired them to do the job."

Pallitser gave me a thoughtful look. Then he said, "What the hell are you involved in, Canon? I have a feeling you're going to shake up things again."

"I hope I will. I hate criminals and I have no love for crooked cops."

"You realize you'll be putting a target on your back. You left plenty of bad feelings behind when you quit the force. This isn't going to help you mend any wounds." He leaned forward and lowered his voice. "The Commissioner has many friends in high places and connections to powerful people who won't think twice about shutting you up by any means they believe necessary. Think about that. Let's face it, you're nobody. Who would care if you suddenly disappeared?"

I had to grin. "I would care and so would my clients, especially the ones who paid me to do a job for them. I actually do have a few friends, which may be hard to believe, and their feelings toward me are genuine. You're right, I may be a Nobody, a mosquito if you will, but even a mosquito can wreak plenty of havoc. If you've ever been in a room at night with a mosquito buzzing around you know what I mean. I'm aiming to do just that—cause havoc. By the way, I almost forgot. I was told that a Julia Titman spoke to you and you gave her my name."

"That's right. Did she get in touch with you?"

"She did. She wanted me to kill her husband. I told her I'm not an assassin. You know who her husband is, right?"

"Of course I do. He's a mobster." His eyes narrowed. "Don't tell me you have an interest in him." When I didn't answer, he said, "Damn it, Canon, you're in deeper shit than I thought. Do you know who Titman runs with?"

"I do. Enrico Ramiro, the head of the Ramiro Family, who, incidentally, is friendly with Commissioner Steelwood. By the way, Julia Titman is the Commissioner's little sister. That makes Frederic Titman his brother-in-law. Do you see where I'm going?"

I left him with that. Driving home I felt much better. Pallitser would find Mekleen and he would investigate him, of that I was certain. He may even locate Meloni. If he hadn't known about Commissioner Steelwood and Titman being brothers-in-law I dropped a bomb into his lap. I decided to visit the Dancing Leprechaun and have a beer.

Or maybe two.

Sonya had already started her shift. She saw me the moment I walked in and came over to talk to me. "Did you pick up your car?" she asked.

Nodding, I said, "Yes, I did. It's nice to be mobile again."

"Just be careful and don't get any more speeding tickets," she said with a smile, but I knew she was worried about me. Not because I might speed but because of what could happen again.

It was a busy night and a bit crowded, even at the bar. I drank a couple of beers and watched the dancers twisting their bodies on the dance floor to music that was nothing but noise to my ears. I've never been a good dancer and had no desire to ever become one. Some of the girls were attractive in their skimpy outfits and some weren't, especially the older women, the ones with their heavy makeup and colored hair. The ones who tried to forget their age by pretending time had left them unscathed and they were still young and sexy by picking up younger men.

"Hi, how about buying a drink for a thirsty girl?"

The voice was familiar and when I turned around I recognized Julia Titman. She smiled and grabbed my arm. "I have a table over there. Come and join me."

I let her pull me across the room, past the dancers, toward a part of the lounge where the music wasn't so deafening. There were a couple of other women sitting at the table. I couldn't miss their extreme beauty. "Sit down," Julia said, pointing to one of the empty chairs. When I followed her invitation, she took the chair beside me. "This is Lews Canon," she introduced me to her companions.

"Hi," one of them said, studying me out of dark, veiled eyes and a smile on her full, red lips. "I'm Doris. Are you Julia's new lover?"

"Hush," Julia said. "He's a detective and not my lover. We're not even friends."

"Oh, really." The woman laughed. "Perhaps he's available then?" She looked at me and fluttered her long lashes. "Are you looking for a good time, Handsome?"

I had to laugh, wondering what this was all about. "I'm always looking for a good time," I said.

"Well, then you've come to the right table. I can give you the best time ever."

"Oh, Doris, stop with this man-eater game already," the other woman chided and turned toward me with a little smile. "She always does this when she's had too much to drink. Don't pay her any attention. I'm Erika, by the way." She extended her arm across the table, offering me her hand.

I took her hand into mine and gave it a slight squeeze. "I'm Lews, but Julia already introduced me."

"Hi, Lews. So you're a detective. Private, I assume?"

"Very," I said, returning her smile. I looked at Julia. "Any reason you brought me here?"

"Yes, a good reason. Doris and Erika are fashion models. I used to work with them. Erika's last name is Cole. She's the sister of George."

When I stared at Erika, she nodded solemnly. "That's right. George was my younger brother." Her face went suddenly dark, all that apparent happiness she displayed earlier gone. "He was murdered and I want those responsible punished."

"The police think he was the victim of a mugging."

"You know about that?" She threw a glance at Julia. "Does he know about you and George?"

Julia gave a small nod. "He knows."

"It seems Julia already filled you in. Then you know who she suspects is behind George's murder. And he was murdered; there is no doubt about that. Are you aware that George was a former Navy Seal? He knew how to defend himself, but there is little defense against a cowardly bullet into the back of your head."

I guess I must have had a blank look on my face, because she chuckled grimly. "That's right. He was shot from behind. It wasn't in any police report."

"The reports said he was stabbed with a knife, but you tell me he died from a bullet?" My eyes searched out Julia. "Did you know that? You never told me."

"I didn't know at the time I talked to you. Erika found out from the coroner. I didn't see his body." She wiped her cheek with a delicate finger.

Doris had been silent the whole time. Now she said, "I guess you're not interested in a brief affair, are you, Mr. Detective?"

"Not right now," I said. "I already have a lady-friend."

"She wouldn't have to know."

Looking at her innocent expression, gave me a chuckle. "Believe me, she would. In fact, I can see her watching me already. She's the bartender." I waved to Sonya, who was looking in our direction. She saw me and waved back. "She's like a hawk," I said to Doris.

"And it's obvious she has her claws in you." Doris laughed and took another sip from her glass. "Too bad. I'm in need of a good man."

"You always are," Julia said. She pulled on my sleeve. "Have you thought about my offer?"

"There is nothing to think about. I told you, I'm not that kind of a guy."

"So you've said. I'll pay you fifty thousand dollars." She spoke low so only I could hear.

Her eyes reflected the light from the flickering flame of the candle on the table, changing their gray-green color to a deep muddy brown. With her red hair hanging loose around her face and her lips half open, she looked like a seductress from some demonic house of temptation.

Fifty thousand dollars! That was a lot of money. Looking into the Face of Seduction, it was hard to resist, especially when she added, "I could be very grateful in many ways." I hadn't realized she had come so close. Her lips almost touched mine and I could feel her warm breath on my face. She smelled of liqueur and mint.

"Hey, Julia, no making out in public," Doris said loudly. "You're supposed to be in mourning."

Julia pulled away. "I want him to kill my husband and I will do anything to convince him to do it," she said, suddenly in tears.

The other two women didn't respond; they just watched us. I could see they were waiting for my reaction. I shook my head. "Listen ladies, there is not enough money in the world that would cause me to kill anyone in cold blood. It would be murder, and I'm not a murderer; neither am I a gun for hire."

"How much did you offer him?" Erika asked.

"Fifty thousand dollars," Julia said.

"I'll give you ten thousand dollars on top of that." Erika looked into my eyes. "And I'll have sex with you as often as you want for one whole year." She wasn't smiling when she said that.

"So will I," Doris piped up. "I mean the sex, not the money."

"You ladies are too much," I said. "I have a feeling this is the alcohol talking. You'll think different in the morning when you're sober. In any case, I'm not interested." I smiled. "That didn't come out quite the way I meant it. Your offer is extremely tempting, especially the part about the sex. It isn't easy to resist three beautiful ladies such as you. Not every day does a man get such an offer."

"That's why you should accept it before we take it off the table," Julia said.

"You know I can't and I won't change my mind. This has to be done the legal way."

"Maybe you should have another drink, something stronger than beer. That might help change your mind." Doris pushed the bottle of wine she had in front of her toward me. Her smile was inviting. "After that you come to my place and I will show you the heavenly pleasure that awaits you for a whole year if you accept our offer."

I glanced toward the bar but didn't see Sonya. "I have everything I need without selling my soul," I said. While I was looking I spotted a bald, overweight man sitting on one of the barstools and I recognized Benny Miller. "Excuse me, ladies, I just saw a friend of mine. I need to talk to him." With that I got up and walked away, glad to have found a diversion.

There wasn't an empty stool beside Miller, so I stood behind him and touched his shoulder. "Mr. Miller," I said when he turned around to look at me.

"Mr. Canon. How are things?" He scrutinized my face. "Got into a fight with one of your clients?" It was easy to see he had already had too much alcohol.

"Not a client, but it may have something to do with your case. I'm not quite sure. By the way, should you be drinking so much already? After all, you've had a heart attack."

"Artificially induced, remember? I'm fine now. What do you mean by what happened to you had something to do with my case? Who did you have a run-in with?"

"One of my former partners, but I think he was hired by your brother-in-law."

"Steelwood?"

"I'm not certain, but I'm trying to find out."

I was looking in the direction of the three women I had left behind at their table. "Come, I want you to meet someone."

He followed me, carrying his bottle with him. The women looked up when we approached

"Ladies, may I introduce a friend of mine? Meet Mr. Miller." Then I turned to Miller and said, "Meet three lovely ladies. That one is Erika, this one is Doris, and then we have Julia." I watched her face, but she didn't give any sign of recognition when she saw Miller, which surprised me.

However, Miller said, "I don't know those other two, but I know who Julia is." He gave her a crooked smile and said, "Hi there, sister-in-law."

Julia stared at him with obvious surprise. "I don't understand."

"I'm married to your sister Angela."

Her eyes went wide. "You're Angela's husband? How long have you been married to her?"

He chuckled. "Too long, much too long."

"And you're still alive?"

"Aren't I lucky?" He took a swig from his bottle. "I was at your wedding, you know, but you probably don't remember me. You're married to Frederick Titman. Are you aware that he is a mobster?" He hiccupped and grabbed the back of the empty chair for support. "I'd better watch my mouth. Maybe I said too much, but who cares? Why should I worry about a man who doesn't even know I'm his brother-in-law? Besides, I'm already in mortal danger from my wife—your sister."

"Why don't you have a seat, Mr. Miller," Julia said.

"Call me Benny. After all you and I are related, Julia, even if only through marriage." He sank into the seat and leaned his elbows onto the tabletop. "I think I had too much to drink. Did you know I'm recovering from a heart attack? Courtesy of my wife."

"Are you saying your marriage is so stressful it gave you a heart attack?" Erika asked, smiling.

Miller chuckled. "Stressful isn't the word, but I don't want to talk about it." He looked at Julia. "How come you never get together with your sister? You've never been to our house, and we haven't had a visit with you. Don't relatives do that? Like visit each other?"

"Normal people do that, I guess." Julia laughed softly. "My family isn't normal. Angela hates my guts. And the feeling is mutual. She tried to drown me once when I was eight."

Miller leaned forward, more than just curiosity on his face. "No kidding, but I'm not surprised. She's a psychopath, you know. She murdered her last husband and..." He stopped talking. "I shouldn't have said that. I have no proof, just suspicions."

"You don't have to stop talking on account of me," Julia said. "I know she's capable of murder. When she was a teenager she used to shoot the neighborhood cats and dogs with her pellet gun. One time she caught a cat and hung it from a tree branch with a noose around its neck. She was cruel then and she hasn't changed. Except now she uses a real gun."

"Why? Who did she shoot?" Miller looked hopeful, possibly expecting some revelation.

"She shot a plumber once who came to fix a leaky toilet. She said she thought he was an intruder. I think she wanted to kill him because he was bragging about the women he dated. Then he asked her out. She never really liked men. When she told my brother about the incident, she was breathless and her cheeks were red. The same way she looked when she hung that cat. I remember it quite well, because it happened on my tenth birthday."

"Did the plumber die?" Doris asked, her eyes wide with some kind of excitement.

"No, she only shot him in the leg. He was going to press charges, but my father, the Police Commissioner, convinced him it wouldn't be a good idea."

"Your father was a persuasive man," I said, remembering how he convinced me to quit the force. "And your brother has the same attractive qualities."

"You know my father and brother?" Julia asked.

"I was a cop for twelve years. Your brother and I went to the Police Academy together. Yes, I know him well. Your father? Let's just say we never saw eye to eye." I was surprised about her not knowing that I had been a cop before I became a detective. I guess nobody ever told her.

I was still standing behind Miller who had taken the only empty chair at the table. I could have looked for another chair, but I was planning to leave the company of Miller and his new-found women friends as soon as an opportunity presented itself.

Julia turned her attention back to me. "Are you on friendly terms with my brother?"

I intended to chuckle but instead it came out like a barking laugh. "Friendly terms? Your brother and I? I'm afraid not. We had a falling-out already at the Academy. Your brother and I were wooing the same girl. I won. I married her."

"I guess he never forgave you for that. Am I right?" She studied my face with great interest. "He doesn't like to lose."

Bitterness rose inside me. "Perhaps it would have been better had he won. My wife divorced me six years ago."

"She's a stupid woman," Doris said, giving me a dreamy look. At least I assumed it was dreamy, especially when she said, "I would never divorce you. You want to know a secret? I've never made love to a redheaded man." She giggled. "Are you red everywhere? I mean…"

"We know what you mean," Erika interrupted her. "Is that all you ever think of, Doris?"

"Not always, but most of the time," Doris said.

I saw my chance to break away and said, "Ladies and Mr. Miller, you'll have to excuse me. I have something I must attend to." I walked away before anyone could make an objection. It seemed Sonya had been watching me, because when I walked up to the counter, she came over. "Who are your admirers?" she asked.

"They are no admirers. One of them is Julia Titman and the other two ladies are just friends of hers. And, of course, you know Mr. Miller."

"No admirers?" Her laughter teased me a little. "It was easy to see even from here that the brunette with the long hair and large boobs was flirting with you."

"Perhaps she was. Her name is Doris," I said, grinning foolishly. "Don't tell me you're jealous."

She reached across the counter and touched my cheek in a quick caress. "Maybe I am, but only a little. Will you stay over tonight again?"

"No, I'll be going home to my place to check up on things. I'll drop in tomorrow night. See you then." I blew her a kiss and then I left.

I walked slowly to my car, breathing in the air. It was warm and humid outside and I could smell the rain.

TWELVE

IN THE MORNING, I called Kabinsky again and told him about my visit with Pallitser. "Pallitser will be doing some investigating. He was quite intrigued to learn that Titman is Steelwood's brother-in-law. Did I ever tell you I have evidence that incriminates Angela Steelwood in the murder of Mildred Stone? Remember, she was the lady who was murdered a couple of years ago. I asked you to look into that file. Did you ever?"

"I didn't get a chance yet, Lews. I have a desk full of cases I'm working on. Stuff that is recent. I can't just drop everything and look at old files. You should understand that."

"Well, I do, Frank. I just wanted to let you know that I spoke to Pallitser. See you."

Disappointed and puzzled by Kabinsky's behavior, I left the office and got into my car. The rain I smelled the night before had finally come, but only as a bit of a drizzle. The temperature had dropped some to make driving in my car without air conditioning more pleasant. Looking at the gauge, I realized the tank was nearly empty so I drove to the garage I always use to get my gas.

While waiting for the tank to be filled, I contemplated my next move. There wasn't much I could do at the moment with any of my cases. There appeared to be some kind of common thread running through them, but I seemed to have arrived at a brick wall.

Sometimes I can do my best thinking sitting in my car. Very rarely I listen to the radio, not finding anything interesting except for mostly advertising and loud music. That gives me time to think.

It is strange and often eerie how most things we encounter are somehow connected and how events influence our lives and future, how one incident leads to another. Most people walk through life and never see these connections; they never realize that every action carries consequences.

My thoughts went back to my time at the police academy, where I fell in love with a beautiful girl. She was not one of the recruits. She worked in the cafeteria. Of course, how things usually are, I wasn't the only one who noticed her. The other man who was trying his best to win her over was Allan Steelwood. He lost.

Steelwood never forgave me for losing out. He and I became enemies. His father was the Police Commissioner and, obviously, he had more advantages than I from the beginning of our careers. Having Allan as an enemy didn't help my advancement in the police force. And all that over a girl!

When my dear sweet wife divorced me after twelve years of, what I thought, a solid and comparatively happy marriage, I was devastated. I had loved her dearly, but I had been blind to the fact that she wasn't happy. Perhaps if I had been an electrician or a plumber, we might still be together, but the family life of a cop is not always ideal and I know I neglected her too many times.

After I quit the force my life was in turmoil. I started drinking more than I had done already before, and one day, out of the blues for me, she presented me with divorce papers. Even though she blamed my drinking as the reason, I realized later that she only took that as an excuse. I found out that she had carried on an affair with our lawyer already for over a year. That hurt, but I knew I had only myself to blame. A neglected wife will begin looking somewhere else and a woman as beautiful as Mary-Ann doesn't have to look for long or too far to find someone who will satisfy her desires.

Not only did she leave me brokenhearted, she also left me broke. Marrying a lawyer did have certain advantages for her, as I discovered.

The judge awarded her our house at the outskirts of the city, all the furniture, and the family car we bought in her name. In addition to that she had already cleaned out our savings account.

Perhaps that was one of the reasons I shied away from making a commitment to Sonya. A man who has been burned does get cautious. I didn't want to get burned again.

A knock against the window ripped me out of my reminiscing. It was the garage attendant. "She's filled up, sir. That'll be forty-five bucks."

I handed him my credit card. I don't like using it too often, but I didn't have enough cash on me. While I waited for him to come back, I watched another guy fill up his car by the self-serve station. Somehow he looked familiar, and suddenly I recognized him. It was one of the cops who had arrested me that day for speeding. Only he wasn't in uniform and the car he drove was not a cop car.

My attendant came back with my credit card. I signed it and then, in a fit of sudden anger, I got out of my car and walked up to the cop. He was so concentrated on filling his tank that he didn't see me coming. When I poked his shoulder, he reacted by pulling the nozzle out of the tank and spilling gas onto the pavement.

"What the hell..." he yelled and turned to face me.

"Be careful with that," I said. "Gasoline is expensive, besides you're polluting the ground and the air."

When he saw me, he dropped the nozzle, his hand moved toward the shoulder holster he had hidden under his open jacket. I stopped him by grabbing his arm and twisting it. "Not so fast, buster. What a coincidence we meet again so soon, *Officer*."

"Let go of my arm!" he grunted.

"Why, does it hurt?"

"What do you want?"

"I want to see your badge." I reached into his jacket and removed his gun before I let go of his arm.

"I don't have it on me. I'm off-duty."

I gave him one of my evil grins. "Off-duty my ass. For one thing, this gun isn't standard police issue. I'll bet you're not even a cop. Show me some ID!" I shoved his own gun into his belly. "Hurry up, I'm a little bit impatient these days and still in pain from the treatment I received at the Twenty-third Precinct. The place sound familiar to you? And I'm more than just a little irritated. I could easily forget myself and put a bullet into your gut. Perhaps you still remember my name. It's Lews Canon and it sounds like exactly what I am."

"Okay, okay. My wallet is in my other pocket. Just give me a chance. Don't go crazy now, buddy."

"I'm not your buddy. You call me that again and I'll smash your head against the hood of your car." I underlined my threat by pushing the barrel of the gun tighter against his gut.

After he had managed to retrieve his wallet, I said, "Now take out your driver's license and read it to me. Once he was done, I asked, "What do you do for a living, Harold Snyder?"

"I'm a cop."

I pushed the gun deeper until he squirmed. "Again, what is it you do for a living? I know you're not a cop."

"All right, I'm not a cop. I'm an actor. Happy now?" He gave me a challenging look. I had to hand it to him, he wasn't cowering.

"How about your buddy?"

"He's an actor, too."

"Who hired you guys?"

He shrugged. "He never gave us his name."

"Wrong answer." I used my other fist to punch him in the ribs. "Hurts, doesn't it?"

He groaned. Then he said, "I'm telling you the truth. He didn't say his name. But I can tell you what he looked like. He was around forty. Tall and slim. Good-looking. Dark hair, dark eyes. And he had a small scar over his right eyebrow."

"Well, that wasn't so hard, was it?" His description of Meloni couldn't have been any more detailed. "Now, give me your wallet!"

"Why?"

"Don't ask stupid questions and give me your wallet."

"I can't give you my wallet just like that. I need my driver's license, otherwise I can't drive." He almost whined and I felt like hitting him across his mouth but contained myself. Instead I grabbed his wallet and shoved it into my pocket. "Why not? You can still drive. Just don't get caught by the cops. I mean real cops."

"What do you want with my wallet? Are you robbing me? If you do, just take the money and let me go."

My laugh probably told him enough. "I'm not a criminal. You can pick up your wallet at the Twenty-third Precinct. You know where to find it. By the way, I'll hang onto your gun for a while. Maybe one day I'll take it to the cops and you can pick it up there. I hope you have a permit for it."

"Hey, I need my credit card to pay for the gas. Give me at least my credit card."

"You should have prepaid before you started pumping." I grinned and clapped him on the shoulder. "Good luck, Harold. Be seeing you." Then I kneed him in the groin.

I left him doubling over beside his car, clutching his mistreated balls. Before I drove away, I took down his plate number, and then I called my old precinct, which was the nearest police station. "Listen, I want to report a theft. There's a guy trying to steal gas at the gas station on Alfred and seventh. This is his plate number..."

Then I headed for the Twenty-third Precinct to deliver the wallet. When I got there, I spotted a young boy playing across the street from the police station and I had an idea. I took one last look at the driver's license in the wallet and wrote down the guy's name and address. Then I removed five bucks from the wallet, walked up to the boy and handed the money and the wallet to him. "Listen, do me a favor. These five bucks are yours if you take this wallet to the cops. Tell them you found it on the street. Don't mention me, okay."

"Sure, Mister. Thanks." He stuffed the money into his pocket and ran across the street. I watched him disappear into the police station and then I drove away, humming to myself. The universe is always fair. Somehow this day was turning out just right.

————

It began to rain more heavily now, but it didn't diminish my happiness. It was almost noon and I had a sudden craving for a hamburger and fries, so I headed for Mama's Big Ones.

One look at the owner and one didn't have to guess how she came up with the name for her restaurant. She was no spring chicken and had seen better years, but she always wore a dress that showed off her giant boobs.

"Hello, Mama," I said when I walked into the place. "I feel like having one of your Big Ones."

She laughed good-naturedly and gave me a wink. "Mr. Canon, do not make jokes like that. Someday I will surprise you and take you up on it." She waddled over to my table and sank into the seat across from me. Taking a serviette from the dispenser, she wiped her forehead with it. "I'm getting too old to work in the kitchen."

"Maybe it's time to hire a couple of young people to take over to do the cooking. Then you can relax and chat with the customers," I suggested.

"I wish I could, but my customers come because I make everything personally. They may not come anymore if someone else does the cooking. People are funny that way, you know. Most of my customers are men and they want me to cook the burgers but they want a young girl like Lindy to serve them. Besides, it would cost too much." She sighed. "I wish I were young and pretty again."

"You're not so old, Mama. And you're still pretty."

Her teeth gleamed white in her dark face and her hearty laughter rang through the room. "Either you are a liar, Mr. Canon, or blind, but I like to listen to your compliments. Makes me feel good. You must be really hungry for my hamburgers. You usually come about once a month, but this time barely a week has gone since your last visit."

"Maybe it's you I missed," I said, winking.

She pushed herself up with her arms. "Oh sure. Next thing you'll be asking me for a date." Laughing, she waddled away.

"Aren't you going to take my order?" I called after her.

"I can't do everything," she called back over her shoulder. "That's what I hired Lindy for."

While I waited for my meal, my phone rang. When I answered it I was surprised to hear Kabinsky's voice. "Lews, I looked into Mildred Stone's file, but there isn't much in there. She was shot. No weapon has ever been found. It's still an open case, but it's pretty much dead. What made you connect her death with Angela Steelwood? What kind of evidence do you have?"

I was going to tell him about the gun, but on a hunch I decided not to; instead I said, "I can't tell you over the phone. The only thing I can tell you is that it's compelling evidence. I'm keeping it in a safe place."

"How about bringing it here and I can have a look at it."

"I will but not today. I'm kinda busy right now." Lindy had brought my order and the hamburger looked and smelled delicious and so did the fries. I wanted to enjoy my meal while everything was fresh and hot. Besides, I was still debating if I should trust anyone with Angela's gun. It was secure in my safe back in the office until I made up my mind.

"Listen, Lews, will you be at your lady-friend's place tonight?"

"Probably not. Why?"

"I'll do some more digging. In case I find something, I want to call you."

"You can always call me on my cell."

"I know I can, but sometimes you don't answer it."

"That's true, but I'll keep it on."

He paused for a moment. "Okay, that's good. Be talking to you." He hung up and I attacked my giant hamburger. Maybe I was wrong about Kabinsky. He was trying. That's all I could ask for.

After lunch I drove back to the office. It was still raining and the humidity and trapped heat in the office made it uncomfortable, but I hadn't planned to stay longer than necessary. I checked in the safe to make sure Angela's gun was still there. Then I wiped the gun I had taken from Harold Snyder with a cloth to remove my finger prints, put it into a plastic bag and stashed it also in the safe. It might just come in handy someday.

I was going to drop in at the Dancing Leprechaun for a beer and to say hi to Sonya but drove home instead. There was still a frozen dinner in the freezer and a few bottles of beer in the fridge and I didn't have to worry about driving to get home should I drink one too many. Besides, my chest was tight and my ribs still a bit sore. I needed the rest.

———

Waking up in the morning after drinking a six-pack of beer is not a pleasant experience. The Scotch I drank between bottles didn't help either. I had a splitting headache and my mouth was full of cotton balls.

My body ached and just to move was a giant endeavor. When the radio on my alarm clock sprang to life and a voice said, "Isn't it a wonderful morning after yesterday's rain?" I was ready to commit murder, but even that would have taken too much effort. I hit the clock with my fist to shut up the bubbly voice. When the phone rang I didn't answer it. Instead I hid my head under the pillow to shut out the world, promising myself never to touch another bottle of beer or hard liqueur again.

However, the phone didn't stop ringing and I finally answered it with a voice that seemed to come out of a rusty radiator. "Hello and go away." I was ready to throw the phone into the laundry basket, but I had sense enough to want to know who called me at this unearthly hour.

"Is this Mr. Canon?" the female voice on the other end asked.

I had no idea who it was, but I said, "Yes. Who are you?"

"Sorry to bother you, Mr. Canon. This is Jenny from the Dancing Leprechaun. Would you by any chance know where Sonya is?"

It took me a moment to gather my thoughts. "She should be home, as far as I know."

"Have you seen her?"

"Not since a couple of nights ago. Why do you ask?"

"She didn't show up for work last night and we've been trying to call her this morning, but she's not answering her phone."

Even through my foggy brain I realized that something was wrong. It wasn't like Sonya at all not to show up for work without a valid reason, and in any case, she would have called to let them know she wasn't coming in should she be sick.

That sudden icy tremor running down my back wasn't because I was cold. My hands were trembling as a great sense of foreboding took hold of me. "Thanks for letting me know," I managed to say before the phone dropped from my clammy fingers.

I stumbled from the bed and into the bathroom. After a quick, cold shower and a couple of painkillers I felt better. Not much but enough to let me formulate straight thoughts. There was no reason to assume the worst. Maybe she decided to take the evening off and go out with her friends and she forgot to let her employer know.

Or perhaps it was that time of the month and she didn't feel like going to work. I called her number but only got her answering service. So I left a message.

"It's Lews. Call me back on my cell. I'm on my way to your place."

I didn't have breakfast, but I wasn't hungry anyway. When I looked at my watch I saw it was already nine o'clock.

The trip seemed to take forever. I must have gotten every red light and all the slow drivers of the city were on the road. Even the pedestrians took their sweet old time to cross the street. When I finally pulled up in front of Sonya's apartment building, I was a nervous wreck. My hands were slick with sweat and my shirt was drenched with perspiration.

I didn't bother with the elevator and used the stairs, taking three with every step. Rushing down the corridor, I finally made it to Sonya's door. I knocked but she didn't answer. With trembling fingers I fished the key to her apartment out of my pocket and managed to insert it without dropping it. I turned the key and pushed open the door, hoping the chain wasn't in place. It wasn't, but it suddenly dawned on me that the lock had been in the open position.

When I saw the upturned furniture and the pillows of the couch on the floor I knew something was terribly wrong. The place was a mess and my first thought was she's been robbed. Looking into to kitchen, I saw the freezer door of the fridge standing open.

When I called, "Sonya!" I heard a moaning sound coming from the bedroom. The door was closed and I rushed to it, my heart pounding, fearing the worst.

Sonya lay on her bed, naked, her arms and legs spread. Her wrists were tied to the headrest with ropes, and her ankles to the legs of the box spring. Her mouth was covered with tape.

When I stormed into the room, she lifted her head and looked at me with wide eyes. The noises she made with her mouth sounded like suppressed screams, but then she dropped her head back onto the bed and lay still. Her face was swollen and there were cuts over her brows. Crusted blood covered both her cheeks.

I rushed to her side and carefully removed the tape from her mouth. Then I untied the ropes. She rolled her nude body into a ball and whimpered loudly. I didn't touch her and let her be, my heart bleeding for her, knowing the agony she must be suffering. She finally stopped sobbing and moved her head to look at me.

"You came," she said in a shaky voice and began crying again.

"Who did this to you?" I swallowed a lump that had formed in my throat. I didn't really have to ask her what happened. I knew.

She grabbed my hand and squeezed it. Her eyes were large and frightened and I felt the anger bubbling up inside me. Whoever did this to this gentle woman would pay. I swore it to myself.

"Who did this?" I asked again.

She shook her head. "There were two of them. I've never seen them before," she whispered.

"I will find them if I have to turn this whole city upside down," I said violently, consumed by rage I hadn't felt for years.

She smiled bravely. "I know you will." She sat up then and clung to me. "I was so afraid for my life," she cried, tears running freely now.

"Hush, you're safe now." I tried to comfort her as well as I could, but words are never enough. I just held her close and let her cry.

After a while she relaxed. "I need to take a shower. I feel so dirty. I don't think I'll ever feel clean again."

I let her go. She got up and went into the bathroom. I heard the toilet being flushed and then the rushing of the water in the shower. There was nothing for me to do but wait, so I went into the living room and started straightening out the furniture. I closed the freezer door, hoping not all her food was thawed and spoiled.

Putting the pillows back onto the couch, I sat down and stared at one of the pictures on the wall.

The safest place in the world is your home it said with golden fancy letters stitched onto a blue, satin background surrounded by a lovely carved wooden frame.

What irony!

Sonya came out of the bathroom, her housecoat wrapped around her slim body. She had three butterfly bandages on her face and she looked much better, except for her swollen, discolored cheeks. She joined me on the couch and leaned against me. "Hold me," she said with a small voice. I put my arm around her and held her. We sat like that without saying a word.

"I'm okay now," she said after a while.

"How can you be? Those bastards raped and beat you," I said.

"Only one of them did this. The other one just watched." She grimaced. "It took me back to the time I was married. My ex-husband, may he rot in hell, watched many times as one of his drunken friends raped me in front of him."

Clenching my teeth, I said, "It makes me sick and unable to understand how a man can do something like that to the woman he loves." My fingers curled, turning my hands into fists. "Hell, if it were up to me I'd have every man who rapes a woman castrated!"

She smiled. "You're a good man, Lews. That's why I love you."

"I love you, too, and I feel terrible for letting you down and not protecting you."

"It's not your fault. You can't be with me all the time."

"What did they want from you?"

"They were looking for something. All they said was *where are you hiding it?* They never indicated what they were looking for."

"That's when they hit you?"

She nodded. "I told them I have nothing hidden anywhere, whatever it is you're looking for."

"Did they take anything?"

"I see nothing missing. Of course, I haven't checked my jewelry yet."

"Can you describe what these men looked like?"

She gave a little hysteric laugh. "Oh, yes, I can, especially the one who raped me. He was big, bald, with a nose like a bulb. And he had tiny ears. His arms were full of ugly tattoos and he wore diamond studs in his ears. Oh, and he had a real high voice."

Shit! I suddenly felt guilty for what happened to her. "I know who that guy is. His name is Jerry Nightingale. He's one of the guys who broke into my office. What about the other one?"

"He was tall, wiry, with a Mohawk haircut. There was a vivid scar running down his entire left cheek. His voice was real deep, and he wore a ring with a crest on his right hand. I'll never forget either of these men."

"I don't know who that guy is, but I have an idea how we can find out. You telling me he had a deep voice makes me fairly certain it is the same guy who was with Nightingale the night they broke into my office. When you feel better, we'll drive to an artist I recently met. He'll draw a picture if you describe the man to him."

"We can go right now," she said, her voice determined and fierce.

"I don't think that's a good idea," I said, gently. "You need to rest and recover from the shock, and we want to let the swelling on your face go down. In the meantime, do you want to report it to the police?"

She shook her head. "No. No police. It will create nothing but problems. In the end it is useless, anyway. They'll do nothing." Her eyes searched my face. "I trust you will do what is necessary."

"These men won't get away with it. I promise you that." I ground my teeth to calm down the anger that was boiling inside me. "You should at least see a doctor. If we go to a hospital, they'll ask questions. I know someone who will be discreet. I'll take you to him. Okay?"

She nodded. "Okay."

THIRTEEN

DR. JHAMIR DIDN'T SAY anything when he saw Sonya, but when he threw me an almost accusing stare with those lemur eyes from behind his thick glasses, I lifted both hands. "I didn't do this."

He removed the butterfly bandages and sewed up Sonya's split skin. He told me to leave the room so he could talk to Sonya in private. She seemed much better when we left.

I stayed with her for the next couple of days, only leaving her for a short time to check up on things in the office. There were no messages on the answering machine. Kabinsky never called my cell or the office. I hadn't expected him to do so, but I had secretly been hoping. It seems I was wrong about my assumption he would make an effort to find out something.

I hadn't seen Nelda since the day she dropped me off at Brandon's garage. She told me she'd be visiting Anton to have her picture taken, and I wondered how that went.

She answered her cell almost immediately. "It's Lews. How's Anton?"

"Anton is fine," she answered, "and so am I. Thanks for asking."

"You didn't give me a chance to ask. How's the picture-taking coming along?"

"He's not taking my picture with the camera. He's painting me."

"In the nude?" I don't know why I said it; it just slipped out, but somehow when I think of a painter painting a woman I imagine it to be a nude picture.

"What does it matter to you?" She sounded irritated and challenging. "Do you think I can't have a picture of me in the nude?"

"Of course you can and I'm sure you look just fine. Listen, I'm not calling you about that. Something unpleasant happened a couple of days ago. Sonya suffered a home-invasion. Two guys broke into her apartment, trashed it and raped her."

"Oh my God! I'm sorry to hear that. Is she okay?"

I chuckled grimly. "As okay as a woman is after being raped and beaten. She's handling it, though; better than expected. Are you still at Anton's place?"

"Actually, we're just having coffee. He's a real nice guy, you know."

"Is he there with you?"

"Yes, he is. You want to talk to him?"

"I wouldn't mind."

A moment later, Anton was on the phone. "Bon Jour, Monsieur Canon. What can I do for you?"

"Mr. Bernard, I need your help. Can you draw a face if somebody describes that person to you?"

"Monsieur Canon, I am an artist. I can do that."

"Great. I wonder if you can do me a great favor. If I bring a friend over to your place would you be willing to draw that picture for us? It is important. I will pay you for it."

"I would be delighted. Come to my studio tomorrow and I will see what I can do. By the way, your partner is a delightful medium." He chuckled. "She told me everything about you and her, Monsieur Canon." He emphasized my name and I had to smile as I suddenly realized he had called me by my real name.

"I must apologize to you, Mr. Bernard, for giving you a false name when I came to you, but I wasn't sure if you would give me any information about George Cole if you knew I was a Private Detective. I guess you know he was murdered." I hoped he wouldn't ask me why I inquired about Cole and I also hoped he hadn't discussed our visit with Julia. I felt bad enough knowing that we were responsible for putting Titman on Cole's trail.

He sighed into the phone. "Oui, I know. What a shame. He was such a beautiful man. I will miss him."

"Julia asked me to find out who murdered him. I haven't had any luck yet, but I'm trying. Can you put Nelda back on, please?"

When Nelda answered, I said, "I may need your assistance in something. I'll tell you everything in person."

The next morning Sonya felt she was ready and we drove to Bernard's place. He greeted us with a big smile and invited us into his studio.

Looking around, I saw a couple of pictures featuring Nelda. There was no mistaking it was her. She wasn't completely nude but almost, and I had to admit, Bernard had done a terrific job of making her attractive. There was one picture depicting a battle between a horde of dwarfs and two giants. Nelda was one of the giants, a savage-looking female, dressed only in a tiny leather skirt, while her breasts were bare. She stood, wielding a huge broadsword, ready to smash it into the dwarfs facing her. I wondered if she actually possessed muscles like that.

Bernard saw me looking and he smiled proudly. "Isn't she magnificent?" he asked. "I've never seen a woman with such beautiful muscles. They are real, as you may already know. She is a perfect model for my pictures. I will make her famous."

Then he looked at Sonya and his smile faded. "May I ask, Mademoiselle, did you have an accident?"

"No accident," Sonya said. "I got raped."

I was surprised to hear her say it so casually.

"Mon Dieux!" Bernard exclaimed. "I am so sorry to hear that. What kind of animal would do such a thing to another person! It is terrible. I hope they find him and he gets punished."

"That's why we are here," she said. "There were two men, but we know the identity of one of them. If I describe the other man perhaps you can make a drawing?"

"It will try my best. Come, and sit down on this chair here and let me get my pad and my crayons."

Sonya took the indicated chair, while Bernard went to get his tools. Then he sat across from her and looked expectantly at her.

Sonya began describing the man in as much detail as she could remember and Bernard drew what she told him. A few times she stopped and took a deep breath, wiping her cheeks with trembling fingers, but she stayed quite calm and I had to admire her for her courage. It couldn't have been easy for her to recall her ordeal, and yet, she barely faltered.

Finally she said, "That's about all I can tell you. I hope it will be enough."

Bernard smiled proudly as he turned the picture he had drawn around to have her look at it. She gasped when she saw it and put her hand to her mouth. "That's him," she whispered. "That's one of the two men."

I looked at the drawing and I had to admit Bernard was talented. Not every artist can draw a picture this accurately from someone's description. In fact, many who consider themselves artists, can't even draw or paint a life-like figure, never mind a face with such detail. In my opinion, splashing globs of paint onto a canvas or drawing a bunch of circles or squares and then giving it a fancy sounding name is not art. Any monkey can do that.

"You truly are an artist," I said. "With this picture we will have no trouble finding this son-of-a-bitch. I will make him pay for what he did to Sonya." I looked at her when I said it and she nodded.

"I'm sure you will," she said in a trembling voice and her eyes moist. Giving me a tiny smile, she reached for my hand and squeezed it.

"How much do I owe you, Mr. Bernard?"

"You owe me nothing, Monsieur Canon. I am happy to do this service for you and your lady. Now, may I offer you a cup of coffee?"

We left Bernard's place an hour later. I took Sonya home and then I drove to the Twenty-third Precinct to talk to Sharon Masters. I decided to go to her rather than to Kabinsky, because I didn't trust him anymore to be of much help.

Sharon was obviously surprised to see me when I walked up to her desk. "Lews Canon, nice to see you. All healed up, and you're looking much better." She smiled. "In fact, you're looking really good."

"Not as good as you," I said with a little chuckle, trying to keep my mind on the light side, but inside I was consumed with an anger that wouldn't go away.

"Well, how nice of you to say that, but I have a feeling you didn't come to give me a compliment." She became serious. "What can I do for you?"

"I need you to find and identify a man for me," I said, taking the picture Bernard had drawn out of its envelope.

She took the picture from my hand and studied it. "What did he do?"

"He violated the woman I love," I said, my voice suddenly hoarse.

She looked at me with understanding, and then she nodded. "Give me a moment. I will try to locate him." She scanned the picture and saved it on her computer. It didn't take long at all until she looked up and smiled. "I have him."

"Who is he?"

"His name is Harry Rosser. He is not a stranger to the police department."

"Harry Rosser?" I repeated, somehow not surprised and my suspicions confirmed as certain things seemed to fall into place.

She must have seen it in my face. "Do you know him?"

"Not personally, but I know someone who does. You're sure that's him?"

"One hundred percent. By the way, this is quite some life-like drawing. Almost like a photograph. Who did it?"

"A painter by the name of Anton Bernard. He is a genius."

"I can see that." Her expression was one of concern. "I'm really sorry about what happened to your friend. I hope she's okay?"

"She's taking it rather well, considering, but I'm not." I spoke harshly. "I want him punished."

"Do you want us to pick him up?"

"No. Not yet. My friend isn't ready to testify. And there is something I need to do first. He was hired by someone and I have to know by whom."

Her face was somber and her voice grave when she said, "Don't do anything rash, Lews. I can see the rage burning in your eyes and I don't blame you for wanting to take matters into your own hands, but don't do it. Let the law handle it."

"The law?" I laughed without emotion. "Remember I used to be a cop? I know how it works. Too many restrictions to follow and too much red tape. Besides, I have a pretty good idea who he works for.

Those are the people I want, the ones the law can't touch; the ones who hide behind the law."

"Who are these people? Maybe I can help."

"I appreciate your offer, but there is nothing you can do. They are powerful people with friends in high places, even in the police department. You can't get involved, Sharon. They'd flatten you like a bug with a steamroller and nobody would protect you. For your own good, don't try to pursue this on your own. I will let you know when I'm ready for your help."

"Let me ask you a question, Lews. Why did you come to me? This precinct is not near your place of residence or your office. I'm sure you have friends in the precinct you worked."

"I thought I did, but you are the only one I trust." I put the picture back into the envelope. "Thank you for your help, Sharon." I smiled. "I would have preferred to take you out for a cup of coffee, but things are as they are. Fate is not always fair."

"Yeah," she said, nodding with a bit of a sad smile. "Fate's a bitch. You take care of yourself, Lews. I hope everything turns out for you and that special woman in your life."

I drove away with the rage Sharon had seen in my eyes churning in my belly. I would get that bastard and I knew exactly where to find him. There was no reason for me to wait, so I headed for Shirley Brandon's beauty salon.

Shirley was busy with a customer, but when she saw me walking in, she came over. "Hi, Lews. Did you find out anything?"

"I'm afraid not, but I'd like you to look at a picture to confirm something." When I showed her the drawing of Rosser, her eyes widened. "Does he have anything to do with Bart's murder?"

I shook my head. "I can't say, but this is Harry Rosser, isn't it?"

"Yes, that's him."

"Good. Has he been in your salon lately?"

"No, but he is due for another haircut." She made a sound of contempt. "That stupid Mohawk he's got only confirms that he is an idiot. He thinks it makes him look tough. Every time I do his hair, I feel like shaving that whole thing off and carve *Idiot* into his bald plate."

"Next time he comes in give me a call. Make sure he doesn't leave before I get here."

"Why, what's he done?"

"He and his friend Jeremy Nightingale broke into my friend's apartment and molested her."

"Oh, my. That's awful! When did this happen?"

"A few days ago. Please, don't mention this to anyone. I don't want him to know that I'm coming for him."

"Are you going to kill him?"

"No, I need him alive to get important information from him, but I may rough him up a little." I smiled wolfishly. "Just a little."

"He deserves more than that," Shirley said. She glanced back at the woman she'd been working on when I walked in. The woman looked agitated. "I'd better get back to her before she walks out on me. I can't afford to lose any customers. I'll call you the minute he makes his appointment."

———

She called the next day. In the morning. "Lews. It's Shirley. He called. He'll be coming in at two o'clock this afternoon."

"Thanks, Shirley."

As it happened, Nelda was also in the office. She knew about my plans. When she heard the name Shirley, she looked up from her computer. "When?" she asked.

"This afternoon."

We parked in front of Shirley's salon at 1:30 to make sure we had a spot as close as possible. Rosser showed up about five minutes before his appointment. Nelda and I intercepted him before he walked through the door into the salon.

"Harry Rosser?" I asked.

He gave me a surprised look. His eyes narrowed and I could see him go tense. "Who wants to know?"

"My name isn't important," I said. "What's important is that we have the right man."

"The right man for what? Actually, I don't care. Now get out of my way!"

He hadn't realized that Nelda was behind him until she shoved her 45 into his back.

"What the hell is going on? What do you want?"

"You, Harry," I said gently. "We want you."

"Do you know who you're messing with?" He spoke with a loud, arrogant voice. "You'll be sorry. I have friends in the police department."

I gave him a hollow laugh. "So you have. I know who you are, what you are, and whose dirty work you do, you conceited punk. Don't try to scare us. Your boss Titman isn't going to protect you now, neither is some high-priced attorney you may have in your pocket, nor are your cop-friends. We're strictly independent and don't have to follow any procedures."

"What are you talking about? You're not cops?"

"We never said we were, but we didn't say we weren't, either. Now —be a good boy and join us in our car."

"I'm not going into any car with you." He winced when Nelda jammed her gun deeper into his back.

"Move!" she said sharply. "If you make a fuss, I'll shoot you and we'll carry you. Take your pick." She punched him in the shoulder to emphasize her order.

I grabbed his collar and twisted it. "Go! I'm losing my patience."

Nelda shoved him into the front seat. She waited until I sat behind the wheel before she took the seat behind Rosser. "Sit still and don't even breathe hard." She spoke harshly. "I have one very nervous trigger finger. The backrest won't stop the bullet."

"Who are you guys and what do you want from me?"

"You'll find out soon enough," I told him. "And now shut up. I have to concentrate on the traffic."

I knew a good place where we would be undisturbed. It took us about half an hour to get to one of the abandoned warehouses in the old industrial district frequented only by vagrants and the occasional couple looking for a place to be undisturbed. Sometimes small gangs of teenagers roamed the area.

Rosser tried to resist when we headed for the old warehouse, but Nelda convinced him he'd be better off to give in to our demands. The place was not really safe inside. Rotten timbers could suddenly decide to fall from the ceiling and the same with the floors, but there was little chance anyone would come to investigate what was going on in one of the empty rooms. It was a perfect place to interrogate somebody who was reluctant to share information.

Nelda tied him to an old metal chair before we began with our interrogation.

"You'd better kill me now before you do anything stupid. If you don't you'll pay for what you're going to do," Rosser ranted. "I'll kill you both myself!"

"I told you before that we're not worried what you or your connections might do to us," I said. "When we're through with you, you will wish you had become a plumber or chosen any other honest trade rather than the one you chose. You will find out the hard way that crime actually does not pay, contrary what some people seem to believe."

"I don't know what you're talking about. Perhaps you should tell me who you are and what you want from me. You want money? I can get you money. Just stop this nonsense and let me go. I promise I won't tell anyone this happened."

"We don't want any money. We want information."

"What kind of information?"

"For starters—who paid you to break into the apartment on 9th street and what was it you were looking for?"

"I know nothing about that."

I smashed my fist against the side of his head. "Wrong answer. I know you were there. Why did you rape that woman?"

"I raped nobody," he rasped, shaking his head.

"But you admit you were there."

"I wasn't." He was stubborn and I knew it would be a long afternoon, possibly even evening.

"Don't be stupid, Rosser. The woman your partner Nightingale raped gave a good description of you and him. There is no doubt you were there. Since you didn't rape her you have nothing to worry about. Now, speak up, what were you looking for and who gave the order?"

"Screw you!" He spit, barely missing my face.

"Let me have a go at him," Nelda said and stepped in front of Rosser.

"Don't kill him," I cautioned. "We need him alive. For a little while, anyway."

"Don't worry. He'll be alive. Painfully alive but breathing." She kicked him in the chest with one foot so hard he and his chair toppled over and skidded across the floor.

Nelda went to pick him up again and brought him back, carrying him and the chair as easily as if he were a little boy. I never knew she was that strong.

"Okay, where were we?" she asked. "Oh right, we wanted to know who hired you."

"Screw you, you goddamn freak," he shouted.

She kicked him again. "Keep this up and you'll be nothing but hamburger meat inside that fancy suit of yours," she said in a calm voice.

"If I tell you will you stop kicking me?"

"I will if you tell the truth."

"Santa Claus hired me." He laughed into her face, which was the wrong thing to do. She hit him in the stomach with her fist. He would have doubled over had it not been for the ropes that bound him to the chair, but he cried out, retching and gasping for air.

"I can keep this up all night," Nelda said. "Only you have the power to stop this."

He held out a long time and I had to give him credit for that, but after an hour of being hit over and over again, he finally saw the light. "All right. I'll talk." His voice sounded weak and I knew he was breaking.

I went close to him and turned on my recorder. "Okay." I said. "First tell me your name."

"My name is Harry Rosser, but you know that already."

"I know, but I just want to make sure I have the right man. Who is your employer, Harry Rosser?"

Nelda had to convince him a few more times during our interview that the smartest thing for him to do was to tell everything, and he did.

According to Rosser, he and Nightingale broke into Sonya's apartment to find the evidence I apparently possessed for incriminating Angela Steelwood. Titman gave the order. The rape of Sonya was strictly Nightingale's idea.

"I never touched that woman. I swear. I'm not a rapist. And neither did I hit her. It was all Nightingale."

He admitted to killing a man in the alley behind the Lucky Millionaire's Casino. His name was Trevor Braintree. He had been a witness in a murder case involving Enrico Ramiro of the Ramiro Crime Syndicate. He also admitted to the murder of Bart Brandon and recently George Cole. There were a couple other killings he talked about. However, he insisted he had never done the actual killing.

"Nightingale did the stabbing. I only held them."

"George Cole was shot not stabbed," I pointed out.

"Yes, he was, but I didn't do it. Nightingale was the man with the gun. I'm innocent of all the charges. I only followed orders. Mr. Titman is the man you want, not me." He grimaced. "You might want to have a closer look at Commissioner Steelwood. He and Titman are close buddies, you know. In fact, they are brothers-in-law. Steelwood is behind it all. He controls everything."

"Would you be willing to testify in court?" I asked.

"No way. Don't make me do that. I'd be a dead man." He seemed hysterical. I guess we had finally broken him.

"You're dead either way. What makes you so sure we won't kill you if you don't agree to testify?"

"I told you everything you wanted to know. There is no reason to kill me. I won't talk to anyone; I promise. Just let me go. You gain nothing by killing me." His belligerence was gone. I felt almost sorry for him. Now he was just a sad excuse for a man, looking pathetic with his hair cut in that ridiculous Mohawk style.

"I can't give you any guarantees, but I could talk to some people who may be able to put you into a witness protection program. You'd have to move away and change your name, but, let's face it, Harry, your career as a criminal is finished either way in this city. What do you say?"

He looked up, the eye that wasn't hidden behind swollen, bloody tissue squinting at me. I could see hope on his bloodstained face. "Can you arrange for my protection?"

"I won't make false promises, but there is a good possibility it could happen. It is the best chance you have to stay alive. You have to face the truth and accept it."

"Okay. I'll take that chance. Just untie me and let me go. Would you have some painkillers? I think some of my ribs are broken."

"They're not broken," Nelda said. "If I wanted to break them I would have hit you much harder and you wouldn't be conscious now, believe me."

He moved his head a little to look at Nelda. "What are you? Man or woman? Are you real or just a figment of my imagination? You look like the devil, but you have the beautiful voice of an angel."

She gave him a wicked chuckle. "I'm neither devil nor angel. Just remember me as the Punisher of Evil."

"The Punisher of Evil," he murmured. "Do you think I'm evil? I'm just trying to stay alive the only way I know how. Did you know my father died in prison?"

"I didn't, but there is no need to give us your family history now," Nelda said. She began untying him. He slumped in his chair and would have slithered to the ground had she not caught him. Helping him to his feet, she said, "Steady now. You'll be fine in a moment. Just relax."

"I'm trying, but my legs are all wobbly." He straightened out his body, still leaning on her. "Everything hurts," he complained with a weak voice. "Can you give me something for the pain?"

"We'll take you to a hospital," I said. "I'm afraid you'll have to wait until then."

He didn't look too good. His complexion was gray. Even the dried blood couldn't hide it. He did need medical attention, but I couldn't find any pity inside me for him.

We dragged him to our car and pushed him into the backseat. As far as we knew, nobody had seen us. I was quite satisfied with the information we gathered. It was all on my recorder. I had enough material to put the noose around a few people's neck.

We dropped him off in front of the nearest hospital and waited until he stumbled through the door into the emergency room before we drove away.

That was more than he deserved.

FOURTEEN

SONYA WAS SATISFIED when I told her that we had located and questioned Harry Rosser.

"Did you kill him?" she asked.

"No. He's alive, but he didn't get away scot-free. Once we convinced him it would be in his best interest to cooperate with us, he was quite amiable. He spilled the beans, all of them. He said he didn't hit you. Is that true?"

"That's true, but he didn't prevent his companion from doing what he did to me. That makes him just as guilty. What about that bastard who raped me? Are you going after him?"

"Nightingale? You bet I will. He's bad news and more dangerous than Rosser. I'll come up with something."

The next morning, I went to see Kabinsky. I took a copy of Rosser's confession with me, but not before Nelda had done some editing by removing our voices and a few other sounds. Another copy was on my computer, but the original recording, the way it had been with our voices and the sounds Nelda's fists and feet made on Rosser's body, was safely tucked away in my safe.

"You look much better today," Kabinsky said when I walked in.

"I look and feel so much better. I have something for you." I handed him the flash drive. "Here. Download this and don't ask me how I got it, just listen to it."

We sat there without saying anything while we listened to Rosser spilling his guts. The whole confession took only twenty minutes, but the material on it was damaging evidence. Kabinsky had no choice but to act upon it. At least that was my assumption.

"Strange, how things work out sometimes," I said. "And it's amazing, how one man's confession can have such an impact on so many people, and how it suddenly ties up so many loose ends. Now we know the actual name of that John Doe who was found in a landfill a year ago. We also know that Bart Brandon and George Cole were not victims of a mugging; they were actually murdered and we know who did it." I bent forward. "And we know the role Frederic Titman played in those murders and, last but not least, we have evidence that our most revered Commissioner Allan Steelwood has more than just a little blood on his hands. What will you do, Frank?"

There was a haunted expression on Kabinsky's face when he looked at me. "What do you think I should do, Lews? This—this so-called confession will never stand up in court. I don't know how you got it and..." He closed his eyes for a moment, "...I don't even want to know. To be honest—you have nothing. Take my advice, throw this confession or whatever you call it away and forget this whole thing. It will be healthier for you and for me." He let out a loud groan. "I wish you would never have brought this or any of the other allegations and conspiracy theories you have to me."

"Rosser is willing to testify in court," I said.

Kabinsky forced a laugh. "Testify? Who do you think anyone will believe? The Police Commissioner or a two-bit hoodlum, who has been in trouble with the law since he became a teenager? Mayor Hudson will certainly stand behind Steelwood and testify to his integrity. There will be other powerful people who will only too gladly speak in favor of Steelwood. This will never even make it to court."

"You can at least pick up Nightingale for the murder of the people I mentioned, can't you? That would be a good start and possibly get the ball rolling. Once you have him in custody, he'll be trying to save his ass by naming the ones behind him."

"Okay, I'll have Nightingale picked up, but I'll guarantee you he'll be out within twenty-four hours."

"I know, I know. Heimi Rosenthal, the lawyer. You mentioned him before. Maybe you should have him picked up, too, while you're at it. He probably answers to either Titman or the Ramiro Family," I said angrily. I tried to stay calm, but the anger inside me was roiling like an agitated kettle full of steaming water and threatening to boil over.

"By the way, where is this Rosser now?" Kabinsky asked.

Lifting my shoulders, I said, "I have no idea. He could be dead for all I know. Not a huge loss if he is, especially since you tell me his testimony is useless. Harry Rosser is a dirt-bag. Maybe next time I see him I will kill him. He may become a threat."

"Don't forget your flash drive," Kabinsky said when I got up to leave.

"You keep it. I have copies."

Angry and feeling powerless, I drove to Brandon's garage.

"Something wrong with the car?" he asked when I entered his shop.

"Nothing wrong with the car. She runs better than ever. I have news about your brother. I know who murdered him."

Brandon dropped the wrench he had been holding. "That means we were right all along. Bart was murdered. Who did it?"

"The guy's name is Jeremy Nightingale. He was hired by Titman to murder your brother."

"So what now?"

I shrugged. "I've been to the cops, but it doesn't look good. He may get away with it."

Brandon smashed his fist into the hood of the car he'd been working on. "Then we have to take the law into our own hands. It's the only way. I will not rest until that son-of-a-bitch is six feet underground."

"I agree with you, Brandon, but we can't lose our heads now." I knew exactly how he felt, but we needed to stay calm. And that included me. "Acting on impulse is the wrong thing to do. This must be planned carefully. You don't want to end up in jail, or worse, on death row."

"Have you told Shirley?"

"No, not yet."

"Don't tell her yet until we figure out how we will proceed from here," he said. "We don't want her to get her hopes up and be disappointed again."

I agreed not to tell her, but what we plan to do and what happens are two separate things. When I walked into my office, Nelda said, "Shirley Brandon just called. She wanted to know if we got anything out of Rosser. She watched as we grabbed him outside her salon."

"Did you tell her?"

"I did. She knows about Nightingale. Why?"

"Well, her brother-in-law thought we should keep her in the dark until we figured out what to do with our information."

"Sorry."

"No harm done. How did she react?"

She shrugged. "She sounded okay, except she wants Nightingale punished, mostly dead. Wanted to know if we had gone to the cops." Her eyes questioned. "How did things go at the cop-shop? Are they going after Nightingale?"

"I'm not sure. Kabinsky clearly did not show any enthusiasm when he listened to Rosser's confession. He thinks we have nothing and should forget about everything. He's scared, how else to explain his behavior?"

"Do you think he's dirty?"

"Frank Kabinsky?" I shook my head. "Not him. He's one of the most dedicated cops I ever knew. We were partners for nearly three years. You get to know a person."

"People change. What's he scared of?"

"He's close to retirement. I think he's more concerned about his own welfare than the welfare of the victims in a crime. How can you blame him? When you work in Homicide you have to harden yourself, and after a while there comes a time when you simply just don't care anymore."

"Is that what happened to you?"

I had to smile. "Are we starting this thing about my age again? First of all I was in Homicide only six years, possibly long enough to become desensitized, I don't know. However, I was only thirty-four when I left the force, a long way from retiring with a pension. I was at the beginning of a career I hoped to pursue for a long time still. I loved my job." Remembering dampened my spirit a little, but I pushed it back into that special place where I filed all my sad memories.

Nelda seemed to sense it, because she didn't comment any further, instead she said, "I printed out a picture of Nightingale. I thought it may come in handy."

"I have a feeling it will. Brandon thinks we shouldn't rely on the police to do anything. He suggested we handle it ourselves."

"I'm afraid to ask what his plan would be," Nelda said.

"I'll have to call Julia and tell her about Cole. Confirm her suspicion that he was not the victim of a robbery and let her know we have the name of the man who murdered him. Also to confirm she was correct in assuming her loving husband hired Nightingale."

"She'll be so thrilled," Nelda said drily.

Julia was more than thrilled. She was angry and offered me money again to assassinate Titman. "I want that bastard dead. And I want this Nightingale dead." She said it quite calmly, but even over the phone I detected the rage in her voice. Rage and fear. "I don't want to end up like George."

"I don't believe your husband will harm you, not physically to the point of murder. He could not risk that."

"I won't take the chance. If you won't do it, I'll find somebody who will." She sounded determined. I was hoping she wouldn't do anything rash. Nothing ever gets resolved that way without dire consequences.

———

It was not really earthshaking news when I read about another murder a couple of days later. Muggings, break-ins, carjacking, and murders were almost a daily occurrence in this city. You read about it in the paper, see it on TV, or hear it on the radio; you shrug, make a comment and forget about it. It is different if the victim is a friend or a family member. Then it's personal and affects you much more. Your whole life can change in a heartbeat.

Even if the victim isn't a friend but a person you know, it has an impact on your life. So it did come as a bit of a shock but not as a huge surprise when Nelda showed me the article.

The body of a man was found last night by a construction worker near the construction site of the new Public Library. He was identified as thirty-four-year-old Harry Rosser. According to reliable sources, he was stabbed to death. The apparent victim of another robbery gone wrong, but Police don't rule out foul play.

"Shit!" I cursed. "There goes my witness. We should have never let him out of our sight. I blame myself."

"What could we have done?" Nelda asked. "Besides, he did need medical attention."

"We could have had Dr. Jhamir treat him. After that, we should have taken him to the Twenty-third Precinct, where they could have put him into a cell for his protection." I punched my fist into my palm. "Damn it! What now?"

"Don't beat yourself up over it, Lews," Nelda warned. "What's done is done. We still have his confession. Something will come up. You taught me that."

"We can pretty much guess who stabbed him and who gave the order. But how did they know about his confession? Unless he was stupid enough to blab about it to someone."

"What if he didn't blab? What if somebody else did?"

"You're not suggesting Kabinsky again? Or are you?" I refused to believe that. Not Frank.

"Not necessarily him but someone who got hold of his report. He must have talked to somebody about it. What about his partner? He does have a partner, no?"

"Yes, he does. I only met him once. His name is Edward Chang. I remember his name, because Kabinsky told me Chang was transferred a couple years back from San Francisco."

"So you don't know him. It's something to keep in mind."

"I suppose so. This is not good, Nelda. Not good at all."

It was getting worse. In the afternoon a couple of cops came for a visit. They had a warrant for my arrest.

I was charged with the murder of one Harry Rosser.

Whoever gave the order to arrest me was quite confident. They took me down to my old precinct. Kabinsky pretended not to see me when I was brought in. Booking went fairly fast. They made me empty my pockets, fingerprinted me, took my mug shot, and put me into a cell.

Nobody came to see me for the rest of the day and I spent the night sleeping on a hard cot, wondering what was going to happen next.

Allan Steelwood came for a visit the next morning. I didn't get up from my cot to welcome him.

"Lews Canon," he said as he stood beside my cot, looking down at me. "Don't bother getting up. I have no intentions to stay longer than necessary."

"Allan Steelwood. Nice to see you again and what an honor to have you personally coming to check up on me. How long has it been? Seven years?"

"Has it been that long? How time flies. By the way, it's Commissioner Steelwood, Canon. Remember that."

I did sit up. Somehow it didn't feel right looking up from a lying position at the man who was never one of my favorite people. In fact, I hated his guts, especially right now. Seeing that grin of superiority on his smug face only enhanced my feeling. "If you want to know my thoughts, it puzzles me to find you in the position of Commissioner," I said, smirking. "But then again—I'm not surprised."

"What does that mean?"

"Come on, Steelwood, we both know you didn't have the qualifications. The only way you could come up in the ranks and become the Police Commissioner was with the help of your father."

"Does it matter how I got this position?" he sneered. "I always knew this would be my job one day; you, on the other hand, were destined for failure from the beginning."

"Who says I failed? I'm quite satisfied with my life." Sure, I was.

"Really? From what I heard you own a shabby detective agency, barely surviving by chasing deadbeat husbands and spying on women who cheat on their spouses. On top of that, you're a drunk. And now you finally sank to the level of becoming a murderer. You call that success?"

Looking at his gloating countenance I had to suppress the urge to kick in his white, even teeth.

"We both know I didn't kill that man. I didn't even know him. What reason would I have to murder a stranger?"

"You state you didn't know Rosser? Then explain to me how you came in possession of a confession he apparently made?" He almost snarled when he said that.

There was no use denying anything. Obviously, he had heard the confession and he probably guessed how I obtained it. "It seems you were notified by Kabinsky. Hmm, I'll have to remember that," I said. "Then you know about the damaging evidence that's on the recording."

"Did you really think you could use that against me? You should have been smarter than that, Canon. No court or judge will even give that piece of fabricated crap a second look. Everybody knows that something like that can easily be faked by anyone. With Rosser dead you have nothing—nothing at all. The only thing you managed is pin a murder rap on your own sorry hide."

"A murder rap that won't stick, Commissioner," I said. "Don't think I'm licked. There are other ways to prove your involvement in this whole affair. Your brother-in-law Titman is a known criminal and I'll find somebody who is willing to testify to that and put him in prison. We'll take it from there."

His laugh and his stance made me want to smash my foot between his legs and crush his balls. It was hard to resist that impulse. He made it almost too easy with his feet apart like that, but I did resist. "Good luck with that, Canon," he mocked. "You can't win against me. Let's face it, you were a loser then and you are still a loser. You couldn't even hold on to your wife."

It was obvious he tried to goad me into doing something stupid, but I played it cool. I wasn't going to give him a reason or the satisfaction of being hauled into a room where a couple of his goons could beat me up again. Not this time.

He bent lower and said in a voice only I could hear, "Let me give you some advice, Canon. Stay away from my sister. I promise you, I will personally end your existence if you don't stop digging into her life or past, and nobody in this city or state will convict me. Nobody will miss you and nobody cares about a loser like you."

"Is this a threat, Steelwood?"

"Just advice you would be wise to heed, but I have a feeling you won't."

I rose from my cot and looked him in the eyes. "And your feeling is correct. I won't stop until I achieve my goal. And don't threaten me again!"

"Or what?" His smile was pure evil. "Next time your girlfriend won't be so lucky just to get raped. She'll be beaten, raped and sodomized; and that's just for starters. Her face will be unrecognizable and no amount of plastic surgery will be able to repair the damage. Even that will not be the end of what's going to happen to her. You want to hear more?"

I wanted to strangle him right there, but I controlled my anger. "You better shut up now, you sick bastard," I said from between clenched teeth. "You or any of your minions lay a finger on her or anyone I'm close to, I will hunt you down and do all the things you mentioned to you. And more. Understand?"

He backed up a little. "Careful, Canon. You're uttering threats against the Chief of Police."

"It's your word against mine. There are no witnesses here, unless you're wearing a wire, and I don't think you'd be so stupid to want to incriminate yourself. As for that other matter? You say I have no leg to stand on to prove my allegations? Neither have you with this murder you're trying to pin on me."

"Well, you're wrong. We have a witness."

"A witness who saw me committing the murder? I'm curious to hear about that one."

"Not the murder itself, but we have pictures of you and your freaky partner abducting Rosser."

"I don't believe you. How would you get pictures?"

"I put a tail on you." He smiled like a politician running for office. "You're not such a great detective after all, Canon. You didn't even spot your tail."

"Even if you have pictures, that still doesn't prove I killed Rosser. What it does prove is the fact that he was with us to confess to the murders. We dropped him off at a hospital. There are records of that. This will work against you not me. By the way, that freaky partner of mine is the daughter of a fine and dedicated police officer who died of cancer in 2010. You may even remember his name. His name was Kevin Pinetree."

"I remember him. He was another one of those do-gooders who

suffer from the misguided delusion they can make a difference in the world by wiping out all evil and all corruption. Maybe that's why he died of cancer," he said mockingly.

"He was ten times the man you are," I said angrily. "So when you speak of him do it with respect."

"The respect you should show me," Steelwood said with a slight edge to his voice.

"You lost my respect a long time ago," I told him. "Now, if you have nothing else you can bore me with I'd like to take a little nap. Go and find another innocent man you can frame."

"I have more. A reliable witness who will testify that you told him you will kill Rosser at the earliest opportunity."

"And who is this witness?"

"You'll see. You will find you have no friends in the police department."

I spent a sleepless night on the uncomfortable cot in my cell. The next morning, I stood in front of a judge.

The name of the judge was Nathan Meloni. The father of the man who gave me a beating a short time ago. My ribs still ached when I moved a certain way.

This did not look good for me and I had a dark sense of foreboding.

He looked up from the papers he had been studying and stared at me over his reading glasses. "For the record, state you name and occupation."

Clearing my throat, I said, "My name is Lews Bullseye Canon. I'm a Private Detective."

He gave no indication that my name was familiar to him. He had to know about me. After all, I was the guy who was responsible for his son going to jail.

"Lews Bullseye Canon, you have been charged with the murder of one Harry Rosser. How do you plead?"

"Not guilty, your Honor."

"Are you presenting your own case or do you seek legal representation? If you do seek legal representation and can't afford an attorney, the State will supply you with one."

"I haven't given it any thought, your Honor."

"Perhaps you should. By the way, this is not a trial. This is just a hearing to determine if your case will go to trial." The gaze of his eyes moved to the prosecutor. "Does the State have evidence or a witness who will testify Mr. Canon committed this murder?"

The prosecutor stepped forward. He was a skinny weasel of a man and I didn't like him, especially when he started speaking with a nasally voice. "Yes, your Honor, the State has evidence."

"What kind of evidence?"

"We have pictures proving that Mr. Canon abducted Harry Rosser for the purpose of murdering him."

"What makes you assume he wanted to murder him?"

"The fact that Harry Rosser is dead."

"And how do you know Mr. Canon committed this murder?"

"We have a recording in which he threatened to kill Harry Rosser."

"Can we hear this recording?"

"Certainly." The prosecutor produced a small recording device. He switched it on.

Harry Rosser is a dirt bag. Next time I see him I will kill him.

Judge Meloni looked at me. "Is that your voice, Mr. Canon?"

I couldn't deny it. It was my voice. I sort of remembered making that statement, but not exactly when and where. "Yes, it is, but if I said that I didn't mean it. Sometimes we say things like that but we won't act upon it. You know, like if a father says to his son, 'You do that again I'll kill you!' Everyone knows the father would never do that. It's just a means of expressing anger."

"I never said that to *my* son and never would have."

I couldn't help but say, "Maybe you should have." Sometimes those word slip past my lips. It's one of my faults.

"What do you mean by that remark?" His eyes stared at me.

"Nothing, your Honor. It's one of those things I do sometimes, saying stuff like that, but they mean nothing."

"I see." He looked again at the prosecutor. "Recordings like that are worthless. They can be easily produced. Do you have a living witness who will testify that Mr. Canon indeed said that?"

"Yes, we have, your Honor."

"Can you produce this witness?"

"Yes, we can." The prosecutor turned and made a sign to one of his associates standing in the back. She went outside and came back a couple of minutes later. Beside her walked a man I knew well. Seeing him caused me to feel disappointed and betrayed.

He didn't look at me when he walked past me to stand in front of the judge.

"State your name and occupation," the judge said.

"My name is Frank Edward Kabinsky. I am a homicide detective."

"Detective Kabinsky. This is just a hearing and you are not under oath, but be advised you can still commit perjury by giving false testimony."

"I am aware of that, your Honor." Kabinsky's voice was flat, without emotion.

Meloni addressed the prosecutor. "Please, play the recording for Detective Kabinsky."

Again I had to listen to my voice, but having seen my ex-partner and one-time good buddy, Kabinsky, I suddenly remembered quite clearly when I made that statement. It was the time when I gave him the flash drive with Rosser's confession. However, I remembered it a little bit differently. Somebody had doctored that recording by removing the word *maybe*. I cursed myself for even uttering such a threat, especially in a police station.

I realized that Kabinsky had recorded our whole conversation that day and probably on other days also.

"Detective Kabinsky, do you know the man who made that statement?"

"Yes, I do."

"Will you testify that he is the one who actually made that statement?"

"I will, your Honor."

"Is that man here in the courtroom?"

"Yes, your Honor."

"Please, point him out to the court and identify him."

Kabinsky turned around and pointed at me. His eyes looked past me when he said, "That's the man. His name is Lews Bullseye Canon."

"Thank you, Detective. Let the records state that Detective Kabinsky identified the accused as Lews Bullseye Canon." Meloni scribbled something onto a piece of paper. When he looked at me again, his face was grave. "Mr. Canon," he said, "do you have anything to say in your defense?"

"No more than I already said, your Honor. I admit that I made that statement in question, but first of all I said *maybe* next time I see him I will kill him. That gives the sentence a different implication. As I stated before, I just said it without actually meaning it. I'm not a cold-blooded killer. There was no reason for me to even consider murdering Mr. Rosser. In fact, it would have not been to my advantage to do so. Harry Rosser was willing to testify in court to confirm what he told me about crimes he committed. Crimes that involved murder, your Honor. Crimes that implicated..."

I couldn't finish my sentence, because the prosecutor cut me off with the words, "Objection! Mr. Canon is the only one on trial here. Whatever he wants to say is irrelevant. He has no right to accuse possibly innocent people with the purpose of diverting attention from the crime at hand—*his* crime."

"Objection noted." Meloni hit the desk top with his gavel. "This court will go over the evidence and decide on a trial date. Hearing adjourned."

"I am innocent of the charge. I'm being framed," I said with a loud voice. Louder actually than I had intended. I could have sworn there was an echo in the room.

The judge gave me one last and annoyed look. "One more outburst like that and I will have you for contempt of court, Mr. Canon. Understood?"

I nodded, steaming inside. I had the sinking feeling that justice would not be served in my case. How can you fight something like this when everyone is against you and if they want your hide?

FIFTEEN

I SPENT another uncomfortable night in my cell. They brought me breakfast, which was actually not bad. An hour after that, a guard unlocked my cell door and told me that I was free to go.

I picked up my belongings and walked to the front desk, puzzled about finding myself free again. I saw a man in a suit standing by the desk, watching me come closer. When I reached him, he said, "Good morning, Mr. Canon. My name is Phillip Roth. I'm your attorney."

"I don't have an attorney."

He smiled. "You have one now. Mr. Miller hired me."

He drove me home to my place. I needed a shower and a change of clothes badly. When I felt human again, I called Miller to verify my attorney's identity.

"How did you know I was in jail?" I asked him after he confirmed that he indeed hired Phillip Roth.

"You partner told me."

"I guess she told you that I've been accused of murdering a guy by the name of Harry Rosser, one of Titman's henchmen."

"She told me all about it. Okay, what's your next move now that you're out of jail?"

"I have to prove my innocence, but in the meantime, I also have to earn the money my clients have paid me. You are one of them."

"Yes, I am. Which brings me back to why I hired you in the first place. What can we do about my wife? Is there any way we can tie her to the murder of Mildred Stone?"

"That may be difficult. However, sitting alone in a prison cell for a couple of days gave me time to reflect and think things over. All my clients have one thing in common: they want Nightingale dead. So does my girlfriend. Would you be interested in coming to a small meeting? I'd like to get you all together and we can do some brainstorming. I have an idea brewing in my head, but I want to run it past all of you."

"When do you want to meet and where?'

"I'll let you know."

I called Shirley. She agreed to a meeting. As did Julia. When I called Brandon, he was also in agreement. "I don't want to meet in my office," I said. "It may be under surveillance. How about if we all meet in your garage?"

"Fine by me. When?"

"How does tomorrow afternoon sound? Two o'clock okay?"

"No problem."

I called the others back and they agreed to come. Then I phoned Sonya. "Where are you now?" she asked after the initial tearful exclaims of excitement to hear my voice and knowing I was free again.

"I'm at home."

"Can you come over? I've missed you and I've been so worried."

"My car is back at the office."

"I'll come and pick you up."

While I waited for Sonya to come, I called Nelda and told her that I was out of jail. "I hope you're free tomorrow afternoon. I want to meet with all our clients at Brandon's garage to discuss strategy. I need you there."

"Sure. I'll be there."

Sonya was at my place twenty minutes later. Covering my face with kisses, she looked at me with a tearful smile. "You look gaunt. Have you eaten?"

I laughed. "I've only been gone a little over three days. And to answer your question: I've had breakfast, but how about going out for lunch?"

"Okay, but not just for hamburgers. I know a little French

restaurant not far from here. We'll have a glass of wine and some French food. I'll take off tonight and we can have a nice romantic evening. How does that sound?"

"It sounds great."

It was a nice place and the food was good, even though I'm not really into French food, but for me it's not always the food. It's who I share the food with. And there was no better company than Sonya.

Her face looked much better and she was so radiant, obviously happy to have me back. Looking at her got my blood boiling inside and I tried not to let it spoil this moment of my own happiness. To think Nightingale had raped her, beaten her, and nearly ruined her beautiful face, strengthened my resolve to have that son-of-a-bitch punished.

Later that night, after we had enjoyed a wonderful afternoon and evening, I decided to tell her about what I was planning.

"I'd like you to come with me to a meeting tomorrow," I said as she lay in my arms, still glowing in the aftermath of our passionate love-making.

"What meeting?"

"I'll be meeting with some clients of mine. We'll be discussing how to punish Nightingale."

She stiffened in my arms.

"I'm sorry to bring this up now, but I thought you might want to be there."

"Are the police not going to do anything about him?"

"It doesn't look that way. I'll be honest with you. There is a good chance he may be coming after me; and possibly you again. I believe he was the one who murdered Rosser. Rosser was stabbed, which seems to be Nightingale's signature. It makes sense, because Rosser implicated him in all those murders."

She turned in my arms and looked at me. "What exactly are you planning to do?"

"I don't know yet. It's up to the group. Whatever the others decide."

"You know how much I want that man punished. In fact, I wish he were dead, but I don't want you to do anything to jeopardize our relationship. I love you too much to lose you. I couldn't bear that."

"I'm just so angry about what he did to you. He murdered three people we know of. Four if we count his companion Rosser. Who knows how many others there are. That guy is a psychopath and he needs to be punished."

"I agree, but I beg you, do nothing rash. The man isn't worth it. Of course, I hate him for what he did, but I won't fall apart over it. I've endured worse than that and survived. Now I found you and I don't want what we have to end in tragedy." She touched my cheek gently. "I love you."

I held her tight. "I love you too. That's why I need to protect you. If it means getting rid of a scumbag like Nightingale it will have to be done."

"I agree, but it will have to be done the right way." She gave me a gentle kiss. "Now, let's get some sleep. You need your beauty-rest."

"I hate the word beauty in connection with me. Let's change that to *handsome*."

She laughed. "Okay, handsome it is. Now go to sleep."

———

The others were already in Brandon's garage when Sonya, Nelda, and I got there. Brandon hung a sign into the window of his office announcing his shop was closed. He had moved the cars he'd been working on into the yard and set up a few chairs to sit on. Brandon sat on a stack of old tires.

"I suppose you've introduced each other already," I said. "All of you know me, of course. This is my partner Nelda and this is my girlfriend Sonya. She has a vested interest in what happens to Nightingale. Most of you know what happened."

"We do," Shirley said, looking at Sonya. "I'm sorry about what happened to you."

Sonya gave her a grim smile. "So am I, but at least I'm still alive."

"I called this meeting to determine what we should do about Jeremy Nightingale." I glanced at Miller. "And there is another matter I would also like to discuss. Mr. Miller is the husband of Angela Steelwood, Julia's half-sister. He might have told you that already."

"No, he never did," Shirley said. "That makes Mr. Titman your brother-in-law."

"That's correct," Miller said.

"So why are you here then?" She gave him a suspicious look.

"My wife has been trying to kill me," Miller said.

"Oh." Shirley sounded surprised but kept looking at him. "Do you want to have your wife killed?"

"Oh, heavens no. I just want her out of my life."

"Then divorce her."

"I can't do that. She'll end up with most of my assets."

Shirley shrugged. "Then you'll probably have to kill her."

"I was hoping for a better solution," Miller said with a little smile.

"Before we get into the real planning stage we should sum up what we have to work with. What do the majority of you have in common?" I asked. Before anyone could answer I carried on. "Let me answer that. It's Nightingale. He is the common denominator here. He murdered Shirley's husband Bart. He also murdered Julia's friend George Cole, he broke into my office and caused a lot of damage, and he molested my girlfriend Sonya. Then he murdered his partner Harry Rosser. Now I have been accused by the law of having committed that murder and may end up in jail for a crime I didn't commit."

"That's true, but how does Mr. Miller fit in?" Brandon asked.

"He is married to a woman he'd like to be free off. If we could tie this all together we may end up with a satisfying solution to everything," I mused.

"I have an idea," Nelda spoke up. "It seems that everyone here wants Nightingale dead. Why don't we try to frame Miller's wife for his murder?"

"Sounds like a good idea, but there is only one problem—she's not going to murder Nightingale," Shirley said. "And as much as I want that bastard dead, I'm not going to do it either." Her eyes rested on me. "Will you, Mr. Canon?" I noticed she hadn't called me by my first name, the way she usually did.

"Hell, no. I'm not an assassin." Glancing at Julia, I said, "I already told Julia that."

"Why? Who does she want assassinated?"

"My husband," Julia answered for me. "Mr. Canon won't do it."

"We could hire someone to kill Nightingale," Brandon suggested.

"Who would you hire?" I asked.

"I know some people. They are a dangerous bunch, but they owe me a few favors. I could get them to do it, but it would take money."

"How much?" Miller asked.

"Twenty grand. Maybe."

"I can put up ten."

"I'll give you ten thousand dollars also," Julia said.

"To kill Nightingale?"

She nodded. "Yes."

"Okay, but how do we get Miller's wife into this?" Brandon seemed to think of something, because he gave her a sharp look. "She's your sister. Are you okay with this?"

"She's my half-sister and I hate her guts," Julia said, almost angrily.

"Well, that solves that." He chuckled. "You are not the only one who hates that bitch around here. We know her quite well. Everybody in this neighborhood does. She wants to have some of the old buildings declared Heritage buildings, which means all the people living in them will be evicted so they can make museums out of them. How can we frame her for the murder, though?"

"I can answer that," I said. "Apparently, she committed murder before. A couple of years ago she allegedly shot a woman named Mildred Stone to death. I have the gun that was supposedly used."

"Not supposedly, Mr. Canon," Miller said. "That's the one she used."

"Great," Brandon said. "All we have to do is have Nightingale shot with that gun and then plant it on Angela Steelwood. Sounds easy enough." He looked over to Miller. "If she's your wife, why is her last name Steelwood?"

Miller made a face and said, "Good question. She's one of those liberated women. Apparently, my name wasn't good enough for her."

"Yeah, I heard about those women. I wouldn't stand for that. If you don't like my name means you don't like me either. I'm proud of my pappy's name." He looked around the room. "So it's settled. We have Nightingale shot and frame that bitch for the murder. All agreed?"

Everyone lifted a hand, except Sonya.

"What's the problem?" I asked.

"Do you people realize that we are plotting a murder here? Does that make us any better than them?"

"Them who?" Brandon asked.

"The criminals who commit these crimes, like breaking into houses, cars, and other places. The ones who commit violent acts like stabbing or shooting people. The ones who commit murder. If we do this we aren't any better than them." She spoke with passion and conviction, and in a way I had to agree with her, but only in a way.

"These are bad people, Sonya," I said. "They need to be punished or they'll do it again. By getting rid of these two, we may be saving lives. I'm quite positive we will. It may even be yours."

"What are you getting out of it besides revenge?" she asked.

"Yes, I'll get revenge, but I'll be sleeping better knowing he won't come during the night and try to hurt you again when I'm not with you."

"This still won't eliminate the threat of Titman or the Police Commissioner. Titman can hire another hit man to do his dirty work for him, and the Police Commissioner will come after you even stronger if he knows you're involved in the framing of his sister."

I knew she was right. "He won't find out about what we did. It's up to all of us to keep our mouths shut." I looked at the others who had been following our conversation with interest. "Sonya is right. We are plotting a murder and we could all land in jail or on death row. All of you must understand and swear that you will never talk about this. Ever! Not even to each other. It must forever stay a secret. You are aware of that, I hope."

"We are and we understand the risk we're taking," Brandon spoke for the others who nodded in agreement. "I for one will never mention it to anyone," he said.

"Neither will I," Shirley echoed his pledge.

"Nobody will find out from me, I swear." Julia held up one hand to underline her promise.

"I swear the same thing," Miller said. "How about you three?"

"Once this is done, it will be forgotten," I said. "It's up to Sonya now if we go through with this." I threw her a questioning look.

I could see the fear and doubt in her eyes, but she nodded. "I'll go along and you don't have to worry about me doing any talking."

"Nelda?" I asked.

Nelda's face was solemn. "It needs to be done. I say let's do it."

"Good." Brandon let out a loud sigh, as if a heavy weight had been lifted from his shoulders. His gaze wandered from Miller to Julia. "You promised ten thousand each. I need it in cash."

"I understand," Julia said. "I'll have it in Mr. Canon's office in a couple of days."

"Same here," Miller said.

"I need a picture of Nightingale and Angela Steelwood." Brandon got up from his pile of old tires and stretched his legs. He smiled. "We want to make sure we'll get the right people."

"I'll get you the picture of Nightingale," I said. "And, of course, Angela's gun."

"I'll take a picture of my wife to Mr. Canon's office." Miller seemed to think of something. "She usually plays Bingo on Friday nights. I can give you the address of the place."

"That would be a great help," Brandon said. "It would make it a lot easier if we don't have to waste time trying to chase her down. It will be a bit more difficult finding Nightingale, though."

We drove home. Nobody spoke much. It's not every day that a group of ordinary citizens plan the execution of another human being. All of us knew we had made the right decision. Sometimes you have to do something drastic to protect yourself and your family.

And sometimes you have to leave your comfort zone and commit an act that may be beyond comprehension of a normal person to keep your mind from going insane.

———

Three days later, I drove back to Brandon's garage. I gave him the two pictures, the address of the bingo hall, and the gun, nicely wrapped up inside a protective plastic bag.

"Make sure nobody touches the gun," I warned Brandon. "Angela's fingerprints are on the gun. The best place to plant it would be in her car's glove compartment."

Brandon smiled. "Don't worry. These people are professionals. They know what to do much better than you and I. The less we know of the procedure the better. Do you have the money?"

I gave him a bundle wrapped in plain paper and inside a plastic freezer bag. "Twenty thousand dollars in small bills, as requested. I hope it'll be enough."

"It will be. We might get it done for less, but this bunch doesn't play games. We don't want to irritate them."

"You're sure they'll do it?"

"Nothin's sure in this world, Lews, but I got confidence."

"Good. I'll breathe easier once this is over."

Then I decided to pay John Pallitser a visit.

"Well, well, if it isn't the Loose Cannon again," he said when I walked up to his desk. "I heard you got arrested for murder. What was that guy's name again?"

"Harry Rosser. I didn't murder him. Somebody is framing me for that murder, and I'm quite positive Commissioner Steelwood is behind it. Did you ever have a look into Steelwood's affairs, Pallitser?"

"No, I haven't. I need a solid reason to do that. I told you that the last time."

"I have a solid reason: *Me*. Steelwood himself came to talk to me after I sat in my cell. He threatened to harm or even kill my girlfriend and me if I didn't stop investigating him, his brother-in-law, who is a known criminal, and his sister Angela Steelwood."

"Those are strong accusations, Canon."

"Strong but true. There is another man who seems to have lost his way."

"And who might that be?"

"Kabinsky. I have reason to believe he's dirty."

He looked at me as if I just told him I was his long-lost brother. "Is this some kind of joke? Kabinsky? I thought you two were pals. What makes you think he's dirty?"

"He sold me out."

"How?"

"He gave false testimony."

"That's not like Kabinsky. He's always been the upstanding police officer." Pallitser looked thoughtful. "Is there anything else you want to share with me? Like why have you been accused of this man's murder? What is your connection to him?"

"I have his confession to at least five murders he's been part of, and he implicates quite a number of people. That's the reason he was murdered." I handed him a flash drive. "It's all here. I gave another flash drive to Kabinsky. I was arrested shortly after. Draw your own conclusions once you've listened to what's on here."

"I'm afraid to ask how you came in possession of this *confession*, Canon."

"Then don't ask. Rosser was still alive the last time I saw him, and that is the truth. I didn't kill him. He was executed for spilling his guts and for the information he had. He was going to testify in court in exchange for protection. The only thing I'm guilty of is not taking him to a police station to give him that protection. He may be alive today. I say maybe. With all the crooked cops I doubt even that." I had a sudden bitter taste in my mouth realizing there were not many people I could trust anymore. I wasn't even sure about Pallitser.

His face was somber when he studied me. "You know, Canon, you and I have had our differences in the past. You never liked me and the feeling was mutual, but if there is one thing I always was sure of, despite your reputation of being some kind of maverick and not very good at following procedures, you always stayed on the straight and narrow. You and Kabinsky made a good team and I was envious about that. That's why it is hard for me to believe what you're telling me about Kabinsky."

"For me, also. But he testified against me at the hearing, and that is a fact."

He sighed. Holding the flash drive in his hand, he said, "I will listen to this and make up my own mind. I'll talk to Kabinsky, if I see the need for it." He grabbed a piece of paper and a pen and scribbled something on it. "This is the name and number of a friend of mine. He's a Federal Agent. Take a copy of the information on this flash drive to him. Do this for your protection." He grinned, but it came out sort of crooked. "And possibly for mine also."

I took the piece of paper from his hand and glanced at it. "Thanks, Pallitser. I won't forget."

Before I rose to leave, he held out his hand. "Good luck, Canon. You'll need it. I must say you do have a knack for falling into crap and you're good at digging yourself deeper into it."

I shook his hand, wondering if I had misjudged him all these years. He was not the kind of man who made friends easily. He came across as a loudmouth and a bigot, but perhaps it was just a front. The fact that he worked in Internal Affairs gave him points in my book.

The name of the FBI agent was Dennis Marrone. I called him after lunch and told him that Pallitser gave me his name. When I asked if we could meet and indicated I had damaging information about Titman and the Police Commissioner, he seemed quite interested and agreed to meet me in an hour.

It took me nearly an hour to drive to the FBI office. The woman at the front desk ushered me into one of the offices and told me to wait.

Looking around, I felt like being in an interrogation room. There was only a desk with a computer and a couple of chairs in front of it. Not much furniture, except for a few pictures of antique cars on the walls.

Marrone came in a few minutes later.

"Sorry for making you wait," he said, holding out his hand. "I'm Dennis."

"Lews Canon," I said.

He grinned. "An unusual name. I hope it doesn't describe you the way it sounds."

"Some people used to say it did," I answered, smiling, trying to make light of it. "I have matured since then."

He took his seat behind the desk. "I made use of the time to check you out while I waited," he said, quite casually. "You're a private detective, Lews?"

I nodded. "Since 2010."

"What did you do before that?"

"I was a cop for twelve years." I smiled. "But I guess you know that also since you checked me out."

He nodded. "I do. Why did you leave the force?"

Here we go, I thought. This *is* an interrogation room. "I stirred up trouble in the police department by exposing a few bad apples. It didn't make me popular, especially not with the Commissioner. He gave me an option—to quit the force or suffer the consequences." I looked him straight in the eye. "I hate corrupt cops. When I swore to uphold the law I meant it."

He smiled. "Pallitser told me that. He also said he didn't like you very much."

"We've never been great friends," I agreed. "I'm curious. What is your connection with Pallitser?"

"We're cousins."

"I hope that's not a bad sign," I said.

Chuckling, he looked at me with an amused smile on his lips. "He also said you had been an outstanding cop with a strong sense of justice. And if he and you had not been mortal enemies you could have been good friends. He also believes in justice and in upholding the law. As do I."

"Glad to hear that." I took out the flash drive. "I want to give you this. Everything you need to know is on this drive. It's the confession of a guy by the name of Harry Rosser. He used to work for Frederick Titman, a known mobster. By the way, Rosser is dead. He was stabbed to death a few days ago. You should also know that I have been accused of his murder and I was arrested for it. I'm out on bail right now until my trial date has been set. I didn't commit the murder and I need to clear my name before I end up in jail."

"I can see your dilemma. Are you going to leave this flash drive with me?"

"It's a copy," I said. "I have another one at home."

"Good. Let me study this and I'll see where it will lead from here." He got up from his chair and walked around the desk. "I'm glad you came to see me. We've had our eyes on this Titman and the people he deals with for a long time. Maybe this will help us with our investigation. By the way, do you have a business card?"

"I do." I fished one out of my pocket and gave it to him. "Thank you for seeing me at such short notice."

"You're welcome." He held out his hand. "Thanks for coming in, Lews. We'll keep in touch."

I drove away, feeling much better. Things might just turn out all right.

A few days later it was in all the papers.

Angela Steelwood, President of the Preservation of Heritage Buildings Society, arrested for murder.

The article went on about how the deceased body of one Jeremy Nightingale was discovered in her trunk after police acted upon an anonymous tip and intercepted her on her way home after playing

Bingo. He had been shot, and the murder weapon, a gun registered to Angela Steelwood, was found in the glove compartment of her car. Miss Steelwood, of course, denied shooting Nightingale. In fact, it apparently came as a shock to her when the body was discovered in her trunk. It also mentioned that she was the sister of Police Commissioner Steelwood.

Miller called me an hour after I read the news in the paper. "Mr. Canon," he said on the phone. "Have you read the newspaper this morning?"

"Yes, I have."

"Then you know that my wife has been arrested for murder."

"I read about it. Sorry to hear that, Mr. Miller. I hope things work out for you."

"I hope so, too. Thank you so much, Mr. Canon. I thought you might want to know."

"I appreciate that, Mr. Miller."

I put the phone down, feeling guilty for being in such an elated mood. Things were starting to fall into place. Nightingale was dead and Angela Steelwood was arrested. But there was still more to do. My job wasn't finished yet.

The next morning, I checked the obituaries from 2015 and searched for Mildred Stone. I found her easily and discovered that she had a son and a daughter, and a sister; all of them living in the city.

I had to be careful to avoid any chance of anyone making a connection between me and the murder of Nightingale, and, of course, the framing of Angela Steelwood that resulted in accusing her of the murder. That was the reason I couldn't go to Detective Sharon Masters. It would have been easy to just call her and ask for the names and addresses of Mildred Stone's next of kin. And calling Kabinsky was out of the question. The man had betrayed me, but I would deal with him later.

I found the address and phone number of the daughter in the phone book. I drove to a public phone to call her, eliminating any danger the call could be traced back to me. When I spoke into the phone, I placed a handkerchief over the mouthpiece.

"Hello, is this Beverly Stone?"

"Yes. May I ask who's calling?"

"My name is Detective Meloni. You may have read in the paper about the arrest of Angela Steelwood, who is accused of the murder of Jeremy Nightingale."

"Yes, I have. What is this about?"

"Before I answer I have to confirm that you are the daughter of Mrs. Mildred Stone who was murdered in 2015. Are you the daughter?"

There was a short pause before she answered, "Yes, I am."

"According to police files, that murder has never been solved. You might be interested to know that we have reason to believe Angela Steelwood may have been the one who shot your mother."

Beverly seemed to exhale sharply, and then there was another short pause.

"Are you still there, Beverly?" I asked.

When she spoke, her voice sounded different. "Yes, I am. Are you sure about that?"

"Nothing is sure, but we want to investigate this possibility. I am not the one looking into cold files, but if you would like to get in touch with Detective Sharon Masters at the Twenty-third Precinct, she will begin the investigation."

"Just a minute. Let me write down the name. That was Sharon Masters?"

"That's correct. When you call her, give her your name and explain to her the nature of your call. Tell her you would like to reopen your mother's case. Also tell her to check the ballistics of the bullet that killed your mother against the gun from Angela Steelwood."

"Should I mention your name?"

"You can, but it is not necessary. Detective Masters doesn't really know me personally. I would suggest you do this immediately to get the investigation going while the case is still fresh. You have nothing to lose, but it will bring you closure."

"Well, thank you so much, Detective—what was your name again?"

"Meloni. Detective Steven Meloni. Have a good day."

EPILOGUE

I BELIEVE that everything in life is connected. Everything that happens causes some kind of reaction. A good deed will spawn more good deeds, and the reverse is true when an evil act is committed. It's like a row of Dominos. Once one of the Dominos begins to fall, the events that follow can't be stopped. Every Domino in that row will fall. The more complicated the pattern, the more Dominos will be affected. An avalanche starts with a tiny snowball but finishes with massive destruction, burying everything in its path.

Angela Steelwood was charged not only with Nightingale's murder but also with the murder of Mildred Stone. Ballistics proved that the bullet that killed Mildred Stone came from Angela's gun.

It took a few months, but in the end Commissioner Allan Steelwood was taken into custody by the FBI, charged with corruption and association with a known criminal organization.

And Frederick Titman?

They say he committed suicide, but that is not true.

A couple of days after the news of Nightingale's murder was published I got a call from Titman.

"You think you're a smart guy, Canon, don't you?"

"Some people say I am. Some say I'm not. I think I am. What's your point, Titman?"

"I warned you to stop it but no, you have to play the big hero. Do you really think you can fight me and the people I'm connected with? Are you really that stupid?"

"Like I said, what's your point?"

"My point? You will find that out. You're dead meat, you son-of-a-bitch! Your girlfriend will wish she were dead when I get through with her. Her pretty face will look like the surface of the moon, nothing but cracks and holes. And that ugly gorilla who pretends to be a woman just because she sounds like one? I'll have a couple of my boys pay her a visit after they're through with your girlfriend and they'll teach her a lesson she'll never forget." His laugh sounded cruel and ugly. "And I'll be there watching everything unfold. Perhaps I'll even join them in the party I'm planning for those two bitches. I'll give them a taste of what a real man is."

I listened to his tirade patiently while I was beginning to boil inside. When he was finished, I said, "Now you listen, you ugly dwarf. The last time I saw you I told you to keep looking over your shoulder or check your fancy limousine before you get in. I may just be sitting in the backseat waiting for you. Remember those words? I meant what I said then but now even more. I do not react kindly to being threatened. The countdown starts now!"

He was talking when I cut the connection. I didn't care what he said, because I knew I had to act fast. I wasn't worried about Nelda. She would castrate anyone who would try to harm her, but I worried about Sonya.

I took the box that I had stored away so many years ago from its hiding place and opened it. Then I strapped on the wide belt with the holster that held my 45. The same model Nelda wore on her hips. It had belonged to her father. Mine was a present from him. He bought both guns at the same time. One for him and one for me.

I inserted six bullets.

Then I drove to the Lucky Millionaire's Casino.

Sitting in my car, I waited for Titman to leave the casino. It was nearly midnight when he finally came out of the building and climbed into the backseat of his limousine. One of his bodyguards sat in the passenger seat, the other one drove the limousine.

I followed them as they drove to Titman's house. The driveway was well lit. As the limousine approached the house, additional lights came on.

His bodyguard stepped out of the car when I drove up the driveway and stopped my car not far behind the limousine.

"This is private property," the guard called to me when he saw me standing beside my car. "You are trespassing."

"Only for a short time until I'm done," I said calmly.

"What do you want, punk?" he said, his hand inching toward his open jacket.

"I'm going to kill your boss," I said.

His hand went for his gun, but I shot him the moment he held it in his hand. I never shoot an unarmed man. He collapsed without a sound.

The driver opened his door and slid out, a gun already in his hand. I waited until he was out in the open completely before I shot him in the head. He didn't make a sound either.

I knew Titman wouldn't be as easy to get, but I knew he had to get out of the car before he could take a shot at me, because of the bulletproof glass. He surprised me when he opened one window and stuck his hand out, firing his gun. It was a mistake. I shot the gun out of his hand. He cursed loudly. Then he shouted, "Canon. I know it's you. Let's talk. There is no need for more violence."

"There never was any need for violence," I shouted back. "You're the one who started it."

"It seems I underestimated you, Canon. Let's have a truce and talk things over. I'll make it worth your while."

"All right. Come out of your car with your hands up," I told him.

He emerged slowly. I watched him closely, not trusting the little bastard, but he came out with his hands in the air. He threw a quick look at his dead body guards. "You're a good shot," he commented. "They were the best."

"I was a sniper in the army," I said. "They trained us well." It wasn't something I wanted to lose much time remembering.

He squinted at me. "What does it take to get you off my tail, Canon?" he asked.

My motive for being here wasn't money, but he didn't know that. "What are you offering?"

"How about twenty thousand dollars? Cash. You can take it with you tonight and this will end it."

Julia had offered me fifty thousand if I got rid of Titman. Her friend Erika would pay me an additional ten plus all the sex I wanted for a whole year. Not to mention her oversexed friend Doris, who was going to match Erika's offer, minus the money. A much better offer. I smiled thinking about that.

Titman interpreted my smile differently. "Not enough? I'll double my offer. What do you say?"

"Let's go into the house."

Before I followed him, I bent to retrieve the guns from the two dead guards. They didn't need them anymore. I also picked up Titman's. He was already at his front door, trying to open the lock. I kept my eyes on him, trusting him only as long as I could see him.

I had, of course, never been to his house before. It was a huge mansion, with expensive chandeliers hanging everywhere. The pictures on the walls were originals, and the statues standing everywhere exquisite masterpieces. The place oozed money. None of it earned legally. There was blood on all of Titman's wealth.

"Is your wife home?" I asked, casually.

He shook his head. "No. She's spending some time with a girlfriend. At least that's what she told me. I don't trust her anymore."

"Why not? George Cole is dead. You got rid of him." I gave him a sarcastic smile. "Do you want me to keep on investigating Julia?"

"Ha, ha, you're a comedian, Canon. By the way, you can't pin Cole's murder on me. You have no evidence."

"I have Rosser's confession. He implicated you."

His smile was contemptuous. "Dead men don't talk. Rosser got what he deserved. He was a two-bit criminal, and an idiot to boot. Who believes what he said?" He gave me a calculating look. "I heard the police arrested you for his murder. This should remind you that I have friends in the police department."

"Not to mention that the Police Commissioner is your brother-in-law," I added. "I'm not really worried. The truth will come out and justice will prevail. Criminals are in reality not very smart. They think they are, but eventually they will always be caught. Sometimes it takes time, but in the end, everything balances out in favor of good. Evil always loses. That's how the universe works."

"Wow! A philosopher. A deep thinker. You missed your calling." He pointed at one of the doors. "My office is in there, as is my safe."

"Go ahead. I'll be right behind you."

His office was lavishly furnished; his desk solid, dark mahogany, his chair huge and covered with rich leather. On the walls hung mounted heads of exotic animals, some of protected species.

"I see you're a hunter," I said.

He just chuckled. "Not really. You wouldn't get me into the jungle, sweating my ass off. I just love those things. I pay others who are stupid enough to suffer hardship so they can shoot defenseless animals." He walked over to the safe resting in one corner.

Before he opened it, I warned him, "I'm watching you closely, Titman. If you have a gun in there, don't even think about trying to use it. You'll be dead before you get it out of the safe."

"No gun, I promise. Just the money. I couldn't even use a gun right now. My hand hurts like hell." I noticed he was using his left hand when he opened the safe and reached in to retrieve a few bundles of money. Moving to his desk, he threw them onto the top. "Forty thousand dollars, as agreed. Take it and leave."

"Not so fast," I said. "Go and sit in that fancy chair of yours."

He threw me a quick look, apprehension in his eyes. "Why?"

"Don't ask questions. Just sit in it!"

He followed my request. I took one of the guns which I had taken from the guards and handed it to him. He stared at it. "What do you want me do with that?"

"Just take it!" I said sharply.

He did and held it in his left hand, not knowing why I gave him a gun.

"Now put the barrel into your mouth."

"What?" He stared, sudden comprehension dawning on him. "If you think I'll commit suicide you must be crazy. I thought we had a deal."

"The only deal we had was that you would pay me forty thousand dollars. There was no mention of letting you live."

"You're a lying bastard, Canon!" he cursed and leveled the gun at me.

When he pulled the trigger and nothing happened, I said, "You didn't really think I'd give you a loaded gun?" Then I shot him in the forehead with his own gun, not in the center, but just a little to his left. He fell backwards into his fancy leather chair and onto the blood-spattered back.

Taking my time, I put the gun, which had fallen to the floor, into my pocket and the one I used to shoot him with into his left hand. I wasn't worried about getting my prints on it because I wore gloves. The only prints on it were his. I scooped up the money, walked over to the safe and took out another ten thousand, and then I closed it. I could have taken more, but Titman and I had a deal. I'm not a criminal. I don't rob people, especially not dead ones. The extra ten thousand were a bonus.

With another look at Titman's still body, I left the room and closed the door. Before I walked out of the house, I made a call.

"It's over," I said. "There are two bodies. Put them into the trunk of the limo and get rid of them, but make sure they're never found. The limo is yours. There'll be ten grand in the glove compartment, as agreed. Give me five minutes to get away."

I locked the door behind me. The house was Julia's now, and I didn't want it to be looted.

I parked my car not far away from the Titman house and watched as another car pulled into the driveway. It's not that I didn't trust the two thugs I hired, but I don't like to leave things to chance. I wanted to make sure they kept their promise and just took the limo without breaking into the house.

The problem when dealing with criminals is that they are not exactly upstanding citizens and not always trustworthy. I didn't know these two. Brandon gave me their phone numbers with the assurance that they could be counted upon to do the job right, and I trusted him.

Once at home, I put the old 45 back into the box, hoping I may never have to use it again. But nothing is ever for certain.

Julia inherited the house and the Lucky Millionaire's Casino. She said she'd probably sell it but not right away.

I visited her in her casino a month after her husband's demise, just to find out how things were going. She had done some redecorating in the office and it looked so much nicer. It had that feminine touch. There was only one guard at the door, but he didn't give me any trouble when I said I was here to see Julia.

She greeted me with a happy smile and gave me a hug. "Thank you, Lews," she said and kissed me on the cheek.

"For what?"

"For saving my life." She walked over to the big safe in the back and took out a package wrapped in plain paper. Handing it to me, she said, "This is for you, as agreed."

"Whatever is in there," I said, "I can't take it. If you think I did something for you to earn a reward, you are mistaken."

"I understand, but this is not a reward for what you assume I'm thinking you have done," she said, still smiling. "This is payment for finding out who murdered George."

"My fee isn't that high," I said.

"We never discussed a fee. Take the money. I can afford it."

As I said, the universe works in mysterious ways. Things always turn out in the end. All it takes is patience and a little bit of faith.

I took the money. In a way, I had earned it, even though I killed Titman not for Julia but to eliminate a threat to me and to Sonya. Erika and Doris, Julia's two friends, came to the Dancing Leprechaun to have a few drinks and, possibly, pick up a guy, but they didn't repeat their offer they made me. They never even mentioned it. Not that I would have taken advantage of it. I had all I wanted and needed with Sonya. Her face has healed up nicely and she looks as beautiful as ever.

I still have no idea what she sees in me.

By the way, Nelda and I moved our office into a different building; one with a working air conditioner and larger windows. The old couch is gone, and I don't miss it at all. We replaced it with a swanky new leather couch. Our desks are made from solid wood and we have two brand new computers with twenty-three-inch screens. Things are looking good.

Another thing I might mention—it seems Judge Meloni was an honorable man after all, unlike his son Steven. He dismissed all the charges against me for lack of sufficient evidence. I'm a free man again.

Spread the word. If you need a good private detective, I'm your man.

My name is Lews Bullseye Canon. You heard correctly.

Lews Bullseye Canon, PI.

The End

THANK YOU FOR READING

Did you enjoy this book?

We invite you to leave a review at the website of your choice, such as Goodreads, Amazon, Barnes & Noble, etc.

DID YOU KNOW THAT LEAVING A REVIEW...

- Helps other readers find books they may enjoy.
- Gives you a chance to let your voice be heard.
- Gives authors recognition for their hard work.
- Doesn't have to be long. A sentence or two about why you liked the book will do.

———

Don't miss out on your next favorite book!

———

Join the Melange Books mailing list at
www.melange-books.com/mail.html

Subscriber Perks Include:

- First peeks at upcoming releases.
- Exclusive giveaways.
- News of book sales and freebies right in your inbox.
- And more!

ABOUT THE AUTHOR

Herbert Grosshans lives near Winnipeg, Canada. He spends much of his free time spinning tales about imaginary worlds and the strange creatures inhabiting them. His first published story "The Anniversary Gift" appeared in *Sweet Revenge* published by Midnight Showcase. Even though he writes in other genres, his love is Science Fiction. He enjoys building alien worlds and societies. Most of his stories contain an element of Erotica. To this date he has published 28 books with Melange Books, not including this one. Please, visit Herbert's websites and blogs to find out more about him and his writing.

Websites: fictitioustales.weebly.com
Blogs: hegro.blogspot.com
hergros.blogspot.com

Pinterest: pinterest.com/herbertg
Facebook: facebook.com/hergros
Twitter: twitter.com/hergros

ALSO BY HERBERT GROSSHANS

WITH MELANGE BOOKS

Rhodar Series

Clouds Over Maridaan

The Xandra Series

Daughter of the Dark

Mother of Light

Goddess of Life

Lure of Seduction

Escape from Paradise

Iceworld

Alien World

Dark World

Stars in Chains Series

Slave

Liberator

Stardogs Series

Return to Redsky

Redemption

Seeds of Chaos Series

Eden's Gate

Hell's Gate

www.ingramcontent.com/pod-product-compliance
Lightning Source LLC
Chambersburg PA
CBHW032046240626
47154CB00003B/1100